Taming the Wildcat
Cowboy Rough Book Four

By

Darah Lace

This is a work of fiction. Names, characters, places, and incidents are either the product of the author's imagination or are used fictitiously, and any resemblance to actual persons living or dead, business establishments, events, or locales, is entirely coincidental.

Taming the Wildcat ~ Copyright 2024 by Darah Lace

All rights reserved. No part of this book may be used or reproduced in any manner whatsoever without written permission of the author except in the case of brief quotations embodied in critical articles or reviews.

Cover Art by Diana Carlile
http://www.designingdiana.blogspot.com

Published in the United States of America

Dedication

To KyAnn Waters, Mia Downing, Nicki Pascarella, B, and N for all the support, encouragement, and miles of plotting. For reading every scene, sometimes twice, because I couldn't make up my mind or get it right the first time. Without you, I never would have written this book.

And for Tori Garcia and my stepdad
for answering all my questions about
law enforcement, uniforms, and other *sheriff stuff*.

Bonus in the Back
Texas Two-Step
Cowboy Rough Book Five

Be sure to check out the bonus scenes from book five in the back of this book.

And for news of Darah's upcoming releases, sign up for her newsletter at:
https://www.darahlace.com/newsletter/

Praise for Darah Lace

SADDLE BROKE

"Hold on to your hats, because *Saddle Broke* is hot enough to start a fire...For a sexy, arousing, and romping good time, don't hesitate to read Darah Lace's *Saddle Broke*. You won't be sorry!"

~Natalie, Romance Junkies

BUCKING HARD

"Darah Lace made a fan of me with her fabulous book, *Bachelor Auction*, and I've been keeping an eye out for more of her work ever since. In this short, sweet story, we're introduced to tomboy Bradi Kincaid, a little girl no more, and pining as always after her best friend, Mason Montgomery. Since coming home, Mason has taken a healthy notice of Bradi, as well...and he doesn't exactly know how to reconcile the fact that his childhood chum developed a woman's body."

~Lynn Marie, Denise's Review

~*~

"I got this one right as I was ready to fall asleep. Told myself I was just going to load it on my ereader and read it later. Didn't happen. Two hours later, I was still reading... This book is a very fast read, without a lot of the tiring running around in circles...Darah focuses on the characters and what they want...Oh, and the "hot, no-holds-barred sex" is excellent, too."

~Emmarae, Romancing the Book

Chapter One

Josh McNamara's phone rang as he took the exit ramp off the interstate just northeast of San Antonio.

Shayna Webber. He needed to change her last name in his contacts.

He checked the side mirror before switching lanes, then pressed the button on the steering wheel to answer the call. "Hey, sweetheart, did you miss me?"

"Watch who you're calling sweetheart." His brother's deep voice rumbled into the cab of Josh's truck. Evan sounded relaxed and happier than Josh had ever heard him.

Chuckling, he made another lane change. "Sorry about that. I didn't know we were in a threesome—I mean a three-way."

"Asshole." Another grumble.

Shayna's melodic laughter settled over him like a worn pair of jeans, soft and comfortable.

He sighed. "Ah, but it feels like old times."

"You're so bad," Shayna chided, but he heard the grin behind her words. "We're on our way home from the airport and wanted to let you know we landed safely."

"That could have been a text."

Evan snorted. "That's what *I* told her."

"But I *did* miss you," she said, "and I've been worried about you. I can hear the lonely pouring off you."

"No need to worry about me, darlin'. I get lots of play."

"I do *not* need to hear that."

He could imagine her rolling those big brown eyes of hers, but he didn't want either of them worrying about him. "How was the honeymoon? Did you even make it out of the room?"

"Oh my gosh, we saw so many beautiful places. There was…"

Her excitement made him smile as he listened to her rattle on about locations he'd never heard of. If anyone deserved to be spoiled, it was Shayna. She was a giver through and through.

When she finally took a breath, she asked, "What are you up to? Sounds like you're driving."

"Just out for a ride." *A long and hard one if I'm lucky.*

"Are you really okay?" Shayna asked. "You sound off."

She knew him too well. He'd have to try harder. "Well, baby girl, since you asked, I think I pulled a groin muscle, and I could use your magic hands."

"My wife's hands are not going anywhere near your dick, and I draw the line at baby girl." The Dom in Evan came through loud and clear. His brother was a possessive son of a bitch and jealous of Josh's close friendship with Shayna. But then, their reunion had been complicated, and Josh had been right in the middle to muddy it up.

"Awe, come on," he cajoled, knowing how to push Evan's buttons in a way he'd be forgiven. "Not even as a thank you for getting you two back together?"

Shayna had been Evan's girl almost a decade ago, and it hadn't ended well. Evan had never been the same, and Shayna... She'd needed a shoulder to cry on. Josh had been that shoulder until she moved with her family to Austin.

Last summer, when he'd fallen from a ladder and broke both an arm and a leg, he found her working weekends at an ER in Austin. After a little begging on his part, she'd come to work as his nurse during the week. Then he'd convinced Evan he couldn't manage the ranch, and since Evan owned half, he should step in. Sparks flew the second they saw each other again, some at Josh's head.

"You'll have my undying gratitude for the rest of my life, asshole, but—"

"Hey," Shayna interjected, a smile in her voice, "stop discussing me like your prized mare." Then her tone turned low, sultry, and not meant for Josh's ears. "Unless you wanna mount me like a stallion and—"

"Fuck me, that's my cue to go, but I'll call you tomorrow, Ev. We need to talk."

He hung up before Evan could ask any questions and slipped into the parking lot outside The Arena, an exclusive BDSM club he'd found in San Antonio only an hour and a half's drive from Stone Creek. If he hadn't already agreed to partner with Buck again, he wouldn't be here. Not when several ranches near his had been the target of cattle rustlers over the last few weeks. But he had his foreman and another hand making rounds to check on the herd, and he'd be home by midnight to help out.

Besides, he needed tonight. To blow off some steam. A guaranteed good hard fuck.

Leaving his coat in the truck, along with his phone, he braced for the sharp teeth of a north wind as he made the short trek to the renovated warehouse. He swiped his membership card through the reader. The door opened, and he stepped into the quiet foyer.

"Hey, Roan," the security guard, called Wrecker because of his gigantic stocky frame, greeted Josh by the club name he'd chosen.

"Wrecker." Josh shook the man's hand. "Take it easy."

The big guy grinned. "I take it any way I can."

Josh laughed. "Don't we all."

"Hello, Sir." Emerald, the hostess at the check-in desk, smiled at him.

Dressed all in black, she was a petite little thing with blonde hair, heavy kohl around big green eyes, and creamy flesh spilling over the top of her corset. Anywhere else, he might have called her darlin' or sweetheart, hit on her a bit, and probably fucked her before the night was through. But this wasn't anywhere else, and she wore someone else's collar. Protocol demanded he respect certain boundaries he might normally cross outside this club.

Sometimes, he felt stifled by all the rules, the control suppressing his easygoing and fun-loving nature. He liked women, liked to flirt with them, to tease, and have a good time. It helped relieve the stress of everyday life on the ranch.

"Hi, Em." He returned her smile but resisted the urge to wink at her. "What'cha got for me?"

"You're in room ten, but Buck hasn't checked in yet, and your sub for this evening—Cherry—is meeting with Wrangler."

He nodded. "I'll be at the bar."

Cherry, huh? Red hair? Virgin sub? He just hoped it didn't mean she was a virgin-virgin.

Josh pushed through double doors into the club and headed to the bar on the far end of the half-acre dungeon. The Arena was crowded, the atmosphere crackling with excitement. A group from Dallas was here for instructional scenes on impact play, like asphyxiation, shibari, and caning.

Not interested.

A little D/s was enough. Voyeurism, for sure. That was what he liked most about ménage. Bondage, not so much, though most of the Doms he partnered with, like his brother Evan who'd introduced him to the lifestyle, and now Buck, wanted their subs tied up like a calf for branding.

For six months, Josh had rolled with the flow to learn about bondage and because their subs enjoyed restraint, but he missed the feel of soft hands on his body, the slide of silky legs entwined with his. At home, he'd found balance with his harem, as Shayna called the buckle bunnies rotating through his screen door. Maybe he'd talk to Evan about feeling torn between this world and the outside.

For tonight… "Rolling with the flow."

In the corner near the bar, he located an empty seating area that gave him a good view of the stage and those watching. Easing into a rawhide chair, he stretched out his legs and listened to the Dom giving instructions as he talked about breath play. Again, not something he wanted to try, but the blonde waiting to help with the demonstration was hot.

As was the redhead sucking her Dom's dick a few

feet away. Josh's cock reached for his bellybutton as he imagined it sliding between her goth-black lips.

A dark figure stepped into his line of sight, blocking his lip-porn and heading straight toward him. He'd been amazed at the number of people he knew or recognized at The Arena, people he never would have expected to be living their best life at the local BDSM watering hole, so he wasn't surprised to see Kane Kilbane among them. Kilbane owned a sprawling ranch fifty miles northwest of San Antonio that made Josh's spread look insignificant.

Kane was a long way from home, no doubt trying to preserve his privacy, like Josh. In a small town, gossip spread faster than a wildfire on the West Coast. Josh's hometown was no different.

He rose to shake Kane's hand. "Hey, man, how's it going?"

"Can't complain." Kane settled into the chair next to his. "You?"

"Doing all right." Josh waited for Kane to explain why he'd sought him out. They didn't run in the same social circles. Kilbane was rancher royalty.

"I heard you're raising horses now," Kane finally said.

"Barely getting started." His pride and joy wouldn't deliver until later in the spring. "We have our first foal on its way."

"I've been thinking about starting a breeding program. Any tips?"

The idea of Kilbane needing tips from him was laughable. While the McNamara ranch was solvent, Josh and Evan were taking things slowly, being careful not to dip too deep into resources that might be needed next year. Josh ran the ranch, but Evan was the money cruncher and kept a tight rein on the purse strings.

Josh shrugged. "I'm learning as I go. All I know for sure is, it's going to take a while to build the kind of horse farm I envision."

Kane grunted his understanding, his focus shifting to the stage. Was he into asphyxiation?

Josh knew better than to ask. Another rule to follow.

Instead, he raised a subject weighing heavy on his mind. "Has anyone out your way been hit by rustlers lately?"

Kane's head snapped around. "Not that I know of. Why? Were you hit?"

"Nah, but several outfits in the county over took it up the ass."

"Fuck." Kane's jaw ticked. "They'll likely make the rounds."

"That's what I figured."

"Do you still brand?"

"Yeah, the old man didn't trust tags, so we've always done both." Josh had carried on the practice after his father died. Tags fell out, animals ripped them off, and thieves could easily remove and replace them. Brands were permanent and still the best way to identify cattle back to their farm of origin.

"You should beef up security," Kane said as he stood. "I'm going to make a few calls."

As Kane walked away, Josh rubbed the back of his neck. He'd already put out feelers for extra hands willing to work nights guarding his herd. As it stood, he only had three. With one man working days, he and the other two weren't enough to guard every pasture. They were forced to ride from herd to herd. It wasn't the best solution, but the larger ranches had picked up every experienced hand. He'd have to expand his search, maybe call the association to see if any of the rangers were interested in moonlighting.

For tonight, there was nothing else he could do…except hope like hell Cherry could clear his head and drain his balls.

****

"How long has it been since you've been out of the scene?"

Harper Quinn turned her attention from the painting of a woman bound in a series of intricate knots to the man across the desk. "A little over a year."

Wrangler, the dungeon master at The Arena, looked at his computer screen again, his dreamy dark eyes assessing. "And you weren't far into your training when you left?"

This interview had gone on too fucking long. She wasn't a new submissive, just rusty, and unless this hot Dom was going to bend her over the desk and cram her full of cock, she was ready to move on.

Telling herself he was only doing his job, that she was lucky to have been granted membership to such an elite club, she grasped the last thread of her unraveling patience. "Three months. Is there a problem?"

"Not at all." He smiled, smoothing the frown from his brow. "I just want to make sure the Doms we've placed you with tonight fit your needs."

She nodded. "I was still figuring out what my needs were when I left."

"Are you sure you want to start with a ménage?"

Her last scene was over a year ago. She'd been

between two cowboys, their names unknown, but she remembered them as Gabriel, a blue-eyed, golden angel, and Lucifer, a dark-haired demon. She'd enjoyed their rough play but hadn't found what she was looking for. The problem was, she still didn't know.

She shrugged and smoothed the filmy shin-length skirt over crossed legs, aware of the bare skin exposed by the slits cut to the top of her thighs but not giving a fuck. She would be naked soon enough anyway. "Picking up where I left off seems as good a place as any."

Like the controlling Dom he undoubtedly was, he didn't take the bait. He nodded, his chocolate brown hair falling over his eyes. Long fingers sifted through the wave to push it back into place.

Like the good little sub she wasn't, she squirmed in her chair, imagining those fingers roaming over her body, filling her pussy—

"May I ask why you left?"

The question was inevitable, expected, but she had no intention of diving into that shit show. "Personal reasons. Nothing to do with my experience as a submissive."

Fucking Blake Enders. Against her better judgement, she'd let him into her life, and he'd wrecked it all to hell—her career, her confidence...and her heart.

That wasn't quite true. Her confidence might have taken a beating, but her heart was only a little cracked and far from broken. Still, Blake had shattered any hopes of advancement in her career with the Houston Police Department.

"Okay, then." Rising, Wrangler gestured toward the door. "If you're ready..."

More than ready, practically chomping at the bit, Harper followed him down the quiet, dimly lit hall. Black tufted walls buffered the sound of stilettos that pinched her toes. Click, click, clicking on the dark unyielding concrete like the echo of a clock on New Year's Eve, promising a clean slate with new resolutions...and new dick.

These were the first steps into her new life.

With the swipe of a card, double doors opened. Music invaded the silence, the hard beat thumping through her body in erotic waves. Adrenaline kicked in as she moved farther into the social area of the dungeon. She'd taken a tour earlier, before the club opened, but the industrial lights had been on and only staff milled about. Now, it was dark, and the place was packed.

She took a deep breath in and exhaled, releasing the tight control she maintained in her everyday life, and assumed the persona of the submissive she'd suppressed for over a year. In this place, she wasn't Harper, former detective with Houston PD and newly appointed interim sheriff of Stone County. She was Cherry, a semi-inexperienced sub with an attitude that needed adjusting, preferably with punishment.

"There are dungeon monitors stationed throughout the club," Wrangler said. "If you need help or have questions, ask one. Do not approach anyone else. Keep your hands to yourself. And above all—safe, sane, and—"

"Consensual," she finished for him. "Got it."

A slow smile slid across his handsome face. "What I wouldn't give to be the one to tame you tonight."

She smiled for the first time since entering the club

and batted her eyelashes at him. "Tougher men have tried."

Shaking his head, he turned and led her deeper into the seductive maze of carnal delight.

Elevated platforms scattered across a large, open space with various scenes of either instruction or entertainment playing out. Intimate groupings of sofas, chairs, and benches wove around the platforms or tucked into secluded corners, allowing a voyeuristic view of the stages.

The décor was different from the club where she'd begun her initiation into submission. Silver House reflected big city glam with black furniture, chrome, and glass. The Arena mirrored the clientele it catered to—Texas ranchers, oil barons, and a few politicians—with natural leather, tables of polished wood, cowhide rugs, and black pipe railing.

In the center of the dungeon, a metal sculpture of an angry longhorn, with his head low and nostrils flared, kicked his back hooves toward the ceiling.

Somebody's compensating for a tiny dick.

As they approached the bar area, the hair at the back of Harper's neck lifted, the warning familiar. Someone was watching her. As a cop, that feeling had saved her life more than once, but here…

Someone wasn't just watching her. Someone was interested.

Ignoring her suspicious nature, she tapped into her female intuition and shifted slightly toward the crowd. Most watched the scene on the stage. Her gaze flitted from one face to the next—a woman with pink hair and a diamond collar, a man in a leather harness holding the woman's leash, two guys petting their sub.

Peering deeper into the shadows, closer to the bar, she almost missed him. Dressed all in black, he blended in, but she pegged him for six-two, two hundred pounds, dirty blond hair—long, lean, and golden. His hooded gaze and distance hid the color of his eyes, but they tracked her every step with an intensity that burned like the Texas sun on a hot summer day.

Wrangler veered through the maze of tables toward the long mahogany bar, forcing Harper to focus on where she was going. He stopped to talk to the bartender but didn't introduce her to any of the darkly dressed men seated there, so she didn't fight the urge to risk another glance at her sexy stalker.

Deep blue eyes locked with hers, stealing her breath. Closer now, she could make out his sharp angular features—the strong set of his jaw, a stern chin, and cheekbones that could cut glass. Something about them seemed familiar. She was good with faces, but the memory niggling at her slipped out of reach.

His gaze dipped to her mouth then lower, taking a leisurely tour of her body. Her nipples beaded as he lingered at the swell of her breasts, and butterflies she'd thought long dead awakened. Their tiny, tattered wings fluttered in the pit of her stomach as he zeroed in on her pussy. Liquid fire seeped from her cunt to coat her thighs.

While his attention was directed elsewhere, she took her own quick survey from his snakeskin cowboy boots, up long, muscular legs encased in black jeans. The denim stretched across lean hips and outlined an impressive package that held its own against a large silver belt buckle.

A black dress shirt hugged broad shoulders, and his

sleeves were rolled midway up sinewy, bronzed forearms. The golden tan, together with wheat-colored streaks winding through blond waves that curled over his collar, spoke of time in the sun.

Hmm. Athlete? Construction? Rodeo Romeo? All of the above?

Done with her assessment, Harper waited for him to finish undressing her with his eyes. When he looked up again, the corner of his full lips lifted into a self-assured smile as if he knew exactly what he was doing to her.

Cocky motherfucker.

He was breaking protocol, but then she was too by encouraging him. He wasn't hers to ogle. She wasn't his. Only the two Doms waiting for her had that right. But Cherry liked playing with fire, and this guy definitely had her in flames.

And that's why your life is fucked all to hell right now.

Ignoring her inner bitch, smart as she might be, Harper raised a brow. He returned the gesture and wagged a finger back and forth between the two of them.

She smiled at his invitation and cast a quick glance at Wrangler. Could she bow out of the threesome to give this hot cowboy a ride?

No. There was struggling with her submissive role, and there was throwing caution to the wind.

She'd already enjoyed his attention more than she should have, forgetting her role and why she was here. This was her first night at The Arena. A session had been arranged, and without justification, she shouldn't—wouldn't—disrespect the Doms waiting for her or risk her membership for a spontaneous fuck.

Disappointment crushing her high, she shook her head and turned toward the stage. The guy on the platform had a woman in a loose choke hold while he talked about the different techniques of breath play—choking, smothering, and strangulation.

"Oh, hell no," she muttered, then caught herself. She'd never yuck someone else's yum, but she'd seen the result of asphyxiation on too many coroners' tables.

"Sorry to keep you waiting." Wrangler broke into her thoughts before she dove down a rabbit hole too dark for tonight's pleasure. "Almost done."

"No problem." She shifted from one foot to another, trying to relieve the ache in her feet. *Fucking high heels better get me fucked good, or next time, I'm wearing boots.*

Enthusiasm waning, she stared at the floor and tried not to regret her decision. Fuck, but her hot stalker made it difficult. She could feel him watching her, tempting her to take one more look.

Fuck it.

She met his gaze straight on with a question she shouldn't be asking. What did he want from her?

Brow spiked, he pointed at her, then put his hand to his throat, forming a collar. Was he asking if she was collared?

Her confusion must have shown because he pointed to the stage, then placed both hands to his throat, squeezed, and stuck out his tongue as if he were choking. A giggle erupted before she could stop it, but she covered it with a cough.

He eased back in his chair, the twinkle in his eyes and a grin that could charm the panties off a nun set the zombie butterflies in her belly free. Which was crazy because funny wasn't her type. She leaned more toward tall, dark, and serious. And she was *not* a fucking giggler.

Wrangler turned from the bar before she could respond. "Ready?"

With a covert wave goodbye to the mystery man who'd kept her wet and entertained, Harper sighed. "Lead the way."

She fell in behind Wrangler, then faltered as he headed into the dark corner and straight for the sexy stalker Dom with a quirky sense of humor.

Chapter Two

Stretching out in his chair, Josh savored the surprise, suspicion, and lust competing for control of Cherry's face as Wrangler introduced them. She'd lowered her eyes and clasped her hands behind her back in typical sub posture, but Josh wasn't fooled. Not after the eye-fucking she'd given him.

Her dismissal? That was just foreplay. She was into him. And from the second he'd seen her trailing Wrangler, with all that raven-black hair falling around creamy shoulders, a stubborn chin that mocked her submission, and tits that made his mouth water, Josh had wanted her to be Cherry. To be his.

"Buck hasn't checked in yet," Wrangler repeated what Emerald had already told him.

"No problem." Josh kept his attention on the thundering pulse in Cherry's neck. Fuck, she was hot. "We'll get acquainted while we wait. Won't we, Cherry?"

The dark lashes fanning her cheeks lifted slightly. "If that is your pleasure...*Sir*."

Sarcasm dripped from the address meant to be said with respect. He'd love to know what mayhem was going on in her head.

Sensing Wrangler's censure, Josh stalled him with a hand. "It is, and you will be."

"Good luck," the DM said and faded into the

crowd.

Not named for her hair—or her innocence if the lust in those dove-gray eyes was anything to go by—Cherry wasn't a typical sub, and he'd bet submission didn't come easy. She was about as docile as an untamed mustang. She was a challenge, and he loved challenges.

Sitting forward, elbows on his knees, Josh crooked a finger. "Come here."

Dainty feet perched on stilts carried her closer until he could make out the slight rise of her pubic bone under her long skirt. The sweet scent of her arousal blended with her perfume to tease his nostrils. His dick flexed, and his mouth watered. Would she taste as spicy as she behaved?

Aching to touch her, he scooted to the edge of the chair so that she stood between his knees. He slipped his fingers inside the slits on either side of her skirt and ran the back of his knuckles over her toned calves.

He glanced up, catching her lowered gaze. "Are you a good girl, Cherry?"

"Yes, Sir." The low, raspy edge in her voice skated over Josh's flesh and into his balls, ramping up his need to hear her beg for his cock.

"Why don't I believe you?" He turned his hands over to palm the silky flesh of her thigh. "Why do I think you're a naughty girl?"

"Do you prefer a naughty girl, Sir?"

Did he? All the submissives he'd enjoyed were well behaved. All but Shayna. She'd been somewhere in the middle, both sassy and sweet, the times he'd joined her and Evan, back when Evan was determined to make sure she could handle another man in their bed.

The women before Josh's dive into BDSM were playful and fun, loving a good romp. So…

"Guess we'll find out." He swirled the finger he'd beckoned her with. "Turn around."

Slowly, she pivoted forty-five degrees, then ninety.

"Stop." While she had great tits, her ass was perfection–small, round, and tight. Josh cradled her ass in his hands and squeezed. He ran his thumbs along the crease of her thighs, then up the seam of her crack. The muscles beneath his hands quivered. "I'm gonna enjoy spanking this pretty little ass."

"What the fuck for?"

With another chuckle, he pulled her onto his lap and nestled her ass against his cock. The heat of her pussy seeped through his jeans. Stifling a groan, he brushed her hair away from her neck and leaned in to nip her ear. "You know exactly what for."

"Mmmmmm." She squirmed against his erection.

He tightened his arm around her waist. "Be still, brat, or I'll turn you over my knee and spank you here."

"Why not go to the room now?" Her slender hands skimmed the length of his forearms. "You can spank me all you want, and Buck can join us when he gets here."

He'd like nothing better, but that wasn't how it worked. "Consider this time alone in the dungeon foreplay."

"That's what I thought we'd been doing," she muttered.

He feathered his lips down her neck to dip his tongue into the hollow of her collarbone. "Are you telling me you're wet and ready for my cock?"

She tilted her head to give him better access. "I'm

saying I don't need any more foreplay."

"I'll decide what you need." Knowing what his sub needed and when she needed it was one of the things he loved about D/s. But he'd always been into making sure his lover found pleasure. Watching a woman writhe and then shatter under his touch got him off almost as much as fucking her.

He waved a hand at the couple on the stage. "What do you think when you look at them?"

"That if he's not careful, he could be facing a third-degree felony and ten years."

Josh smiled at the slip. He doubted she realized how much she'd just revealed. A lawyer, maybe? Paralegal? Some type of law enforcement professional? He couldn't ask her questions like he would if they were on a date. Instead, he draped her legs over his spread thighs, opening hers wide and leaving them bare as the front panel of her skirt flowed like a waterfall between them, the hem pooling on the floor.

"If breath play isn't your thing"—he'd figured as much by the way she'd wrinkled her nose at them earlier—"how about the couple on the couch to your left?"

The pair he'd watched earlier were fucking now. Skirt around her waist, the redhead straddled her Dom, riding his cock in an unhurried rhythm as he sucked her nipple into his mouth. The woman's head fell back, her spine arched.

Cherry's breath shuddered, and the pulse under his lips quickened even as she relaxed into him.

"Now we're getting somewhere." Josh caressed the creamy flesh of her outer thighs down to the knee. "See how her pussy stretches around his dick, how her juices glisten on his shaft?"

Diverting his fingers over her knee, Josh started a slow journey up the inside of her thigh. A faint mewling sound and the slight shift of her pelvis let him know she liked what he was doing and where he was going, but he stopped shy of the sweet treasure hidden by her skirt.

With a featherlight caress, he eased his fingers under the flimsy material to find the hollowed-out spots between her thighs and her pussy. He trailed his index fingers into the depth and out the back, taking a trip over the curve of her ass, then swooping back again.

"Fuck," she whispered on a long exhale. Her head lolled against his shoulder, but she continued to watch the couple while he watched her.

"Don't worry, little brat, I will." He groaned just thinking about sinking into her hot, wet cunt. "I'm going to fuck you until you scream my name."

"I don't know your name."

He started to remind her his club name was Roan, but he didn't want her calling out that name as she came. Another wave of irritation rippled through him, but before he let his struggle to mesh both worlds spoil the night, he inhaled a calming breath and counted through his exhale.

Fanning out his thumbs, he traced the seam of her swollen lips in rhythm with the slow fuck going on a few feet away. "Then I'll fuck you until you can't remember your own."

"Oh god."

Josh closed his mouth over her neck and bit down, gently then a little harder when she didn't complain. Her ass ground into his dick, and he was half-tempted to whip it out and fill her pussy. Her skirt would hide them. Not that he really gave a fuck who watched right now.

"Excuse me, Sir." The bartender's matter-of-fact voice came from somewhere to his right.

Cherry tensed, but Josh countered her reaction by grazing her clit.

"J.J.?" Josh's tone came sharper than he'd intended as Cherry's hips lifted for more pressure and he retreated to the shallow dip, refusing to let her take charge.

"Emerald asked me to let you know that Buck is here and he's waiting for you in the room you reserved."

"Thank you." Josh stroked his hands down Cherry's thighs to her knees. He didn't want his time alone with her to end. He didn't want to share her. Whether it was Cherry or his recent frustration with straddling both worlds causing his sudden reluctance, he couldn't say, but she'd come for a threesome, so... "Are you ready, brat?"

"Am I—" Her eyelids fluttered then opened. Perfectly arched brows dove into a V. "Can you finish what you fucking started first?"

As much as he wanted to, he shifted her legs between his and stood, taking her with him. "Your begging needs improvement. Try a little more sweet and a lot less sour next time."

To his satisfaction, she wobbled and leaned into him, and even with high heels, the top of her head only came to his chin. A grin pulled at his lips that he didn't bother to hide. "Don't worry, brat. We're done with foreplay."

****

Still under the intoxicating influence of Roan's touch, Harper let him steer her down the hall, his fingers laced with hers. What the fuck had he done to her?

He'd barely touched her, and she'd turned into a fucking rag doll, pliant and eager for him to do whatever he desired. It had to be the dungeon. She'd never played there, always starting out in a private room where the only stimulus was the scene in which she participated.

But thank fuck, as he stopped at the door to Room 10, the aggressive energy of suppressed need and the urge to push limits began to surface.

His hand hovered over the keyless entry, yet he didn't swipe the card. Had he changed his mind?

Before she could ask, he shoved her against the door. His hard body flattened hers against the cold metal, his forearms bracketing her head. "I have to taste you."

His mouth slanted over hers, his tongue parting her lips. Fisting her fingers in his hair, she met the thrust of his tongue as he explored the well beneath her tongue, the caverns of her cheeks, and the roof of her mouth. Her heart pounded, stirring her zombieflies into a frenzy.

Harper strained against him, lightheaded at his untethered urgency to devour her. She hadn't been kissed like this in a long time. Blake had been a good kisser, but he never made her forget who she was. Fuck.

Fighting the stupor invading her brain, she bucked her hips and tugged his hair.

A groan rumbled from Roan's chest, vibrating

through the thin fabric covering her breasts, making them tingle. Large, calloused hands fanned her face as he pulled back. "You even kiss like a fucking brat."

She opened her mouth to tell him to go fuck himself, but his grip on her jaw tightened.

"I'm not complaining." He dragged his thumb over her lips, parting them until the rough pad met teeth. "Just hoping you fuck like one."

Adrenaline unfurled all the way to her core, kicking the need for his dominance up another notch. Had she finally found a Dom who got her? "Guess you're about to find out."

She tried to bite his thumb, but he was too fast, sliding his fingers into her hair.

He closed in for another kiss. "Count on—"

Harper nipped at his lips, hard, and the rest of his words and a chuckle dissolved into a bone-melting assault on her mouth. With a grunt, he jammed a knee between her thighs and ground his cock against her belly.

Was he going to fuck her in the hall while Buck waited on the other side of the door? The thought stirred heat in her core. She bucked against him, needing more, needing his hands on her, everywhere— her tits, her ass, her pussy.

But when his fingers untangled from her hair, they closed around her wrists and squeezed until she was forced to let go of his hair. He slammed her hands against the door above her head and broke the kiss.

His eyes were as dark as the deepest ocean, lust sparking through them like sunlight on water. He gathered her hands into one of his, then wiped the back of the other over his mouth and came away with a smear of blood. "You like to play rough, do you?"

She licked her lips and tasted the metallic evidence of his words. Maybe she'd gone too far, but she'd made up her mind when she'd decided to give BDSM another try. This time, she wasn't holding back. "What can I say? I'm generous. I like giving back."

Roan's bark of laughter surprised Harper as he released her. He stepped back to look her up and down with a cocky smirk that said he could handle whatever she dished out. He twined his fingers with hers. "Let's get to it, then."

Excitement dancing in her veins, Harper tried not to think about how good her hand felt in his as he led her into the playroom. It was much like any other—a St. Andrew's Cross, a spanking bench, and a big inviting bed.

A man, presumably Buck, stood off to one side surveying a cabinet of toys and torture devices. He'd already stripped down to black dress pants. Nice ass. He was bulkier in muscle than Roan, not as tall, and with his dark hair cut military short, he had an air that reminded her of a cop, which made her a little nervous. She didn't need one of her own finding her here.

Releasing her hand, Roan closed in behind her. "This is Buck." His hands skimmed along her arms, soothing and stimulating at the same time. "Buck, meet Cherry."

Buck turned around, an easy smile playing at his lips. "It's nice to meet you, Cherry. Sorry I'm late."

His accent held no hint of the deep drawl that flavored Roan's speech or her own but rather a twangy clip of Australian.

Buck's gaze fell to Roan's hands on her arms, then

swept over her shoulder. Some kind of acknowledgement passed between them. She'd seen it a year ago with the two Doms in her last scene. Roan would be the dominant partner tonight. He'd staked his claim.

Harper would have rolled her eyes at the show of testosterone, but Cherry relished Roan's reluctance to hand her over to another Dom. She'd have been happy to have spent the night alone with him. Ménage was an experiment, not a necessity, but he and Buck were obviously partners, so maybe it was something he needed.

Roan's touch slipped away as he skirted the bed to sit in one of two chairs against the wall. Elbows propped on the arms, he steepled his fingers. "Take off your clothes."

Instinct and twenty-eight years of trained aggression threatened to overwhelm her. Relinquishing control went against her very core, but she had learned. As a submissive, every surrender of that control freed her softer, more feminine side and eventually led to a higher plane of intense pleasure.

Reaching behind her, Harper tugged at the knot of her halter top. His hot gaze followed the material as she peeled it from her skin, damp from the exertion of their hump fest in the hall. The scrap of fabric fell at her feet, but her hair covered her breasts. She brushed it behind her back and arched, giving him an unobstructed view of one of her best features. Men loved her nipples.

His lazy grin proved he was no exception. "Like ripe cherries."

Hiking a brow, she returned his smile.

"Now, I get the name." He flicked a finger at her

skirt.

With a darting glance at Buck who stood on the other side of the bed, she tugged the zipper at her back. It slid with ease, and the garment slithered over her hips and down her thighs, floating to encircle her feet. She stepped out of it and waited for further instructions.

This was the easy part—submitting to direction for the simple things, like undressing. To Cherry, submission was a game of power. She just wasn't sure how much Roan and Buck would allow. BDSM was built on anticipating a set of behaviors negotiated beforehand, but they hadn't done that yet.

Roan began unbuttoning his shirt, giving her a peek at the dark golden hair dusting his chest. "Shoes off."

Thank god. She was used to boots or sneakers, and these five-inch motherfuckers were killing her instep.

Buck gathered her clothes and hung them on hooks she hadn't even noticed. Having him perform that task for her felt strange as if the roles were reversed. Usually, she was undressed and kneeling in the center of the room before her Dom arrived.

Rising to face the wall, Roan tugged his shirt from the waist of his pants. The black fabric slipped from one shoulder, then the other, revealing taut flesh that rippled over muscle with every move like water over river rocks. A scar slashed across one side of his back, reminding her of the knife wounds that some gang members wore as badges of honor.

He hung the shirt next to hers and unbuckled his belt.

Harper licked her lips, eager to see what else he had to offer.

"Safeword?" Buck asked, dragging her attention

from Roan's beautifully hard body.

"Wild—" She cleared her throat and swallowed the saliva flooding her mouth. "Wildcat."

Roan snorted, and her gaze flew to meet his knowing blue eyes over his shoulder. "Fitting."

"Does our kitten have claws?" Buck asked, moving back to the wall of torture to inspect a pair of cuffs.

Roan thumbed his lower lip and folded himself into the chair again. "Not sure about the claws yet, but she definitely bites."

With a sigh, she lowered her head and looked at her fingernails. No claws. Never had them. Growing up, she'd been too busy trying to stay one step ahead of her brothers to worry about manicured nails, and later, she kept them clipped short for her job.

"Hard limits?" Buck asked.

She dropped her hands to her sides. *Here we go.*

No matter the Dom, her answer always brought displeasure. "No anal."

The room grew quiet except for the thud of Roan's boots hitting the floor, but she could imagine the silent conversation taking place between them.

"A ménage with no anal?"

"Fuck that."

"Call Wrangler for a replacement sub. This one's broken."

Roan's bare feet appeared in front of her. His thumb and index finger gripped her chin, forcing her to look up. Anger blazed in his eyes. His jaw ticked.

Yep. There it is.

Her heart dropped to her stomach. Why did the thought of him turning her away sting? She barely knew him.

His grip gentled. "Did someone hurt you, little wildcat?"

Harper blinked at the direction he'd gone. No one had ever worried about her, only the pleasure she denied them.

"N-no more than I've asked for." She couldn't explain the irrational fear that gripped her the first time she'd tried anal sex. Her partner had barely touched her there, and she'd freaked out. Then she'd been more unsettled by her violent reaction than anything he'd done and refused to try again. "I don't know why it scares me."

"Don't worry, luv," Buck said, approaching them. "There are many other things we can do to you."

Roan's free hand snaked around her middle, hauled her flush against him, and lifted her with no effort at all until her toes came off the floor. The buckle of his belt was cold against her belly, but his skin was hot and smooth except for the hair feathering his chest and tickling her hardened nipples. She braced her hands on his shoulders, loving how the deltoid bunched and flexed beneath her fingers.

"The last thing we want is for you to be afraid." He threaded his fingers into the hair at her nape and dipped his head to capture her lower lip with his teeth. Slowly, he dragged at her lip until it slipped free. "I'd much rather have you hissing and clawing like a wildcat."

She shivered, trying to find some hidden meaning in his words. Was he inviting her bratty behavior?

Fuck, she didn't need encouragement. She needed the spanking he'd threatened.

Buck strapped a harness of some kind around her hips, but she couldn't think as Roan's tongue traced her lips, then flicked past them to leisurely investigate the cavern of her mouth. She moaned into the kiss. Into Roan's fingers fisting into her hair. Into the ridge of his cock fitting perfectly against her clit.

Her breath hitching, Harper mimicked his actions, battling his tongue in a struggle for power. She drove her fingers into his golden locks. Cool. Silky. Begging to be pulled. She didn't hesitate.

A growl rumbled through him, which only made her bolder. She wrapped a leg around his and ground against his thigh for relief. The friction sent a delicious jolt of desire from her clit into her core. It wouldn't take much to—

He lowered her and eased out of the kiss. Whimpering, she tightened her hold on his hair to keep his mouth on hers.

A deep chuckle peaked her frustration as he unwound her leg from around his. "Enough, brat."

His determined lips left hers but blazed a path along to the swell of her breast.

"Oh god, yes," she hissed. "Do it. I need…suck it."

But he denied her the pleasure of his mouth. Why? Because she demanded it? Did he want her to fucking beg? She clenched her jaw to prevent the plea from spilling out.

Roan dropped to his knees, his mouth continuing its descent across the plane of her belly. His callused hands roamed to settle on top of the harness at her hips. Another set of hands grazed her ribs, then cupped her breasts as Buck pressed in behind her. His thumb flicked the nipples Roan had refused. His cock—when had he removed his pants?—poked the base of her spine. She wasn't sure whether to shove her ass backward or thrust her hips forward.

Blue eyes scanned up her body, stalling to watch Buck knead her breasts before rising again to focus on her face. Roan's tongue circled her bellybutton above the wide leather strap. "Spread your legs for me. Show me how wet you are for us."

She widened her stance and felt the proof of her lust trickle down her thighs.

Buck's lips stopped their exploration of her shoulder. "I'll bet she's dripping."

"Fucking soaked." Roan's nose teased the crest of her mound, and his nostrils flared as he inhaled deeply. "And she smells like heaven."

That cocky grin she couldn't help but find charming and sexy as hell stirred something inside her, something foreign. She'd played at submission, but never really felt a burning need to please...until now.

Fuck that.

"I told you I didn't need more foreplay." She tugged his hair, trying to bring his mouth to her mound. "Can we get on with the fucking?"

His tongue made a tsking sound as he shook his head. "And here I was, about to eat some pussy, but now..."

He nipped at her pubic bone.

Her hips jerked, and she yanked harder. "Asshole."

Roan's grin just widened as he wrapped the straps of the harness around her thighs, but the flat of Buck's big hand landed a stinging swat on her ass.

"Motherfucker," she yelped. "That hurt."

"Be happy for that little reward because if you keep it up, you won't get another one." Buck arms were quick as they wound around her. His fingers fit like manacles on her wrists. "Let go."

She searched Roan's face, waiting for instructions. He didn't seem to mind her bad behavior. In fact, he almost seemed to regret the slight nod he gave her, but she loosened her hold and let Buck crisscross her arms at her chest.

"Now be a good girl," Buck said, "so we can make you scream."

Roan flicked his tongue over her clit, then winked and reached for something on the bed. Was he flirting with her again? Or promising a different kind of punishment, promising he wouldn't leave her wanting? He was the most playful Dom she'd ever come across. He definitely marched to a different beat.

He buckled leather cuffs around her ankles and attached a spreader bar. When he stood, he placed a quick kiss to her lips. Buck shifted his hold to her upper arms so that Roan could bind her wrists in another pair of cuffs.

Once they were secure, Roan rubbed a thumb over her bottom lip. "On your knees, little wildcat."

Chapter Three

Cherry's quick intake of breath whispered over Josh's thumb, and the pupils of her eyes dilated, leaving only a thin ring of pale gray. Her tongue snaked out to lave the tip, and his cock tried to fight its way out of his jeans.

He groaned, wishing she was licking his dick and not his thumb. Maybe he should rethink having her suck Buck's cock first.

Buck moved to sit on the edge of the bed. "Come, luv."

Too late.

Her lashes fluttered several times at Buck's command, then understanding dawned and disappointment flickered across her face just before a mask of compliance fell into place. She'd wanted to be on her knees for *him* not Buck.

A streak of possessiveness tightened Josh's chest, but he shrugged it off as the lingering effects of the call from Evan and Shayna. He'd been trying to shut down the envy that had clawed at him since they'd gotten back together.

He wasn't lonely. His bed never stayed empty for long. Shayna teased him all the time about having a revolving door. Still…

Next time—*and there would be a next time*—he'd have Cherry alone. While he liked to watch, the chemistry between them didn't leave room for anyone else.

With another quick kiss, he helped her to her knees in front of Buck. Squatting behind her, Josh drew her arms back and connected the wrist cuffs at the base of her spine.

"Okay?" he asked.

She tested the restraints and nodded. "It's fine."

The lie sounded pretty on her lips but made him frown. Like an untamed filly fought a bridle, Cherry struggled with bondage, and he doubted she even realized it. He'd remove the cuffs, but reading the needs of his sub wasn't his only job as lead Dom. He had to consider his partner, too, and Buck needed her restrained.

Somehow, he had to get her all worked up and past her discomfort.

With an internal sigh, he gathered her against his chest and murmured in a low coaxing tone that only she could hear, "Good because I want you to be comfortable when I watch your pussy swallow his cock."

"Fuck." She clamped her knees shut and rubbed her legs together.

"No, brat." He pried her knees apart. "Keep them open, so Buck can see the pretty pink pussy he's about to fuck."

And he'd be damned if he'd let Cherry get off by herself. He planned to be balls-deep in her pussy when she finally came.

He snagged her lip with two fingers. "But first, I want to watch him fuck your dirty little mouth."

Josh eased two fingers over her velvety tongue,

half expecting her to bite him, but she sucked them deeper. Buck's groan drowned out his own. Her body lost some of its tension, and a soft whimper hummed through his fingers and straight to his balls.

He glanced at Buck stroking his cock, then back to Cherry. She watched Buck through heavy eyelids.

"I want to see your lips stretched around his dick," Josh rasped, plucking her taut, red nipple.

"Mmm." She sucked harder and rocked her hips.

"I want you to take him to the back of your throat." He pushed his fingers deeper. "I want this filthy mouth so full of his cum you can't swallow it all."

Buck's hand pumped faster. "Bloody hell, Roan."

"Can you do that for me, wildcat?" Josh asked, ignoring Buck's agitation. *First, he's late, and now he's in an all-fired hurry.* "Can you be a dirty girl?"

"Mmmhmm."

Josh opened his mouth over the bite mark he'd left on her neck earlier in the dungeon and sucked hard, matching the rhythm of her hot mouth on his fingers as he branded her with his mark. He'd give her a few more before the night was through.

When she stopped fighting the pain—and his Dominance—and merely trembled, he eased the pressure, brushed his lips over the bruised skin, and ran the flat of his tongue up her neck to just below her ear. "Cherry?"

"Hmm?"

"If you do all that I ask, all that Buck asks, I promise to give you what you crave."

Her hips undulated, and she pushed back against him.

With a chuckle, he removed his fingers from her

mouth and nipped at the tender flesh below her ear. "You don't have to remind me, brat. I know what you need."

Rising, Josh adjusted his cock and, feeling her gaze follow him, returned to stand beside the chair that would give him the perfect view. He crossed his arms over his chest and jutted his chin at Buck.

Cherry tossed her hair over her shoulders and gave her attention to the man in front of her—or rather his dick. Her tongue sliced over her lips, wetting them, and Josh's cock once again strained into the denim holding it prisoner.

Dick in hand, Buck scooted closer to the edge of the bed, and Cherry bent forward. Her tongue snuck between her lips to capture a bead of pearly fluid at the tip of his cock. He gathered her hair on top of her head so that he and Josh could watch her take him into her mouth.

Josh groaned. "Fuck, yeah, just like that. Take it all."

She obeyed the command, sliding down the shaft, making Buck's dick disappear before gliding back up. Down again, she took him deeper, her gaze seeking Josh's as if needing his approval.

He gave it to her as he ground the heel of his hand along the length of his cock. Her eyes heated, prompting him to unzip his jeans and shove them down, along with his boxers. His dick sprang forward and into his palm. He slid his thumb over the tip, spreading pre-cum around the ridge.

She shuddered and sucked harder, hollowing her cheeks on Buck's cock.

"Fucking hot," Josh said, slumping into the chair

without missing a stroke.

Buck's grip on Cherry's hair forced her attention back to him and the task at hand. She sure as fuck knew what she was doing as she regulated her breathing in unison with the upstroke, holding it when Buck blocked her airway on the down.

"Oh yeah, that's good." Buck sounded as if he'd eaten gravel. "Do that again, luv."

Over and over, she sucked him deep. Saliva dripped from her chin. Her eyes watered, and every three or four strokes, she glanced at Josh to…

What? Make sure I'm watching, that she's pleasing me? Or fucking tying me up in knots while I wait for my turn?

She angled her head, and Buck slid down her throat again. This time the muscles in her neck relaxed as she held him there and swallowed. Tears trailed down her cheeks in rivers of mascara.

Buck's nostrils flared with every heaving gulp of air. He was close.

Josh squeezed the head of his cock, imagining her throat tightening around it.

With a guttural growl, Buck shoved her off his dick and stood over her. She stared up at him, her eyes flashing triumph, her hair like black ink spilling down her back as she thrust out her tits.

Mesmerized, Josh held his breath, ready for Buck to shoot his load. He'd have rather watched her swallow Buck's cum, but this was a hot break in the fucking routine Josh'd grown bored with—a blow job each, then fucking their sub, either together or one at a time.

Buck swooped her off the floor and placed her on the end of the bed, facing the headboard. He smacked her ass then smoothed a path to the pale flesh between her shoulders and forced her face into silk sheets. He wasn't just breaking routine; he'd blown it all to hell.

What the fuck?

Josh sat forward, white knuckling the armrests, not liking where things were headed. With any other sub, he wouldn't care that Buck was taking control of the scene. Josh had never considered himself a true Dominant.

But jealousy churned in his gut as he took in Cherry's pale body, bent over, ass in the air, hands behind her back. Her breath rushed in and out, shallow but even. Her eyes were closed, her red lips swollen and parted. Fucking beautiful…and *his*.

With a growl, Josh launched out of the chair.

Sensing his movement, Buck's gaze slid toward him. His hand stilled, and he offered an apologetic smile before lifting a brow in question.

Get the fuck out.

That was what Josh wanted to say. Buck acted like he had somewhere else to be anyway, but…

Josh looked at Cherry. Hair a mess, cheeks flushed under smudged mascara, and…*fuck*. Those silver eyes were now open and assessing, waiting for him to make a god damn decision.

She wants this. Signed up for it. She's primed for fucking.

Resigned to wait a little longer, he gave the go-ahead nod.

"Do. Not. Fucking. Come," he grumbled at her. If he allowed her to come at all tonight, *he* would be the one so deep inside her she'd taste his fucking cum.

Buck rolled on a condom and lined up with her

entrance. The head of his cock squeezed into her pussy.

"So bloody tight." Buck grabbed onto the harness's handles and slowly pulled her toward him as he eased his hips forward.

"*Fuck*." Josh envied every inch that disappeared into her glistening, pink cunt.

"Can't... Fuck it!" Buck withdrew and slammed into her.

A garbled cry wrenched Josh's focus back to Cherry's face. Her body rocked forward and back with the driving force of Buck's thrusts, but she continued to watch Josh, luring him closer.

At the edge of the bed, he palmed his dick and caught Buck's rhythm. "Do you know how fucking turned on I am right now? How good your pussy looks stretched around his cock?"

She snagged her bottom lip between her teeth.

"Jesus, she just squeezed the fuck out of my dick." Buck pistoned faster.

"She likes dirty talk." Josh squatted next to the bed and brushed sweat-dampened hair from her face. "And you like Buck cramming you full of his cock, don't you?"

She bit down harder, her lip turning white around her teeth. Any harder, and she'd draw blood.

"No, brat." He dragged her lip free with his thumb. "Save that for me."

"Save...what?" she asked around Buck's hammering thrusts, a guarded uncertainty creasing her perfectly arched brow.

He leaned in to lick the indentions she'd left on her mouth. "Your bite. Your fight. Your cum. Everything you—"

"*Fuck.*" Buck buried himself deep, his spine stiffening, the roar of his release echoing around them.

What the fuck? He's done? Already?

Something was definitely off. Buck normally took his time.

Not that Josh gave a good god damn, right now. The only thing he could think about was Cherry—tasting her, hearing her scream as she came in his mouth, and feeling her cunt fist his dick.

The second Buck slumped over her, Josh stood. "Sharpen your claws, wildcat. It's my turn."

****

Harper released a long breath of relief as Buck pulled out and moved aside to dispose of the condom. He'd fucked her good and hard, and she'd been on the verge of orgasm, every naughty word from Roan pushing her closer. Only the need to please Roan, to wait for his permission kept her from coming all over Buck's thick cock.

For some reason, the need to please Roan scared her more than her overwhelming attraction to him. He wasn't like the other men in her life, certainly not like any Alphahole Dom she'd played with, but his ability to read her sexual cues and his willingness to fulfill them added to his appeal.

No, no, fuck, no. A relationship—even here at the club—was out of the question, and whatever this connection was between them seemed to be heading in that direction.

I can't fucking do this. Not again.

Her safeword rose in her throat, ready to spew, yet as Roan took Buck's place behind her, she bit down on her lip and braced for penetration. She wanted that monster dick of his. Besides, she might be all wrong about him. He might be full of shit when it came down to understanding her kink for rough sex.

He ran a hand over her ass, and his fingers teased their way along the underside of one cheek. His lips trailed his touch. His teeth sank into one fleshy globe.

"*Motherfucker!*" She hunched forward to escape Roan's sharp bite and the pain that speared through her glutes. Icy-hot pleasure rode the wave of pain and crashed into her pussy. "Oh god." The flat of his tongue lapped across the bite as two fingers sank deep into her cunt. She jerked, then shoved against his fingers, her inner walls clamping tight. "More."

"Uh-uh-uh." He withdrew his fingers and nipped at her ass again. "Mmm, finger-licking good." He made a smacking sound. "Bet it's better from the source."

Harper moaned, and her pussy clenched in anticipation of him finding out.

He chuckled. "Don't worry, brat. I'm really hungry, and I'm going to drink every drop when I eat your greedy little pussy."

A droning buzz pulled her attention to the other side of the bed, but the device in Buck's hand wasn't a vibrator. He raised his phone to his ear and paced out of her line of sight. "Yeah?"

Are you fucking kidding me? A phone?

"What the hell, man?" Roan voiced her complaint aloud as he removed the ankle cuffs and spreader bar, then unbuckled the wrist cuffs.

She hissed as her arms fell to the bed, but whatever stiffness she felt didn't stop her from pushing onto her elbows.

"Take it slow," Roan said.

Taming the Wildcat

She rolled her shoulders. "I like the pain, remember?"

"Sorry, mate, but I have to go." Buck appeared beside her, buttoning his shirt. "I apologize for being a distracted wanker tonight, Cherry, but an emergency calls."

What was he? A doctor? Maybe on call? That would explain why he was allowed to have a phone in the rooms.

"Perhaps I can make it up to you later in the week." Buck glanced at Roan as he tucked his shirt into his slacks. "Or maybe not."

A second later, the door slammed behind him.

"Does he do that often?" she asked. When Roan didn't answer, she twisted a look at him. A frown marred the beautiful angles of his face. Shit. With his partner bailing, did he not want to finish? "Does this mean we're done?"

"Do you want to be done?" His brows dove deeper. "You're here for a threesome."

"So are you." She held her breath, hoping he'd want to stay with her and more than a little pissed that his response meant so much when only moments ago she'd thought about ending it. But he'd promised to fuck her until she forgot her name.

Knowing she was going to regret it, she said, "If you're okay with only me, I'd like you to keep your word and fuck me into amnesia."

His forehead smoothed as his sexy grin slipped into place. "I'd like nothing more, but first—"

He grabbed her ankles, startling a yelp from her as he flipped her onto her back and dragged her toward the end of the bed.

Oh, hell yeah!

Then he was kneeling with her legs draped over his shoulders. Palming her ass, he lifted her toward his face, closed his eyes, and inhaled a long breath. "You smell as good as you taste."

Lust spiked her blood, making her dizzy. She wiggled closer. "I thought you said you were hungry."

Stormy blue eyes met hers. "Starving."

Harper flung her arms wide to the bed. "Then why the fuck are you wasting time talking."

"I'm waiting on you, brat."

"I'm right here."

"Mmm, I see." His tongue swept across his lips, then he inclined his chin toward her outstretched hands. "If I'm taking you for a ride, you need a better grip."

Oh my god, yes.

Harper drove her fingers into his soft sun-streaked hair, savoring the satiny texture as they curled into fists and gave a slight tug toward her center.

"That's a good girl." He didn't resist, letting her guide him where she desperately needed him. He lapped at her opening, gathering juices, eating her as if he was—

"*Fuck.*" She jerked against his tongue as it swept upward through her folds. "Starving."

Roan grunted and sucked at her clit.

Fire streaked down her thighs. The drumming of her heart pounded in her ears.

"Roan?" It was the closest she'd come to begging.

Two fingers glided into her wet passage, the tips finding her G-spot, then retreating as his talented mouth left her.

"No," she whined.

"How bad do you want to come?" he muttered, his lips grazing her clit.

A shiver dotted her skin with goosebumps. "So fucking bad."

His fingers eased back in, filling her, stretching.

Harper moaned and gave his hair another yank.

"I like it. I like winding you up." He nibbled at her folds, then sucked the spot he'd bitten. "Not the pain, but the wild, almost feral resistance to submission that drives you. Your need to make me work for it."

Roan had known her for only a couple of hours, yet he understood her better than she understood herself. He actually fucking got her. But she'd have to figure out what that meant later because, right now, she teetered on a cliff, so close to that sweet cavern of bliss.

Digging her heels into his back, she arched off the bed and tried to force an angle that would catapult her over. "Work…harder."

"I'd demand you to say please, but your body already has." He grunted. "*Besides,* I can't wait to watch you fall."

His tongue and his fingers found their targets at the same time, then again and again.

"Yes…yes…" The coiling heat erupted from her center, and the world around her closed in until only the pleasure and the man giving it to her mattered. Every nerve ending sparked. Her muscles convulsed as a river of hot lava raged through her. "*Roan!*"

He didn't stop until the last aftershock ended and her body melted into the bed. Only her chest rose and fell, her lungs screaming for oxygen.

"Beautiful." Roan gently pried her fingers from his hair and took one last lick. "Fucking beautiful."

In the next instant, his hands claimed her waist, and she flew as he tossed her higher on the bed. He crawled over her, trailing open-mouthed kisses on her knees and the inside of her thighs. He stopped to nip at her mound before continuing across her abs.

Harper reached for his head to push him down on her clit again, but he caught her wrists and continued his climb. She tried to dodge his tongue when he reached her ribs, but he was determined, and she couldn't hold back a laugh.

She shook her head. "Not an erogenous zone."

Poised for another lick, he glanced up at her from beneath dark golden lashes, that damn grin sliding across his face. "I like that."

"What?"

"Your laugh." Keeping his eyes locked on hers, he lowered his mouth again.

"Don't you d—"

His tongue swept her ribs, then teeth grazed the skin. Her body jolted, and a squeal of laughter escaped. He closed his mouth over her skin again and sucked lightly, then harder.

Her laughter faded into a moan as the tickling sensation gave way to the invisible threads linked to her cunt. He repeated the action on the underside of one breast, then the other. She squirmed to get his mouth on her nipple, but he bypassed it and kept moving up licking, biting, and sucking, reigniting the insatiable ache in her pussy.

Motherfucker.

His mouth hovered over hers, and his cock nudged at her opening. He laced their fingers beside her head. "I want your pussy squeezing my cock when I make you come again."

Desperate for relief, Harper craned her head to whisper against his lips, "Any time you're ready, cowboy."

His mouth slanted over hers, his tongue demanding entrance. She welcomed the penetration, though she ached for it elsewhere, and tasted herself as she sparred with him. Circling her hips, she tried to impale herself on his dick.

A hand flattened on her hip, pinning her down. Hadn't he just said he wanted to be inside her? Why was he holding her back?

What is he fucking waiting for?

Oh shit, he was waiting for her. Roan was giving her what she needed, just like he'd said he would. Something—or someone—to fight against.

One foot braced on the mattress, she thrust her hip against his hand, her palm against his shoulder, little good that it did. Adrenaline fired her blood at the resistance, and with a growl, she shoved again, using the force of her weight to roll him to his back. He carried her with him, his hands settling on her waist.

Pushing off his chest, she sat up to straddle him.

"Fuck, yeah. Ride me, wildcat," he said, positioning her over his cock.

When he'd stood beside her, pumping that monster cock, it had been bare. When had he put on a condom? The thought was fleeting as he slowly lowered her, and the broad head of stretched her opening.

Resting her hands on his chest, she shuddered as she adjusted to his thickness then bounced to take more. His fingers dug into her flesh, keeping her progression to one leisurely inch at a time. Sweat dotted his brow.

The ripple of muscle under her fingers hinted at the strain on his control.

Harper admired the strength it took to maintain it. Cherry wanted to fucking break it.

"Easy," he rasped.

"No…not easy," she said around heaving breaths. "I want…every fucking inch. Hard. Fast. Now." She raked her barely there nails across his pecs. "Hard."

His body jerked, cramming her full of his cock, the crown bumping her cervix. A jolt of pleasure/pain rippled through her. Her inner walls contracted.

He grunted. His jaw ticked.

"Move, damn it." She dug in her nails.

Air hissed between his teeth as he recaptured both her wrists. Blue eyes narrowed on hers then fell to the marks on his chest. The quirk of his lips belied the growl that slipped past them. "The wildcat has claws after all."

Never one to pass up an opportunity to gain the advantage, she rocked back and shivered as the crown of his cock bumped her cervix again. Tilting forward, she angled her clit against his pubic bone. She closed her eyes as delicious tingles swirled in her core. "Yes."

"That's it," Roan murmured, his deep voice a caress.

He placed her hands on his chest again as if she hadn't just left her mark there, as if to say he trusted her not to leave more. Or maybe he was just offering her leverage.

He grabbed her ass, encouraging her to move. "Take what you need."

She rose on her knees, then slid down his cock, savoring the friction, the fullness, the nudge at her G-spot, the grind against her clit. Picking up speed to match the building pressure, she rode him harder, faster.

Almost there…

****

Cherry's nails stabbed into his flesh, but Josh didn't care. The pleasure washing over her as she came was worth every second of pain. Head thrown back, black hair mussed, flushed cheeks, smudged mascara surrounding eyes scrunched tight, red lips slack, those little mewling noises that crawled right into his balls. Her full creamy tits jiggled with every bounce on his dick, and that tight little cunt clutched him like a wet, velvety glove…

Reining in his need to come with her, he continued to thrust through her orgasm. He wouldn't last much longer, but he didn't want to come until he gave her one more.

When the spasms wracking her body ebbed and she went limp, he sat up, crushing her against him, then relaxed his hold so that she could catch her breath. He peeled a shank of damp hair from her cheek.

So wild. So fucking beautiful. Like a dark angel falling from heaven.

He groaned. What the hell? When had he become a poet?

Her head lolled back, and a breathy sigh drew his attention to her red lips, swollen from his kisses and dry from her rapid breaths. He traced her bottom lip with his thumb, then with his tongue.

Her pussy contracted around his dick, making him chuckle and grind his teeth.

"Greedy little wildcat." Josh drew back to fan his

fingers around the column of her slender neck. The bones beneath his touch were small, delicate, like the rest of her, yet there was a strength about her, both physical and mental, that once again made him wonder who she was outside the walls of The Arena. "Don't worry. I'm not done with you yet."

Her pulse fluttered like the wings of a hummingbird. The bruise of his bite stood out against her porcelain flesh. His cock twitched and his fingers flexed around her throat as the same overwhelming drive to possess her, to mark her again, spiked his blood.

With little effort and no resistance from Cherry, he rolled her onto her back, her body soft, her will yielding to his. Her whimper seeped into his chest as her arms circled his neck. He tensed in anticipation of more hair pulling, but her fingers explored his back and shoulders, and her thighs splayed wide to make room for his hips, welcoming his dominance.

He centered his weight on his elbows and knees and lowered his lips to hers. She opened for him, her tongue sparring with his. Need flared hotter. He had to move.

He'd meant to go slow, to give her time to reach another high before he pushed her over the edge, and to enjoy the ride, but after the first long slid out, with the walls of her pussy tightening around him like a satin vise, he was lost.

His dick took over where his brain failed. Every stroke demanded another. Nothing else mattered. He needed to come, but he didn't want the pleasure to end.

Don't. Come. Don't. Come. He repeated the mantra over and over, trying to stave off the tingle in his spine as he hammered into her. Sweat beaded his brow and upper lip and forged a trail down his back. His muscles burned. The next brutal thrust drove her up the bed.

Growling, he gripped her shoulder with one hand, her ass with the other, to pin her down.

"Yes," she hissed into his mouth.

Josh lifted his head and gulped for air. *Don't. Come.* "Not yet."

Her broken cry floated around him like a beautiful melody as she arched into her climax, her pussy contracting in unrelenting spasms, as if trying to milk him into release.

Don't. Come.

Her short fingernails cut into his shoulders.

"*Fuck,*" he roared, his back bowed into the pain. Heat raged through his body. His dick swelled. One more driving plunge into her hot depths, and he careened head over ass into an orgasm. Cum spewed from his balls and erupted from his shaft, filling the condom until there was nothing more to give.

Their breathing evened, and his muscles loosened, crushing her into the mattress, but he couldn't move. Didn't want to. Didn't want to lose the connection with her.

Jesus, what the hell was wrong with him? And why was he still so fucking hard?

Reluctantly, Josh eased to one side and collapsed on the bed beside her. He'd take care of the condom when his mind stopped spiraling.

He'd fucked a lot of women and never felt like this. Why was this one any different? But then he'd felt something different about her from the moment he saw her. He was pretty sure she felt it, too.

He glanced at her from the corner of his eyes. She was staring at the ceiling.

"You okay?" he asked. When she didn't answer, he turned on his side. "Cherry?"

"Who's Cherry?" she asked, her lips, more bruised than before, curling into a smile that didn't reach her eyes.

For a second, he didn't understand her question, and then he remembered his promise to fuck her until she forgot her name. He grinned as he removed the condom and tossed it in the waste basket on the other side of the nightstand.

Head in his hand, he propped on one elbow and trailed a finger over her nipple. "Give me a few minutes—" He laved the taut bud. He hadn't paid homage to these beauties yet. "—and I'll make you forget everything else."

"I don't doubt it." She sighed as he took her into his mouth and sucked. Her small fingers wove into his hair, lightly holding him to her for a moment before her hand fell back to the sheet. "But I have to go."

His hand stilled on its path over her abs. "We have the room all night."

"But you don't have me." Gray eyes connected with his. "I start a new job Monday, and I have a lot to do befo—" Her brows dove into a frown. "Fucking hell, why am I telling you all this?"

"Because I'm irresistible?"

She snorted.

Tugging her closer, he loomed over her and nipped at the generous swell of her tit. "A good fuck?"

She shrugged. "Meh."

He lifted a brow. "What's your name again?"

She laughed. "Okay, I'll give you that one, but I really have to go."

Cherry slid out from under his arm and out of bed. Josh watched her tiptoe around the bed to where Buck had hung her clothes. The hickey under her breast sent his fingers over his chest. The rise of welts and the breaks in the skin made his dick jump. She'd marked him, too. He wanted more.

But he shook his head, resigned. *Not gonna happen.*

He needed to get back to the ranch anyway. Cherry had done exactly what he'd hoped she would. She'd made him forget the ranch, the threat of rustlers—he smiled—his name.

Rising, he joined her and grabbed his jeans off the floor.

Her gaze slid in his direction then away. "You don't have to leave on my account."

He shoved one leg into his jeans, then the other. "I'd rather sleep in my own bed."

The zipper of her skirt whirred, and he had his T-shirt halfway over his head when she said, "I'm sure there are other subs whose memories you can erase."

Was she kidding? Sure didn't sound like it. He stuffed his head through the hole to look at her. Her expression, though a bit strained, was void of humor. Was she jealous? Or indifferent? Or cutting him loose?

Josh jammed his arms into the shirt and yanked it down his torso. He grabbed her upper arms and gently pulled her close. Her face was blank, her emotions shuttered, but she didn't shy from looking directly at him.

"You've got me all wrong." Though did she really?

In his rodeo days and the not so recent past, he'd rotated buckle bunnies in and out of his bed, sometimes three or four in one afternoon.

But he'd changed over the last six months, and he had a feeling Cherry could change him forever. Did he want her to? Maybe. Whatever the fuck he was feeling, he liked it. But did she?

"I want to see you again, if not tomorrow night, since you have stuff to do, then another night." He thumbed the corner of her mouth. "The question is, my little wildcat, do you want to play with *me*? No Buck. No other Dom. Just me?"

Chapter Four

Cum spurted across Josh's belly as hard jolts of fiery pleasure coursed through him in waves. Images of Cherry on her knees and sucking his cock encouraged his hand to squeeze tighter, to pump faster, until he lay spent, his breath ragged, his body damp with sweat, regardless of the early morning chill.

The sun crept over the trees, filtering into his bedroom. He should have been up and out to check on Star again, but he couldn't get Cherry out of his head. No matter how many times he tried to exorcise the memory of her soft, milky-white skin against his and those gray eyes that sparked with a challenge.

He ran his fingertips over the crescent-shaped cuts on his chest and smiled. "Little wildcat."

She'd been on her knees for Buck the night before last. *Tonight, you'll be on your knees for me.*

His dick hardened, but he sat up and swung his legs over the side of the bed. He didn't have time to take care of it, and his hand was a poor substitute for Cherry's pussy.

Fifteen minutes later, he stood inside Star's stall, staring at the fresh pile of healthy manure and smiling like an idiot. An exhausted idiot.

He never thought he'd be happy to be mucking horse shit, but Star was the first mare in what he hoped would become a horse farm, and she'd come down with colic. The vet had been out yesterday, and they'd been treating her with fluids to break up the impaction. By late evening, she seemed to be feeling better, but the vet suggested checking on her every other hour for bowel movements.

"Hey, girl. Looks like you're on the mend." Josh ran his hand along her rounded belly. She wasn't due to deliver until May, but he couldn't afford to have anything go wrong. "You keep this up, and maybe Cal can get you some breakfast. Would you like that?"

The horse whinnied.

"How about a nice mash?" Josh dug his phone from his back pocket to check the time. "He should have been here by now."

His phone buzzed in his hand. Rusty Harris appeared on the screen. He was going to have to give him—Cal and Mark, too—a big raise. With Josh watching Star all night, Rusty and Mark had been out riding herd on their own.

"Yeah?" Josh answered, closing the stall door behind him.

"You need to get over to the south pasture." Rusty's usual brisk tone sounded rougher than Josh had heard it in a while. "The corner along the county road."

Josh shrugged into his coat as he stepped into the cold morning air. "What's up?"

"Rustlers."

The word was a fist to the gut, stopping him just outside the barn. "You sure?"

"I'm sure."

Josh hung up and broke into a sprint, ignoring the twinge in the leg he'd broken almost a year ago. He climbed into his truck and peeled out of the drive. God dammit, he should have hired more hands, been out there with them last night, something.

He and Rusty had moved as many of the cattle as possible to the south pasture, but there wasn't enough grass to sustain the whole herd. They'd both thought that, if they were going to get hit, the north pasture was the most likely target because it was off a main highway.

They'd been wrong.

"Son of a bitch." Josh banged a hand on the steering wheel.

Fifteen minutes later, he pulled onto the shoulder behind Cal Jessup's truck. Cal stood with Rusty on the other side of the fence next to Rusty's horse, Calico.

As soon as Josh killed the engine, he was out of the truck and striding toward the downed fence. "What d'ya got."

"I was on my way in," Cal said, "and found a half dozen cows wandering on the road. I was surprised when I saw our tag on 'em and then the cut in the fence." He pointed to the herd in the distance and held up the barbed wire with a clean cut. "I got 'em back in and called Rusty."

"Where's Mark?" Josh asked.

"I sent him back to the bunkhouse to get some sleep," Rusty said around a chaw of tobacco.

Josh nodded. "Cal, you head on in. Star needs looking after. Give her some mash."

"Will do." Cal dug in his pocket, pulled out his keys, and held them out to Rusty. "Take my truck. I'll ride Calico back in and give him a good rubdown. He deserves it after working hard all night."

"Thanks." *Definitely raises all around.* Turning to

Rusty, Josh said, "What are you thinking?"

"Here." Rusty aimed a gnarled finger at the trail where the tall grass was bent. "Looks like a small trailer, maybe a twenty-footer."

Josh scrubbed the back of his neck. "How many?"

"Near as I can count, only about ten."

"Ten?" That didn't make any sense. Why risk getting caught for so little? "Why would they come all the way out here for ten head? Unless the highway is too visible."

"Maybe something spooked 'em." Rusty jerked his chin at the Mill's place. "It's possible Walter saw something. Or maybe Reed. Want me to ask?"

Josh looked toward the red brick ranch house at the top of the next rise and shook his head. "Leave it for the sheriff."

Reed Mills would have called him if he'd seen anything. They'd been friends since kindergarten. But his grandfather would have helped the thieves load McNamara cattle and shown them where to find more. The old man was bitter and bat-shit crazy. Josh didn't want Rusty on the wrong side of a shotgun if Walter caught him on his land.

"I'll call the sheriff's office. They can send someone to talk to him or Reed." Stalking back to his truck, his blood rising, Josh added, "In fact, I'll go talk to Jenkins myself."

"Jenkins ain't the sheriff no more," Rusty hollered. "He retired, and they appointed an interim…"

Josh didn't hear the rest as he slammed the door and started the engine. Jenkins had grown lazy the last few years. Maybe the new sheriff would get off his ass and do his fucking job.

His phone pinged on the console. Wrangler's name popped up in the notification bubble.

Dread sat like a cannonball in Josh's gut. There was only one reason the DM at The Arena would be texting him.

Fuck me, could this day get any worse?

He mashed the button in the steering wheel to listen to the message.

Wrangler: Cherry cancelled. Is there another sub you want to play with?

****

Harper sat in the lumpy black leather chair behind a massive 1970's metal desk that took up most of the small office she now called hers. Beige brick walls, bare except for aerial maps of Stone County and the state of Texas, closed in around her. Bent and beat-up aluminum blinds covered a large window with a view of the outer office and the open door with gold letters that still read Sheriff Tom Jenkins.

Heat blasted from the vent overhead. Fuck, the whole state was under a winter advisory, but she was being roasted alive.

Sweat beading her forehead and between her breasts, Harper tugged at the collar of the turtleneck under her brown uniform shirt. She hadn't chosen the high-necked shirt because of the weather but rather to conceal the massive hickey Roan had gifted her two nights ago.

Despite the heat, she shivered as memories of the wicked things he'd done to her seeped unwarranted past barriers she'd erected to protect herself.

What the hell was I thinking?

She hadn't been thinking. That was the problem.

When he'd asked her if she wanted to see him again at the club, her brain had screamed *"Fuck no!"* but her body had melted against his hard, warm body as his mouth teased her jaw and her neck, and she'd caved, promising to meet him tonight.

But now…

She didn't have time for distractions, even delicious ones like Roan. And it wasn't just the deliciousness. His ability to read her wants and needs beyond the physical scared the fuck out of her. He was fucking relationship material, and that was not in her plans.

Taking out her phone, she looked at the message she'd sent to Wrangler after a sleepless night.

Harper: Can't make it tonight? Please offer my apologies to Roan.

Wrangler: I'll take care of it.

Her thumbs hovered over the screen as regret shuddered through her. She couldn't ignore the tingle peaking her nipples and the liquid fire dampening her panties. There was a chance it wasn't too late, that Wrangler hadn't acted on her text. What would it hurt to retract her lie?

She closed her eyes and felt again the warmth of Roan's hands when he'd walked behind her through The Arena. The way he'd tucked her close, guiding her through the crowd, then nuzzled her ear, insisting on walking her to her car.

"It's dark out there. You shouldn't walk alone."

She'd almost laughed, but telling him she'd been trained in self-defense and took down bigger guys than him on a daily basis would lead to more questions she wasn't prepared to answer. Still, she had to admit, begrudgingly, that she'd liked the illusion of his protection. The way he'd drawn her against his side, bearing the brunt of the icy wind with no coat while she'd been bundled up in hers.

And how he'd taken her keys to unlock her car and used the cold as an excuse to weave his arms inside her coat, press her against the car, and kiss her stupid one more time before she climbed behind the wheel.

God, the man could kiss…and fuck like a beast.

And he gets you like no one ever has.

But then, he'd smiled that sexy grin, waggled his talented fingers at her, and trotted off across the lot to a black four-door pickup, his license plate shining in the streetlamp. The numbers and letters had automatically logged into her memory before panic sliced through her like a knife through butter. If he wanted to find her, all he had to do was run her plates. Fresh perspiration beaded her upper lip just thinking about it.

With a groan, she laid her phone aside and reached for the four messages stuck in a neat row to one side of her desk. The hen-scratch on the notes was illegible and did nothing to steer her thoughts from Roan.

Was that truly what her triggers boiled down to? Someone who liked to play a little rough? Someone to give her just enough freedom while maintaining control? Was all the exploration of BDSM for nothing?

I never needed all the whips and chains and extra dicks? Just one man to spank me, hold me down, and tell me I'm pretty?

"Fuck." The rollers on the chair squealed as she pushed away from the desk and to her feet. Pausing in the doorway, she blotted sweat from her forehead with the sleeve of her shirt and assessed the outer office.

Two desks belonging to the night deputies, Keith Dollins and Dylan Ackerman, sat back-to-back. A larger desk, she'd learned when she arrived, was normally manned by Chief Deputy Sheriff Curtis Mealer, but his chair was vacant. Off to the right was a single jail cell, empty at the moment except for a wall of boxes, and separating the office from the waiting area was a counter and a rail with a swinging gate. The security around here needed updating.

As she wove through the desks, the tap of her boots on the tile floor had the head of Sheriff's Dispatcher Price swiveling in her direction. The curvy, young—early twenties—blonde greeted her with sparkling blue eyes and a pink-lipped smile. The top three buttons of her uniform were unbuttoned, showing off the generous swell of cleavage behind a white, lace-trimmed cami. "Morning, Sheriff."

Biting her tongue, Harper nodded. There would be time for change and redirection later. Her position as appointed interim sheriff could be temporary. Only the election in May would determine whether she stayed on or had to find another position. She had four months to make a name for herself, one that could rise from the ashes of her mistakes.

For now, she had to get a feel for smalltown life in Stone County. "Price."

"Call me Kelsey," she said. "Can I get you some coffee?"

"No, thanks, and you don't ever have to do that. For me or for them." Harper jerked a thumb over her shoulder toward the desks. "Where's Mealer?"

"He's making the rounds by the school."

Harper frowned and held her ponytail off the back

of her neck. "Right."

He hadn't said anything about an agreement with the school when he'd introduced himself earlier and shown her to her office. Not that he'd said much at all. She wasn't sure if he was naturally quiet or if experience—he was in his mid-forties—kept his mouth shut until he got to know her better. Or did he resent her for taking the position as sheriff?

No, Zeke had told her they'd offered the job to Mealer first, and he'd turned it down.

She sighed inwardly. She wasn't the only one with adjustments to make. Everyone here, the town included, was probably as nervous about her as she was about them.

"I can't read these." Harper handed the blue slips of paper to the girl and plucked at the front of her shirt, peeling it from her damp skin. It wasn't any cooler up front.

Taking the messages, Kelsey's smile faltered. "That's not my real handwriting, I swear." She laughed, sounding a bit uneasy. "Sheriff J used to fuss at me because I never got all the information, but people talk fast when they're scared or stressed. I came up with my own shorthand. I just forgot to transcribe these for you."

"I see," Harper said, impressed by the girl's initiative and ingenuity. "How long have you been here?"

"Ten years."

No way was this girl twenty-eight. She couldn't be more than twenty-two or twenty-three.

Kelsey laughed again, her eyes dancing with mischief. "My aunt worked dispatch for over thirty years, and I hung out here after school until my mom got off work at the bank. Aunt Kay gave me stuff to do after I finished my homework—filing, running errands, stuff like that. Later, when I needed a job, Sheriff J paid me to help answer the phone, type up warrants, and eventually, help with dispatch. Aunt Kay retired when I graduated high school three years ago, and he offered me the gig. Said I was already trained. So, really only three years full-time."

Harper wasn't sure if Aunt Kay or Sheriff Jenkins was the mastermind behind the plan for Kelsey to fill the position or if they'd just lucked into her. But three years, fresh out of high school… The girl was younger than she thought, and her enthusiasm made Harper feel old.

Maybe because in the eight years separating them, every fucking rung on the ladder Harper had managed to climb was hard fought, and she'd seen some categorically horrific things along the way. She was cynical and jaded and…fucking burning up.

She ran her finger around her collar for the hundredth time. "Do you know where the thermostat is? It's like a sauna in here."

"As a matter of fact…" Kelsey practically skipped across the room, reached under a shelf lined with binders, and indicated the thermostat. "That was Sheriff J's number one rule. No one touched the gauge but him. The man's skin is paper-thin. He was cold all the time." She laughed again. "We learned to wear lighter clothing."

Hopefully, that explained the amount of cleavage on display, and she wouldn't have to talk to Kelsey. As a woman, it was difficult enough working in a "man's" field without adding a sexual element. They would never take Kelsey seriously. But then maybe she was happy with her position and wasn't looking for advancement.

The phone rang as Harper headed back to her office and unloaded the few things she'd brought from the cozy little craftsman she'd rented on the outskirts of town. A new nameplate that read Sheriff Harper Quinn, a half dozen books pertaining to law enforcement, and a lucky rabbit's foot. The nameplate was from her youngest brother, the only one who didn't condemn her for exchanging her blues for browns.

The good luck charm was a gift from her first partner, a man who sounded a lot like Sheriff J and Aunt Kay rolled into one. He'd been resistant, at first, to having a female partner, but before she'd moved up the ranks with his encouragement, Zeke Haley had become a mentor and more of a father than her own dad. In fact, Zeke was the one who'd recommended her for this job. He was an old college buddy of the mayor's father.

Kelsey tapped on the glass of her door. "Here you go."

Harper tossed the rabbit's foot in the top drawer of her desk and rested a hip on the edge. Taking the messages from Kelsey, she glanced at the transcribed and neatly written messages, times and dates included, once more impressed.

"Thanks." Noticing the one on top was from the mayor, she added, "Can you call the mayor's office and make an appointment for me to meet with him this afternoon?"

The mayor's office, as well as the judge's and

district attorney's, were in the courthouse across the street. She needed to make herself known and thank the mayor for what she considered a favor to Zeke.

"Sure." Kelsey bobbed her head.

"And what's this one about? Mrs. Butts? Someone is leaving their cigarette butts in her yard?"

"Not cigarette butts." The girl grimaced. "At least once a week, someone rings her doorbell and leaves a picture of a butt, as in buttocks, on her porch." She shrugged. "It's been going on for as long as I can remember. We've told her to get a doorbell with a camera, so we'll have a video of the pranksters, but she thinks the doorbell will read her mind."

Harper fanned her face with the note, which offered little help. "Seriously?"

"And that leads to her next complaint and message number two." Kelsey ticked off a second finger. "She's convinced aliens are using mind control on her dog because it barks at her when she watches TV. It probably just needs to take a dump. Dylan told her to tie a foil hat on the dog's head."

A flush of pink stained Kelsey's cheeks when she said the deputy's name. She'd have to keep an eye on that.

"And this one?" Harper asked, seeing a third note from Mrs. Butts. "Someone's snooping in her mailbox?" Mail theft was prevalent with the elderly.

Kelsey waved a dismissive hand. "I know what you're thinking, but we've looked into it, and it's just Jody, the mailman, delivering the mail. Honestly, I think Mrs. B is lonely and wants someone to talk to."

"Maybe." She'd have to pay a wellness call to make sure Adult Protective Services didn't need to get

Taming the Wildcat

involved. A lot of elderly were left on their own and didn't know about or resisted the resources available to them.

Harper looked at the last message. Josh McNamara called to report stolen cattle. "Did Mr. McNamara give you any specific details?"

The girl blushed a brighter shade of red. "No, just that he's on his way in." She fanned herself. "As if it isn't hot enough in here already. That man'll burn the building to the ground. He's hot as fuck."

Harper smiled at the girl's exaggeration, then checked herself. No need to encourage her. One cute deputy was enough of a distraction. "When Mealer gets back, tell him to come see me, and can you get me the shift reports from the past week?"

"Sure."

Once more alone, Harper flopped into the squeaky chair—soon headed for the dumpster—plunked her elbows on the desk and buried her face in her hands.

What the hell have I gotten myself into? A skeleton crew, alien mind control, and a bunch of asses.

"Here are the files," Kelsey announced, startling her.

Harper lifted her head as two manilla folders landed in front of her. "That's everything from the last week?"

Kelsey nodded and opened her mouth to say more, but the phone rang, and she hurried back to her desk to answer it.

The first file included a one-line incident report regarding a routine traffic stop for speeding—a non-resident of the county passing through Stone Creek. The second was a minor vehicle vs. deer accident. Was this what her life had come to? Twiddling her thumbs all day waiting for someone to run a red light in crazy town?

"Sheriff?" Kelsey said from her door. "Wendy Johnson called to report a commotion going on next door. Leon Hargrove is drunk, beating on his front door, and screaming at the top of his lungs. His wife locked him out again."

"Is this habitual behavior for him?" Harper unlocked the side drawer of her desk, pulled out her Glock, and stood, sliding the weapon into the holster on her hip.

"Nah, it's just... He lost his job a few months ago. He's trying really hard to find something else, but..." Kelsey shrugged. "Anyway, it happened one other time a couple of weeks ago."

"Is he violent?" She grabbed the keys to the sheriff's vehicle and her phone, then draped the brown Sheriff's Department coat in the crook of her elbow. She was still too hot.

"I don't think so. I haven't heard that from the guys."

With Kelsey following, Harper strode through the front office and pushed her way through the swinging gate. "Get Mealer on the radio. Tell him to meet me there." She paused at the front door. "Can you take Mr. McNamara's statement?"

A sly smile lifted Kelsey's lips. She unbuttoned the fourth button of her shirt and spread her lapel wider. "Don't worry. I know how to entertain Josh."

Harper shook her head. She almost felt sorry for Josh McNamara. She'd definitely have a chat with Kelsey about the dress code and, especially, the code of conduct. But it would have to wait. The situation with Leon Hargrove wouldn't.

A wall of cold hit her as she stepped out the door, down the sidewalk to the black SUV marked Stone County Sheriff, and into her comfort zone. Adrenaline surged through her veins. Sitting behind the wheel was better than sitting behind a desk any day, but maybe she'd have the best of both worlds.

Just like you would with Roan if you weren't such a pussy.

Chapter Five

Pulling up to the address Kelsey had provided, Harper put the SUV in park. It smelled of old man cologne and cigarettes, courtesy of the former sheriff. The street was busy, but the house was quiet, no sign of Leon Hargrove. Protocol demanded she wait for Mealer, but Leon could be in the house beating his wife.

Harper waited for traffic to pass before she grabbed her jacket from the passenger seat and stepped out of the vehicle. The front door of the house opened as she rounded the vehicle. A young woman wearing fuzzy purple house shoes and a thick, pink bathrobe ran toward her. Her eyes were rimmed red, and her hair was a tangled mess, but overall, she appeared calm.

After donning her jacket—she'd finally cooled the fuck down—Harper pulled on a department baseball cap and approached the woman on the sidewalk. "Are you okay? Is he in the house?"

"He left," the woman said, her words turning to steam. She gestured down the street in the direction Harper had come from. "Probably down at the park. He goes there when he's stressed." She blew into her cupped hands to warm them. "He didn't have on a coat."

Harper hadn't seen anyone as she'd passed the park. Even if she had, she wouldn't know Hargrove from Adam. "Does that happen often?"

"No, but he deals—dealt—with a lot of pressure with his job. Now, he deals with the pressure of not finding one." She lifted her arms and let them drop against her sides. "He's either overqualified or doesn't have the experience they're looking for. It's hard on a man, not being able to provide, especially when we're barely hanging on to our house. I understand that, I do, but..." Fresh tears welled in her eyes, and she used the cuff of her robe to dab at them. "Drinking isn't going to help."

"What did Mr. Hargrove do for a living?" Harper asked.

"He sold athletic equipment." Her lips wobbled in an attempt to smile. "He played football in college, a linebacker. He was a potential number one draft pick until he blew his ACL."

"And you are?"

"Ashley Hargrove. I'm Leon's wife."

"Can you tell me what happened this morning?"

"He came home drunk. That's what happened. Like he's done the last two weekends." More tears flowed. "I can't deal with it. I don't know where he goes, who he's with, though I don't think he'd cheat on me, but that would be preferable to picturing him dead in a ditch and..."

A sob hitched in Mrs. Hargrove's throat, and Harper gave her a moment to collect herself before she asked, "Has he ever hurt you? Is he violent when he's drunk?"

"No!" she shrieked as her head snapped up. "Leon would never hurt me or anyone else. Ask around, and folks'll tell you. Leon's big and he looks mean, but he's really sweet. A big teddy bear."

"What happened when he got home this morning?" Harper could guess but needed to hear it from Mrs. Hargrove.

"I had the locks changed and his bags on the porch. I…" Another sob.

Harper glanced at the two suitcases by the front door.

"When he couldn't get in, he knocked," Ashley continued. "I told him to find somewhere else to sleep it off and not to come home until he was ready to choose between me and the drink." Her brows dove into a V. "He started beating on the door and hollering how he was sorry, but he's still drunk and I've had it. I love him, but I can't watch him destroy himself like my daddy did."

"Thank you, Mrs. Hargrove." Harper smiled, trying to reassure her. "I'll go down to the park and have a look."

"Please don't hurt him."

"Don't worry." Harper circled the car, knowing her advice would go unheeded. She opened the driver's door, then looked at Ashley Hargrove over the hood. "Do you want me to bring him home?"

The woman shook her head vehemently, broke into tears again, and ran back to the house.

Harper had seen this a thousand times. Homes and families broken by unemployment and alcohol or drug abuse. Only the names and faces changed.

Once she called dispatch to report her relocation to the park, Harper made a U-turn. Traffic was picking up with people trying to get to work or kids to school as she eased into the parking lot. Tall trees and strategically placed foliage blocked her view of most of the area, but what she could see was clean and well-manicured. A far cry from some of the city parks she'd seen.

She pulled up Leon's driver's license photo. His wife wasn't kidding when she said he looked mean. The shaved head and thick downcast eyebrows didn't help. Six feet five inches. Two hundred sixty pounds.

Fuck. She'd been trained to take down assailants his size, and she'd done it before, but it would be easier with help, and she preferred her bruises given with orgasms.

Like the ones Roan gave me Saturday night.

"Ugh." Harper grabbed her radio to ask Kelsey what the hell was taking Mealer so long when Leon stumbled out of the bushes and toward the street.

Jumping out of the car, she called, "Mr. Hargrove."

Either he didn't hear her or chose to ignore her as he wove along the shoulder of the road.

"Leon," she yelled louder and jogged closer, careful not to get within reach.

Swinging around to face her, he teetered to one side, and a black truck swerved to avoid hitting him.

Shit. She couldn't wait for Mealer.

With a quick check behind her for oncoming traffic, Harper crossed into the lane, lunged for his forearm, and yanked him toward the shoulder. He didn't resist, but his boot hung on the curb. He flailed, the force of one meaty arm sending her flying. She landed face down on the soft Bermuda grass instead of the sidewalk and had a nanosecond to be grateful before the bulk of his weight came crashing down on top of her.

Air whooshed from her lungs. Her vision blurred, not that it mattered since she couldn't see fuck with her face buried in dead grass. The sound of boots scraping the sidewalk grew louder. Mealer?

About fucking time.

"Leon, get off her." The gruff voice sounded familiar, but she couldn't see who it belonged to.

Leon shifted, and she was able to turn her head to one side. Brown leather boots that had seen better days stepped out of her line of sight. Not Mealer. His standard issue boots were black...like the truck parked on the side of the road...with plates she'd memorized.

Fuck, fuck, fuck. Roan. He'd found her.

He'd done exactly what she suspected he might. Looked up her plates and hunted her down. Why? One possibility after another darted through her mind like tumbleweed batted by the desert wind. Psycho stalker obsession? Extortion? Complete exposure? Or worse—interest in more than she could give.

"Get...the fuck...off me...you...big ass...motherfucker." She tried to squirm out from under Leon, but he was too heavy.

Great. Now, she looked not only incompetent but weak.

With a boot to the shoulder, Roan pushed Leon off of her and onto his side. Oxygen rushed into her lungs as she struggled to her hands and knees and rested her forehead on the ground, not ready to face Roan or the reasons he was here.

She swiveled her head away from Roan and stared into Leon's confused, bloodshot eyes as he took in her face for a heartbeat, then her badge and, finally, her gun. Her radio had come unclipped and was who knew where.

The big lug shifted his gaze to the man standing behind her, and his face split into a goofy grin that corroborated his wife's description of the teddy bear she loved. "Hey, man, whatcha you doin' here?"

"I'm looking for Sheriff Quinn." Anger tinged the deep voice that stroked her clit and dampened her panties, regardless of the fear gripping her. "Kelsey said I could find him chasing your ass down. Is he here?"

I'm going to fucking kill that girl.

Not only had Kelsey offered up Harper's whereabouts, but she'd broken a half dozen confidentiality laws and recklessly put a civilian in harms' way. Roan could have walked into a dangerous situation looking for her.

Wait. He'd said *him*.

Roan wasn't looking for Harper, the woman, or Cherry from the club. He thought the new sheriff was a man. Why did it make her feel better to know he hadn't tracked her down, that he was looking for the sheriff?

Defeat dragging at her, she closed her eyes. This was not at all how she expected her first day on the job to go. Somehow, she had to get rid of Roan until she could regain control of this shit show and pull herself together.

When she looked at Leon again, his head bobbled as if he couldn't hold it up much longer, and his eyes rolled toward Harper. Even in his drunken haze, Leon had the clarity to poke at the badge on her chest. "Ish yer lucky day, dude. I foun' her for ya."

Fucking hell. Teddy bear or not, Harper wanted to shove her boot in his mouth.

"Her?" Roan's disbelief made her cringe, but then

she hadn't made a good impression and she *was* on all fours with her ass in the air.

A laugh gurgled in her throat, but she choked it back. She'd been in this exact position for him two nights ago. Would he recognize her ass?

Dry brown Bermuda crunched beneath his boots as he stepped in front of her. "*You're* Sheriff Harper Quinn?"

Harper sighed. There was no getting out of this one.

"I am." She pushed up and sat back on her heels. Again, the irony of her current position at Roan's feet wasn't lost on her as she lifted her gaze to gorgeous, blue eyes that flared with recognition.

Shock and confusion were quickly erased with the anger she'd heard earlier in his voice but only for a moment before fine lines crinkled the edges of his eyes, and a slow smile lifted one corner of his mouth.

He stuck out a hand. "Need some help, *Sheriff*?"

"I got it." Gingerly, she struggled to stand. A stab of pain in her hip stole her breath but she ignored it as she straightened. Her pride hurt more than her body.

"Are you okay?" Roan asked, his hand at her elbow. "I know firsthand the damage Leon can do. We played football together in high school."

Cheeks flooding with heat, she shrugged him off and reached behind her back for the handcuffs hooked to her belt. "I'm fine."

"Sher'ff?" Leon lumbered to his knees but swayed as if he might fall again. "Can I go home now?"

Roan steadied Leon until he gained his balance.

"I'm afraid not, Mr. Hargrove." Harper held up the handcuffs.

Leon hung his head and placed his hands behind his back without her asking.

"What are you arresting him for?" Deputy Mealer appeared at her side as she snapped the cuffs around Leon's thick wrists.

Now you show up.

Searching the street, she located Mealer's car behind Roan's truck. "Public intoxication."

Mealer smoothed a hand over his beard. "You sure you wanna do that?"

Teeth clenched, she wanted to ask if he'd questioned Jenkins. From under her lashes, she stole a peek at Roan's pinched brows and wondered if he, too, questioned her decision. Ignoring both men, she guided Leon toward the deputy's cruiser.

The deputy dogged her heals, and she could feel the heat of Roan's presence as he, too, followed.

"This'll be a lot of paperwork when we could just take him home," Mealer persisted in his complaint.

"I'm aware," she snapped. She could tell him Ashley Hargrove didn't want her husband there, but why kick a man while he was down.

Once she had Leon settled into the backseat, he looked up at her with big brown, teddy bear eyes full of remorse. "I'm shorry to be sho mush trouble."

"You'll be fine, Mr. Hargrove." She shut the door and pivoted toward the deputy. Her hip complained, and she bit back a string of curses as she leveled Mealer with her best don't-fuck-with-me glare. "Take Mr. Hargrove in, and I'll deal with him after I talk with Mr.—uh…" She looked at Roan, not really wanting to know his real name.

"Josh McNamara."

Of course.
She sighed inwardly. "Sheriff Harper Quinn."

He held out a hand, his expression void of recognition as if he hadn't had his head between her legs and then fucked her to multiple orgasms two nights ago. "It's nice to meet you, *Sheriff.*"

****

Aware of the deputy watching them, Josh wondered if he noticed Cherry's hesitation as her gaze slid to Josh's extended hand.

No, not Cherry. Harper Quinn. Sheriff Harper Quinn.

She tucked her small hand into his, and a current of lust zinged up his arm. He was already hard, had been since the moment she looked up at him, her mouth even with his crotch, but his cock managed to stretch another inch behind his zipper.

"Mr. McNamara." She shook his hand, her grip firm, and all he could think about was how it or her lips would feel around his dick. "If you'll head back to the station, I'll be happy to talk to you about your missing cattle."

"Stolen," he corrected. "Not missing."

She turned a raised brow back to Mealer.

The deputy looked like he wanted to argue. Instead, he nodded and circled the vehicle.

Tension crackled between them as they waited for Mealer to pull away from the curb. Josh took the time to study her. He couldn't believe he hadn't recognized her right away.

Long black hair hung in a loose ponytail down her back, the tips and a few stray wisps around her face lifting with each gust of the wind. A piece of grass stuck out behind her right ear. Her cheeks were flushed. From the cold or because she felt the same heat of attraction he did?

Unable to stop himself, he cupped her jaw and thumbed away the tiny bead of blood forming at a scratch inching across her pinkened cheekbone.

Her cherry-stained lips softened and parted for a fraction of a second before they thinned again. She batted his hand away, her gaze full of fear and darting around them. Without a word, she struck off down the sidewalk.

"Harper," he called out then stalked after her.

Harper. The name was hard on the tongue, edgy, tough, but it fit her better than her club name. He had guessed she might be in law enforcement. Then he'd thought he lost her. And here she was, sheriff in his hometown. If he hadn't been up all night with a sick horse and hit by cattle thieves, he might consider himself a damn lucky bastard.

She scooped a radio off the ground where she'd fallen, along with a baseball cap that read Stone County Sheriff Department across the front. She shoved the cap on her head as if she donned armor and kept walking toward a Stone County SUV.

"We need to talk," he said, keeping step with her.

She shook her head. "I'm not doing this here."

"Would you rather *do it* at your office?"

"Fuck you." She spun on the balls of her feet to face him, her gray eyes, as dark as a thunder cloud, scrunching into a grimace. Again, her hand pressed to her hip. She drew in a deep breath and exhaled slowly. "Look, I'm not fucking up my first day on the job with personal issues. Come back to the station, and we'll talk about your stolen cattle. That's it. We have nothing else to discuss."

Josh bristled at the dismissal. "Nothing to discuss?" He looked down at her shirt to see the proof of her lie. "Your nipples say otherwise."

She rolled her eyes. "That's from the cold, asshole."

Trying not to touch her, he stepped closer, half expecting her to back away. Instead, she held her ground, her chin raised stubbornly.

"It's not the god damn cold," he spoke quietly, "and I'll bet if I stuck my hand down your pants, your clit would be swollen and wet with your juices."

"Fuck you," she repeated, but the words were breathy this time and the storm dilating her eyes raged with lust not anger. Nor did she bother to deny his claim.

He smiled. "I'd love to."

A shiver quaked through her, snapping her gaze from his mouth to his eyes. Hers narrowed. "I'll see you back at the office."

Josh didn't follow her but watched her walk away, or rather her ass as it pendulumed in a rhythm that made his balls tingle.

She slammed the car door a little too hard, and his grin deepened, then slipped when he remembered why he'd come looking for her.

Fingers curling into fists, he headed toward his truck. He'd been frustrated as hell when he'd gotten to the sheriff's office only to find the sheriff had been called out. Kelsey had easily volunteered the sheriff's location and that it was "just Leon on a weekender."

Irritated that he'd been left to cool his heels with a

babysitter nearly half his age and flaunting assets he wasn't interested in sampling, Josh had left to hunt down the new sheriff and get the ball rolling toward finding his livestock. A deputy could have handled Leon. His cattle were worth thousands, and they could be sold or slaughtered or halfway across the country by now. All that in addition to his failure to guard against rustlers and letting Cherry slip through his fingers.

Now though…

He flexed his fingers and relaxed his jaw as he climbed into his truck. His cattle were still gone, and he might not ever get them back, but unlike this morning, he knew exactly where to find his spitting-mad wildcat any god damn time he wanted to feel the sharp sting of her claws.

Josh was halfway back to the square in the middle of town when his phone rang. Evan's name popped up on the screen.

"Hey," he answered.

"I got your message," Evan said. "What's going on?"

"I'm waiting to talk to the sheriff." *About more than rustled cows.*

"What's the hold up?"

"Long story." One he didn't want to get into. "Rusty's securing the area until the sheriff can get there."

"I'll be there as soon as I can."

"There's no reason for you to be here. Nothing you can do."

"I can light a fire under the sheriff's ass."

Josh chuckled. He'd like to see Evan trying to get the upper hand with Cher—Harper. But the thought of

Evan's hands on his little wildcat—upper or lower—darkened his mood.

"What's so funny?"

"Nothing. I got this."

"I'll call the insurance company to start a claim."

Josh would rather find out who took his cattle and get them back. Fucking thieves. But he couldn't tell Evan that he liked the idea of working with the new sheriff to find them. That he liked doing *other things* to her, too. They were the perfect fit. At least he thought so. She might have different ideas. Why else would she have cancelled on him?

"Josh? You there?"

"Yeah. Sorry."

"What's up…besides the rustling? You seem off. You're usually busting my balls about something or another."

"I…" Josh sucked in a deep breath, and the words rushed out of him on an exhale. "I don't think I'm going back to the club."

Not without Harper.

Now that he'd voiced his decision, he knew it was the right one. For him.

"Did something happen?"

"It's what *didn't* happen." He sighed. "Don't get me wrong. It's hot. I like some of it. But there's too much control. I miss the spontaneity, the fun, laughing during sex."

"You don't have to be hardcore to enjoy the club."

"I figured out that much recently." Should he say more? "I met someone."

"And?"

"And I don't know. It was different. Better." A

strange combination of easy and controlled. A sharing of power rather than an exchange...for the most part.

"That's a good thing, right?"

"I just don't know if it was *better* for her. We were supposed to meet tonight, but she bailed."

"Oh."

"Yeah, oh." Josh braked for a redlight.

"And you don't know who she is," Evan said flatly.

"Umm, yeah, actually I do."

"You do?"

As the light turned green and Josh accelerated into the intersection, he almost smiled as he pictured the shock on his brother's face. During the early days of Josh's initiation into BDSM, Evan had lectured him over and over about the importance of anonymity.

"Yep."

"How did— Never mind. The problem is simple then. Talk to her."

Josh scowled at the screen. "Sounds like something I said just a few months ago."

"Best thing I ever did was listen to my big brother."

"And don't you forget it." The courthouse came into view. "I gotta go."

"Okay, then. Keep me posted."

"Will do."

"And talk to her."

"Yep." Josh hung up, the tension in his shoulders creeping into his neck. He could talk to her until he was blue in the face, but would she talk to him?

A minute later, he slipped into a spot beside Harper and met her as she stepped onto the sidewalk. The wind nearly pulled the office door off its hinges when he opened it for her, then it resisted when he tried to close it.

"We'll talk in my office," she said, kneeing the swinging door and holding it for him to pass through.

"Um, Sheriff?" Kelsey blocked his entry with a flirty smile, then shifted to face Harper, her ass brushing against his hip. "Mayor Radcliff is waiting in your office."

Funny how two days ago, he'd have enjoyed a flirtation with the girl, but she was too young for him, and now, the only woman he wanted rubbing up against him was Harper. He retreated a step, but it was too late if the finely arched brow hiking up Harper's forehead was any indication.

"Why's he in my office?" she whisper-shouted.

The sexy rasp of her voice triggered the memory of her cursing Buck for a swat to her ass, and Josh's palms itched to feel the heat of her reddened flesh. This time, though, he'd be the one to put it there.

"I'm sorry." Kelsey blinked. "I tried to get him to wait out here, but he insisted and he's the—"

"Mayor," Harper interjected, her tone softening. "I get it. Not your fault, Kelsey." Her gaze darted across the room. She watched Mealer trying to get Leon into a cell before he passed out, then turned back to Kelsey. "Call Ashley Hargrove to let her know her husband is safe."

"Yes, Sheriff."

As soon as Kelsey was back at her desk, Harper turned an apologetic smile on Josh. Yanking at her turtleneck, she gave him a glimpse of the mark he'd left on her Saturday night. Lust grabbed him by the balls, but uncertainty clung to him. He still didn't know why she'd cancelled.

"I'm sorry, Mr. McNamara. Would you mind waiting just a moment?" She indicated the bench in the reception area. "This won't take long. I'm sure the mayor will understand your cattle come first."

"I'll wait." He wasn't fucking happy about it or the formal tone she used on him as if they were strangers, but he found it hard to say no when his dick was trying to launch out of his pants. He leaned forward to whisper, "But you'll owe me one, preferably on your knees."

"You're a dick," she hissed and shooed him on the other side of the rail.

He didn't bother to hide his interest in her ass when she slipped off her coat and entered her office. If this thing between them continued, and he planned to make damn sure it did, everyone in town would know she was his, and that she wore his brand.

And he'd start with the fucking mayor. Radcliff was a connoisseur of women and had his fucking hands all over her.

Chapter Six

The mayor wasn't at all what Harper expected. He'd risen when she entered her office, and her brain began cataloging his stats. Six foot. A hundred and eighty-five pounds. Blue eyes. Black hair, cut short up the sides and long on top, deliberately styled to hang over one eyebrow. A hint of gray painted his temples. Hmm, late thirties.

He extended his hand. "Sheriff Quinn. I'm Bradley Radcliff, mayor of Stone Creek."

"Mayor Radcliff." She took his proffered hand.

He smiled, his lips pulling wide, the top as full as the bottom, which came across as seductive. The charcoal suit wasn't designer, but he wore it like a runway model. To say he was attractive would be an understatement.

His free hand closed over her elbow as he shook her hand, and she altered her last thoughts. She'd met men like him before. Groping politicians, smooth talkers, manipulators who assumed every woman was flattered by their attention.

Extricating herself from his grip, she laid a hand on her sore hip. "I'm afraid I'll have to reschedule. Mr. McNamara"—she gestured with her other hand to the man who tempted her more than she'd like—"has had some of his cattle stolen, and I really need to get out to his place to take a look around."

"I understand." But instead of leaving, he folded his slender frame into one of the chairs in front of her desk. "This won't take long."

The exact words she'd just said to Roan.

Taking Radcliff's cue, Harper removed her gun from the holster and tucked it into her desk, then sank into her chair and tried not to think about the ramifications of knowing Roan's real name, of him knowing hers, and how they were going to coexist in the same small town.

"Zeke warned me that looks can be deceiving."

His blunt compliment tugged at her last nerve. "I always listen to Zeke, Mayor Radcliff."

He chuckled. "And so shall I, Sheriff."

She slid the messages and both case reports she'd left out earlier to one side and waited for him to say more. When he didn't, she asked, "What can I do for you?"

"My dad went to college with Zeke," he said, ignoring the prompt that said she was done shooting the shit. "He's like an uncle to me. He got me out of more than a few scrapes when I was young and stupid."

Through the window, movement caught her eye. Kelsey handed something to Mealer, then settled against the counter, no doubt using it as a tray for her tits so that Roan could see what she was serving up. Harper hadn't missed the ways she'd sidled her ass up to him like a hound in heat.

She's probably been banged more than a snooze button on Monday morning.

Regret immediately sliced through Harper. Slut-shaming? Really? And a fellow female officer, at that.

Fuck, you'd think you were jealous or something.

Her gaze shifted to Roan. To his credit, he didn't seem to notice Kelsey's tits or her chatter, which chipped at Harper's resolve to keep him at a distance. Instead, he watched her and Radcliff, his mouth pulled into a frown.

Harper refocused on the man who was essentially her boss and found him studying her, his eyes hidden by long, thick lashes. A smile slipped easily into place, perfect teeth gleaming. "We can exchange Zeke stories another day. Perhaps lunch?"

"I'll have Officer Price contact your office." *And arrange a meeting in his office.* Lunch would have the town speculating about her relationship with the mayor. She'd learned her lesson with Blake.

All business again, he sat forward. "Let's get to the reason for my visit... I hear you've already had an adventure in the park." He laughed, the sound like rich bourbon.

Fuck, she could use a drink, and it wasn't even noon.

"Don't worry," he went on. "They're all a bunch of busybodies with nothing better to do, but you might want to keep a low profile if you want to get reelected. May will be here before you know it."

Harper folded her arms over her chest. "I'll keep that in mind, Mayor."

"Please, Harper, call me Bradley." He stood. "May I call you Harper?"

She stood and skirted the desk. "Of course, Mayor, er—" *Motherfucker.* "—Bradley."

"Listen, Harper." He rested a hand on her shoulder. "I wouldn't put too much time into this rustling. You won't find them, and it will just drain city resources."

He held up a hand. "I'm not saying to ignore it or not to investigate, but Josh has insurance. I'm sure of it."

How the fuck did this guy get elected in an area where most of the residents were farmers and ranchers if he didn't at least pretend to care about their livelihood?

He stepped back. "One more thing. Would you *please* stop by Mrs. Butts' place on your way out to the McNamara ranch? It's on the way, and it will only take a minute."

"I planned to get by there, but it'll probably be tomorrow." She still had to deal with Leon and meet the night shift.

"Hmm, I'd really appreciate it if you could do it today." It wasn't a request. "She's been calling all morning, demanding to see you, and Mary Lou—my secretary—is threatening to quit if I can't get her to stop."

Harper gave him a smile as fake as the one he wore. "Of course, I'll do my best."

"Wonderful!" He clapped his hands together. "I'll owe you one."

Glad it's not the other way around. I am not getting on my knees for you, asshole.

As she walked him to the front, Kelsey scurried back to her desk, leaving Roan where he leaned against the counter and glared at the man behind her.

Harper swung the gate wide, but Radcliff stopped in the opening, blocking her path. "I'll see you later, *Harper*."

His practiced smile and the way he said her name, as if they shared some intimate secret, made her cringe. She nodded, not trusting herself to speak.

He moved on, pausing beside Roan. "Sorry to hear you lost some cattle."

Roan pushed away from the counter with a growl. "I didn't *lose* them."

Radcliff laughed and slapped him on the back. "So you didn't." He pointed to Harper. "I'm sure the sheriff will do everything she can to find out what happened."

Hypocritical motherfucker.

"Come this way, Mr. McNamara." The sooner both Radcliff and Roan were out of her office, the better.

Carrying his coat over his shoulder, Roan sauntered toward her, his boots eating up the dingy green tile. She kept her gaze from traveling higher. She'd already noticed how his faded jeans hugged his hips and cradled his dick. And so had her damn pussy.

Fuck, she'd been wet since before he threatened to stick his hands down her pants. But she wouldn't tell him that.

"Sheriff?" Mealer's chair rebelled with a loud creak as he rocked back. "You want me to start booking Leon. You said you wanted to handle it, but..." He looked at Roan.

She still wasn't sure what to do with Leon, and he was already passed out. "No, I'd like you to head out to Mr. McNamara's place and start processing the scene. I'll be out as soon as I can."

"Roger that." Mealer grabbed his coat and hauled ass toward the door.

"Your deputy doesn't seem to like paperwork."

She'd have laughed because she thought the same thing, but Roan's warm breath on the back of her ear teased goosebumps down her neck. Her nipples tightened into hard buds, and heat coiled in her lower belly. And yep, more cream coated her panties.

Suppressing a moan, she led him into her office and put her desk between them. She indicated the two chairs across from her. "Have a seat."

He draped his coat over the back of one chair and sank into the other, a leg stretched to the side. He smoothed a hand along the edge of the metal desk. "Do you know how hard I am right now? How much my dick wants to sink into your pussy?"

Her gaze snapped to the open door, and her cunt contracted, a tingle zipping to her clit.

"She can't hear us." He leaned forward. "But do you really care? I'll bet I could fuck you right here, and you'd love every second, knowing she was watching or that anyone could walk in. Maybe even your arrogant, piece of shit mayor."

"Not that it's any of your business, but that piece of shit mayor is my boss." She swallowed the anger lodged in her throat and the flurry of zombieflies trying to eat their way out of her chest. Yet she couldn't deny the truth of his words or how wet they made her. Or that Roan's jealousy made her giddy. She didn't want him to be jealous. Didn't want to be jealous of him. "And I told you, I am not having this conversation while I'm working."

"When then?" he countered, his eyes glinting.

"I don't know. Tonight, maybe."

That seemed to settle him. She hadn't pegged him as a hardcore Dom. Had she made a mistake? Was that what this was? He wasn't jealous. Merely possessive.

"I still have a room booked at The Arena."

"No," she barked and wished she hadn't when Kelsey tilted a questioning glance at her. More guilt for thinking hateful thoughts about the girl bubbled up at her obvious concern. Harper smiled and shook her head.

But Roan was right. They needed to talk. She had to know if he was going to out her, and she needed to make sure he understood that nothing else could happen between them. Those damn zombieflies died again midflight and dropped to the pit of her stomach as she formed her next words. "You should go to the club, work off some steam. Otherwise, if you want to talk, I'll call you when I'm free."

His jaw ticked several times. "Fine."

"For now, I'll need a statement." She yanked at the heavy drawer to her left, found the form she needed, and held it out to him. "Fill this out. I'll have Kelsey type it up while we head out, and you can come back in later or tomorrow to sign it."

"That's it?"

"No, that's not it." She slapped the form and a pen on the desk in front of him and pushed out of her chair. "We'll canvas the neighbors to see if they saw anything—"

"There's only one," he snipped.

"—and I'll call TSCRA. They will probably take over the investigation, but until they do, we'll do everything we can to give you some answers."

Texas and Southwestern Cattle Raiser's Association assisted with the investigation of livestock theft and other ranch-related property losses, including saddles, tractors, and trailers. She'd never worked with them before, but they would likely send out one of their rangers.

Roan grunted but picked up the form.

"Excuse me a moment." Pulling at her collar again, Harper escaped to the bathroom and splashed cold water on her face. The thermostat setting had nothing to do with the fire simmering under her skin. Her office had felt small and confining this morning, but with Roan's big frame filling the space—and filling her head with erotic images—the walls had fucking closed in on her.

No matter what she told him, she couldn't deny the way her body revved just hearing his voice. She'd gone from zero to sixty on the lust-ometer the second their hands touched at the park. She'd wanted to melt against him and wrestle him to the ground all at once. Even if they were alone, she couldn't afford to show how weak he could make her.

Blake had made her weak, and her father had pointed it out every chance he got, warning her that Blake would drag her down. He wasn't strong enough for "a woman like" her.

"Your blood is as blue as mine. Your brothers', too," he'd said. *"You're smarter than them, though. One of the youngest detectives on the force, and if you keep it up, you'll climb the ranks fast. But not with that bastard Enders between your legs. He has too much ambition. He'll hold you back to make himself look good, then climb over you to take what's yours."* Then he'd ruined the only compliment she could remember him ever giving her, albeit a crude and backhanded one. *"Don't shit where you eat, girl. If you need to scratch an itch, find someone outside the force."*

As much as it killed her to admit it, he'd been right about Blake, about everything. But this wasn't the time to wallow in self-loathing.

Must not show weakness.

Bracing her hands on the sink, she stared at her reflection. Fuck, she was a mess.

With hurried fingers, she plucked several pieces of grass from her hair, freed it from the elastic band, and finger-combed it back into a high ponytail. There was nothing she could do about the scratch on her cheek without calling attention to it.

Weakness.

On the way back to her office, she stopped to check on Leon. "What the hell am I going to do with you?

"Doesn't matter," Leon muttered, startling Harper. He sat up, holding the sides of his head. "She doesn't want me no more, Sheriff."

At least he wasn't slurring anymore.

"I can't even get a job at the feed store." He stared at the boxes stacked against the wall opposite the bunk he sat on. "She doesn't like it when I drink, and I don't know why I did it. Just wanna forget for a while what a failure I am, I guess."

"Everything will be okay," she said, not really believing her own words. She didn't think he did either. "Just try to get some sleep and then we'll figure it out."

She turned around and slammed into a hard wall of muscle. The citrusy scent of Roan's cologne swirled around her, making her dizzy with desire. So much for cooling off.

Harper flinched as his hand settled on the tender flesh of her hip where she'd landed on her radio when she fell. It was bruised, for sure, but nothing to worry about.

He re-settled his hand higher on her waist, his thumbs stretching along her ribs toward her breast.

"You okay?"

Pain, panic, and pure pleasure swirled into a tornado of emotion and indecision. It would be so easy to move in closer and lay her head on his chest, to let him wrap her in his warm strength, to soak up as much of it as she could. She'd complained, if only to herself, about how little action she would see in Stone County, but she hadn't wished for all hell to break loose in one day.

Weakness.

"I'm fine." she grumbled, ducking to one side and out of reach. Luckily, Kelsey had her back to them, and Leon probably wouldn't remember seeing the intimacy of Roan's touch. Not like she would. "You startled me. That's all."

Roan held out the form, his gaze assessing as if he heard the lie for what it was.

Fear.

"I'll give it to Kelsey, and we'll head out." She took his statement and crossed the room to Kelsey. "I need you to type this up for Mr. McNamara to sign once we get back."

"Sure." Kelsey leaned sideways in her chair to peek around Harper as she accepted the paper.

Harper glanced behind her. She'd expected Roan to follow her, but he was still at the yellow line outside the cell, feet braced apart, arms folded across his chest. The low timber of his voice carried across the room. She couldn't make out what he said, but Leon perked up and nodded vigorously, then winced and pressed a hand to his temple.

"I'm sorry about earlier," Kelsey said.

"It's okay." Harper pulled her focus back to the

dispatcher. "People like Radcliff like to throw their weight around just to show they can."

"I'm not talking about that." She jutted her chin at Roan. "I mean when I, um, flirted with Josh." She shrugged. "A girl's gotta try."

She really didn't have time to get into it, but since Roan was occupied, and Kelsey had opened the window...

"I get that he's attractive, but—" Harper started to point out the girl's unbuttoned shirt and found it done up almost to the top, not a thread of lace in sight. *Good.* "—you represent the department. The men will never see you as an equal. You won't have their respect."

"He's not interested in me anyway." Kelsey laughed, and Harper wondered if she'd heard a word she'd said. "That man can't take his eyes off you. He watched you like a dog guards his bone the whole time you were in your office with the mayor. And the way he checked out your ass..." She fanned herself. "Mmm, girl—er, Sheriff, sorry—you need to climb on that and take him for a ride."

Before Harper could assure her that would never happen, Kelsey leaned to one side, a professional smile replacing her naughty grin. "Oh, hey Mr. McNamara." She patted the statement on her desk. "I'll get this all typed up for you. It'll be ready when you two get back."

He nodded but his eyes held Harper's. "Ready?"

She wanted to ask him what he'd said to Leon that made him less miserable. "I just need to get my coat."

Once again in her office, she grabbed her Glock and their coats then made sure he preceded her through the gate this time. No more ass watching in front of her co-workers.

As he held the front door open, Kelsey caught her eye and winked conspiratorially, giving her a thumbs up.

Jesus Christ, this job was going to kill her. Or she was going to kill someone. It was just a matter of when.

And who's going to be first.

Chapter Seven

Harper bumped along in front of Roan's truck, their tires crunching on the pea gravel of the long winding drive leading to Mrs. Butt's house. He hadn't been too happy when she told him she had to make one more stop and she'd meet him at his ranch.

"What? Is it time for a coffee break?" he'd growled in one breath. In the next, he'd agreed to follow her wherever she was headed and wait outside. "I've got over two hundred acres, sheriff. You'll never find the right place, and going all the way to my house will take too long."

Stopping alongside the hedges in front of Mrs. Butt's house, she killed the engine and checked her rearview. Roan was already out of his truck and heading her way, a brown felt hat crushing thick blond waves over his ears. She lowered the brim of her cap and called in her location, aware of his impatience as he hovered outside her door, his hands in his pockets, steam billowing from his mouth.

Harper didn't blame him. She'd let Radcliff bully her into putting him off. That, and part of her wanted to punish Roan for making her want more of him. Seeing him outside The Arena screamed a catastrophe in the making.

Cold nipped at Harper's nose and ears as soon as she opened the door. It was getting colder by the minute. She'd barely gained her feet when Roan captured her wrists and twisted her hands behind her back. His hard body slammed her against the back passenger side of the car, making it rock with the force. He jammed a knee between her thighs.

"What the fuck do you think you're doing?" She pushed against him with her upper body.

"All morning, you've been leading me around like a bull with a ring in his nose. I'm done waiting." Roan lowered his head until the brim of his hat tapped the bill of her cap. "We're not going anywhere else until you tell me why."

"Why what?" The fog of her breath mingled with his.

"Why did you cancel?" He relaxed against her, and the hard length of his dick mashed her sore hip. His thigh shifted against her clit.

Pleasure and pain swirled through her. She bit back a moan and tried to break his hold on her hands. His fingers clamped hard around her wrists, adding to a rising need for more.

"I was looking forward to coaxing a half dozen or more orgasms out of your pretty pussy tonight," he drawled, "only to have Wrangler ask me who else I'd rather play with since you weren't coming. At least, not the way I wanted you to."

Jealousy was a green-eyed bitch, and she dug her nails deep into Harper. "I'm sure you have a lot of women waiting in line."

"Careful there, wildcat. You almost sound jealous." His eyes narrowed. "That's the second time you've insinuated I'm a fuckboy, and I don't like it very much."

"*Pbbsst.*" She rolled her eyes. "I know a player when I see one."

"But you like the way I play, and *I* like the way *you* play. Why shouldn't we enjoy each other?" He adjusted his grip to secure both her hands in one of his and shoved the other inside her coat. Cupping her breast, he ran a thumb over her traitorous nipple that grew taut and heavy at his touch. "Tell me. What are you afraid of?"

"Nothing," she lied against his lips and bucked against him half-heartedly. Her brain was shutting down, her body taking over. Fuck, she wanted to *play*. "I told you we'd…talk tonight."

"No. Not tonight." He traced her lower lip with his tongue as he worked the buttons of her shirt open to her waist and shoved her turtleneck up to expose her bra. "Now."

"The sooner we get this wellness check done, the sooner we can get to your ranch."

"Then tell me what I want to know."

Once more, Harper bucked against him, nearly moaning when his thigh rammed the seam of her jeans against her clit. Liquid fire seeped from her cunt, and her knees weakened. "I already told you I was starting a new job."

"Bullshit. We all have jobs." Rolling his hips again, he pinched her nipple, and damn him and his satisfied smile, she tried so hard to hold back a moan and failed. "That's it. Don't hold back."

"Get…the fuck…off me," she breathed when she wanted to beg him to do it again. Fucker knew what he was doing.

"Come on, wildcat. You know how this works."

His mouth slid along her jaw to that sensitive spot beneath her ear. "Use your safeword if you want me to stop."

Heart hammering, she parted her lips to say the word that would end whatever this was between them. But when he yanked down her bra, the sound of tearing lace foreign yet wickedly seductive in the quiet countryside, and sucked her nipple into his hot mouth, all that came out was, "Someone might see. Mrs. Butts—"

"Isn't getting out of the house in this weather," he said, lifting his head. Crisp air stung her breast and a shiver rolled through her as his hand roamed over her ribs then lower to skim her belly just above her belt.

Her stomach contracted under the slight graze of his knuckles. Sweet Jesus, his touch was lethal. Everything about him was dangerous.

"And we're parked behind the hedges." He looked around. "Unless you're worried about a few cows." The buckle of her belt gave way to his expert handling, then he attacked the button of her jeans. He lowered the zipper.

The weight of her Glock and radio dragged at her waistband, widening the gap for him, giving him more room to play.

The tips of his fingers skated under the lace of her panties. "Besides, we've already established you don't really care. And fuck me, neither do I."

"Oh god." Harper panted, wriggling toward his fingers, aching to have them inside her."

"I need to see how wet you are, how much you want me."

"Stop talking and just fucking do it."

A half growl/half chuckle hummed into her mouth as he meshed his lips to hers in a leisurely kiss and parted her folds with his middle finger. The rough pad rode over her clit on its way to her opening, and this time her hips jerked of their own volition.

His finger sank deep, and their moans mingled as their tongues battled for dominance. He pulled out and doubled up on the next thrust, two fingers filling her, stretching her inner walls.

The hand holding hers loosened and journeyed up her back, its mission unclear. From a dark, blurry corner in her mind, reason suggested she take advantage of her freedom. Yet she didn't balk when he removed her chances of escape by winding her ponytail in a fist tight enough to sting her scalp.

He was right anyway. She'd craved the rush of adrenaline that came with her job. Her craving for him was just as dangerous. She wanted this, him, the possibility of getting caught. What the hell was wrong with her?

Nothing a good orgasm won't fix.

****

Josh felt the moment Harper submitted. Her mouth softened, her back arched, and when she dropped her hands from around her back, she didn't push him away. Instead, she dug her fingers into his jacket and hauled him closer.

Once again, he was reminded of the last yearling he'd broken—with patience and whispered words of encouragement rather than brute force. It took longer, but the animal's spirit remained intact.

He didn't want to break Harper. He enjoyed her passion, the fight to remain his equal rather than his submissive. But he knew enough to realize that, if he let her exert resistance to his dominance, like the young filly, she'd wear herself out, learn to trust him, and allow him to take control.

That didn't take long.

Gently pulling her ponytail, he ended the kiss to look at her. Every time he did, it was like taking an arrow to the chest. So hauntingly beautiful.

Baby-fine hair framed her face like black filigree. Equally black lashes fanned flushed cheeks. Bare red lips, pouty from his kiss. Her creamy tits rose and fell with every breath, tempting him to taste them.

And her pussy…

Josh had almost forgotten why he started all this. Besides his own obvious need to touch her. But he'd been wrong. Forcing her answer with sex would break her…and sever the connection between them. He'd be damned if he stopped, though. If she slipped and told him what he wanted to know, fine. If not, he'd at least remind her how good he could make her feel.

"You're fucking drenched." He shoved his cock against her hip and drove his fingers into her, hard.

She gasped. "Need to come."

"Shh, it's okay. I've got you." Josh eased his fingers, slick with her juices, from her tight sheath and circled her clit. The little kernel was swollen and hard, ripe for an orgasm. "You are so perfect."

He was tempted to fuck her right here. He doubted she'd say no, but later, she'd resent him. Besides, he didn't have a condom, hadn't expected to need one until tonight. Watching her come apart with only his fingers would have to be enough.

The velvety heat of her pussy contracted around his

fingers as he stroked in and out and rotated the heel of his hand against her clit.

"Oh god, yes," she hissed. "Don't stop."

"I won't. I want to watch you come." He increased the speed of his thrusts and the tension of his hand in her hair. "I want you to call my name."

"Roan," she whispered, her head craning back against the window of the SUV.

"No, Harper," he whispered. "Josh."

The pulse at the curve of her slender neck fluttered. Her breathing had quickened, and tiny spasms signaled her climax.

"Say it," he rasped. "Say my name."

"Josh."

"Again." He crooked his fingers and found her G-spot. He rubbed it once then backed off. "Say it again."

"Josh."

He smiled and curled his fingers forward again. "Come for me, wildcat."

A silent cry parted Harper's lips, her body stiffened, and her pussy milked his fingers as he fingerfucked her through an orgasm. He could do this all day, just to see her like this. His dick was hard enough to chisel stone.

The scent of her feminine perfume just about did him in as he withdrew his fingers and lifted them to his nose. He started to lick them clean but stopped short of his lips. Instead, he painted her juices across one taut nipple. A shiver rolled through her as he bent to have his first taste of her since Saturday night. It seemed a lifetime ago.

Sweet. Tangy. Fucking incredible.

A mewling noise erupted from her throat as he

drew her into his mouth. She released his coat and secured a tight grip in his hair, knocking off his hat. He grunted as he pressed the hard bud against the roof of his mouth and sucked.

"Motherfu—" She was coming again. "Yes...yes...*Jo-osh*."

Pre-cum leaked from his cock, wetting his jeans, at the way she dragged out his name. God dammit, she was going to make him fucking come in his pants.

When her fingers loosened and her hands fell to her sides, he straightened and gently unwound her hair from his fist. He took her hands in his and straightened, kissing each fingertip. "You're fucking amazing."

"Mmm...you're...fucking...crazy," she said, her breathing not quite evened out yet.

Josh watched her face as reality ate away at the pleasure he'd given her. A deep inhale, a long exhale, and when she opened her eyes, the walls were up again.

She looked down at the damage he'd inflicted on her bra and her gaping jeans and frowned.

"I'd say I'm sorry," he offered, "but I'm not. I'll buy you a new one."

She sighed. "You got what you wanted. Now, let me go, so I can do my job."

"Not everything." Josh grinned and pressed the palm of one hand to the bulge in his pants. "I'm a patient man, but now, you owe me two."

That got him a smile but no retort. He was wearing her down.

She wasn't the same woman from the club, the one who'd taunted him with a sultry smile and a naughty mouth. This woman was all business...or had been until he'd coaxed her inner wildcat out to play.

He was definitely on the right track.

****

Harper's hip hurt like a motherfucker, and her legs went limp as Roan—Josh—eased his weight off her to scoop up his hat. The fog of lust began to dissipate, and with that...came regret. This couldn't happen again.

"What are we here for anyway?" he asked, cramming his Stetson on his head.

"*We* are not here for anything," she said, buttoning her shirt over her torn bra. Fuck, that was hot. She tucked the tail of her shirt in her jeans and shivered as her fingers met her saturated panties. Fucking hell. "I'm here to do a wellness check."

He frowned. "On Ellie?"

With a glance in the window behind her, she yanked the band from her crooked ponytail and combed her fingers through the tangled mess before pulling it back up again.

He picked up her cap and brushed the mud off. "Sorry."

She tossed it in the front seat.

"If by Ellie you mean Mrs. Elmira Butts," she said, walking away and up the front walk, "then, yes?"

Josh fell into step beside her. "Why?"

"I need to make sure she's safe out here by herself."

"Ah, she complained about the ring and runs again?"

"Among other things," she muttered.

He laughed. "She might have her moments, but that woman is as sharp as a tack and could run rings around you and me both."

"It's those moments I'm worried about." She

climbed the wooden steps to the porch and rang the doorbell.

He leaned a shoulder against the doorframe, a sheepish grin plucking at her heart. He was so damn sexy when he smiled. Hell, was there a minute of the day when he wasn't sexy?

"I should confess, Sheriff," he said, his gaze settling on her badge. Or was he looking at her boobs? "I might have rung her doorbell a time or two in my youth."

"I could see you being a little shit."

He gaped in mock innocence. "Who me?"

She shot him an if-the-shoe-fits glance and rang again.

"Actually, at the time—I think I was ten or eleven—I was trying to impress a girl. Texas Tallulah Taylor."

She snorted. "I should have guessed." She pictured him as a boy desperately trying to win the heart of a prepubescent girl named Texas. "Did it work?

"Nah, she only had eyes for Will."

"Awe, bless your little shit broken heart." She meant it sarcastically, but her heart melted a little more thinking about how hurt he might have been by the girl's rejection.

She aimed a finger at the bell again, but he waved her off and knocked so hard the screen door shook on its hinges. "She won't answer the doorbell because of all the little shits. She'll only answer a knock."

"You couldn't have told me that before?" she asked, not feeling as sorry for him anymore.

His grin stretched wider. "Guess I'm still a little shit."

"Or a big dick."

"You think I have a big dick?"

The door swung open, saving her from having to admit she did. But it didn't stop the flush of heat warming her cheeks.

A small woman with white hair that clung to her head in tight curls frowned up at Harper through the screen. "I'm not buying. Take your wares elsewhere."

"Mrs. Butts, I'm Sheriff Harper Quinn," she said, trying to keep her tone professional. "You called and said you wanted to see me."

"You don't look like no sheriff I ever saw." Then her gaze drifted over Harper's shoulder where Josh now stood, and her face lit up like a Christmas tree. "Josh, honey, what are you doing here?"

"We came to see you," he said, close enough that his deep voice vibrated through Harper's coat and into her back.

Mrs. Butts unlocked the door and pushed it open. "Come on in, boy, and bring your girl with you."

"I'm not his—"

"You're a pretty thing," Mrs. Butts said, sizing Harper up then pulling her in for a hug.

Not accustomed to affection, Harper stiffened. "Um, thanks."

The woman let her go to hold out her arms to Josh. Stepping close, he gently wrapped his arms around her frail frame and kissed the top of her head.

As he released her, she wrung the towel. "Are you okay? Jody told me about your cows. Rustling is bad business."

Harper wasn't planning to stay long enough to take off her coat, but Josh didn't give her a choice when he reached over her shoulders to peel back the lapels.

"I've got it." She pivoted to one side to finish removing her own damn coat.

Josh shrugged out of his jacket and hung it and his hat on a hook on the wall. "Jody's the mailman, Ellie."

"Yeah, you gotta watch him, ya know." Mrs. Butts' head waggled from side to side. "He's always reading my mail."

He took Harper's coat from her and hung it beside his. "And speaking of cattle...I saw some in your front pasture.

Mrs. Butts wagged the towel in her hand "Those are Aaron Peterson's. Jody told me he had more cows than grass, so I told him to tell Aaron to bring 'em over here. I have more grass than God."

"So, you're leasing your land?" Josh asked.

"Nah, just being neighborly. I don't need his money, and he can't afford it anyway. Not with that oldest of his in college and three more to go."

"Mrs. Butts, can we sit down for a minute?" Harper asked, taking advantage of the lull in their conversation.

"You go right ahead." Mrs. Butts patted her hair and smoothed her worn blue sweater. "You'll have to excuse me. I've got a bun in the oven."

Harper cut a glance at Josh. The woman had to be in her eighties. No way could she be pregnant. They must have caught her in one of her "moments." Then it hit her, the aroma of freshly baked bread and a hint of cinnamon.

Mrs. Butts laid a hand on Josh's arms. "Come help me in the kitchen." To Harper, she added, "He loves to ice my buns."

With rushed but spry steps, the older lady hurried

toward the back of the house.

"Be right there, Ellie," he called and pulled Harper against him, his hands squeezing her ass as he gave her a quick peck on the lips. "I'd love to ice your buns."

Then he was gone, leaving Harper with her mouth open and an image she couldn't erase.

To get her mind off the man she wanted to smack one second and fuck the next, she made a round of the front room to her right. It was clean and tidy except for the yarn and knitting needles on the floor next to a worn brown recliner.

Pictures lined the mantel and every other surface. Some were professional shots of children, probably standard school pictures. Some taken in studios. Others were candid, most of them with a younger Mrs. Butts and children of various ages and eras.

"That's me," Josh whispered against her ear, making her jump. He pointed to an image of a reed-thin boy of five or six with white-blond hair standing next to Mrs. Butts and a man. *Mr.* Butts? "And this one."

Her gaze swung to the framed picture of five boys, approximately ten years old, all with dirty clothes and faces, their eyes full of mischief. A whole gang of little shits.

The same scrawny boy grinned back at her from the middle of the group, then Josh's finger slid to the smaller boy with his hat pulled low to hide his eyes. His grin was reminiscent of Josh's. "That's my brother, Evan." He indicated the next boy with brown hair and big brown eyes. "That's Reed Mills. He was my main man. And this is Noah and—"

"In here, honey," Mrs. Butts yelled from the dining room. She laid a platter of iced cinnamon rolls on the long, mahogany table. "Would you like some coffee?"

Harper shook her head, wanting to ask why Josh would be in pictures on Mrs. Butts' piano. Were they related? No wonder he was so defensive of her. "That's not necessary, ma'am."

"It's no trouble." She disappeared into the kitchen again.

Josh latched on to Harper's hand and led her to the dining room. "You have to try these."

Her heart stalled then kicked into overdrive as he intertwined their fingers. Before she could extract them, he released her and pulled out a chair then sat beside her.

Steam rose from the glazed bun he dished onto a plate and placed in front of her. "Ellie makes the best cinnamon rolls in Texas."

She pushed the plate away. "This isn't a social call."

"Not for you maybe." Shifting toward her, he slung an upper arm over his chairback, his hand resting on hers. "She'll be offended if you don't eat."

"Here you go." Mrs. Butts carried a tray into the room and set it on the table. She handed Harper a steaming cup of coffee and poured a glass of milk for Josh. "Josh likes milk with his buns."

"Thanks, Ellie." He served a roll to Mrs. Butts, who stood at the head of the table wringing the towel, and dished out one for himself.

Resigned to humor both Mrs. Butts and the man watching her expectantly, Harper pulled her plate close and cut into the pastry. "Mrs. Butts—"

"Please call me Ellie, honey." She looked at Josh, her eyes full of adoration, then back at Harper. "You're one of the family now."

Harper waited for him to set the elderly lady straight, but he merely encouraged her with a wink. "Go on. Eat up."

Harper shoved the fork in her mouth. A burst of buttery goodness roused her palate, followed by an explosion of cinnamon and sugar and an underlying hint of salt. "Mmm, this is really good."

"Ha! I told you." Josh beamed with pride as if he'd made them himself. "Best in the state."

Ellie clapped her hands in short bursts. "I'm glad you like them. I made them hoping the sheriff would drop by this morning, but I'd rather you had them." She ruffled Josh's hair and sat in the chair at the head of the table next to him. "I'm happy to see you settling down."

"Ellie," Josh said over the brim of his milk glass. "Harper *is* the sheriff."

"I thought you were bringing a plumber. My sink's leaking again." The woman squinted at Harper, then smiled and patted Josh's hand. "It'll be nice having a plumber in the family."

Some of Josh's amusement faded as worry wrinkled his brow and the corners of his eyes. He stared at Ellie, as if finally seeing some of Harper's concerns.

Her heart aching for him, Harper set her fork down and wrapped her numb fingers around the hot, coffee mug. "Do you have any family nearby, Mrs. Butts?"

"Of course." But she shook her head, and her expression turned wistful. "My Bernard and I were never lucky enough to have children." Then she indicated the menagerie of photos on the buffet behind her. "But my family is all around me. I see them every day, and they visit often."

Harper hid a frown behind the rim of her cup. The woman talked in riddles. Or was it confusion?

Ellie used the table to push herself from the chair. "Since you're here, I wanted to show you something."

As soon as Ellie left the room, Josh said, "There are seven markers out back by the big oak—five stillborn and two that didn't make it past the first week."

Harper couldn't imagine being pregnant once, much less seven times. She'd thought about having a child with Blake for about a half a second but thankfully dodged that bullet. She'd been too focused on building her career back then. Now, she was too focused on saving it.

She sipped at her coffee, letting it warm her insides as she glanced at Josh and then at a picture of Mrs. Butts holding an infant. Maybe if she'd have had a woman like Ellie in her life growing up, a mother or a grandmother, she might feel differently. There would have been a support system to help her raise a child and still keep her career—

What the hell?

One fucking morning with the man and her hormones were on a rampage.

Said man finished his cinnamon roll and gulped at his milk, which left a frothy white mustache on his upper lip. Should she tell him?

"Ellie was a nurse," he said, "and midwife for thirty years. She helped deliver my parents. And she babysat me and my brother and every other kid in town. She's a part of everyone's family."

Relief lowered Harper's shoulders. That made sense but didn't diminish her concerns about Ellie's mental instability.

He shrugged. "Why are you so curious about her family."

"I want to make sure she has someone to look after her."

"You don't have to worry about Ellie." He pointed to the photos around the dining room then swung the arm on the back of her chair to encompass the living room as he finished off the milk. "Her family takes care of her."

"You being one of them?"

"Yes." He smiled, the milk mustache making him look adorably ridiculous.

She bit back a laugh, her lips twitching. "Um, you might want to…" She pointed to his upper lip. "Milk mustache."

His brows wiggled. "Do I look like I've been between your legs?"

Harper rolled her eyes again and searched the doorway to make sure Ellie hadn't heard. "You did *not* just say that."

Josh chuckled and wiped the milk from his mouth as Mrs. Butt's bustled back into the room.

She laid a thick binder on the table. "Here you go."

"What's this?" Josh asked.

"Evidence." Ellie rubbed her hands together. "I kept them as proof. They're all in date order."

Josh chuckled. "Uh-oh, I'm in trouble now."

"Don't worry, boy. I took yours out and burned them." She peered at Harper. "He always came back and apologized after he rang my bell."

Harper choked on her coffee and set the mug aside as Josh ducked his head.

"Oh, don't be shy," Ellie continued. "Josh did chores to make up for hurting my feelings." She ruffled his hair again and pointed to the binder. "If these other heathens'd owned up to their meanness, I mighta burned theirs, too."

Harper almost groaned. She didn't want to know what she'd find inside, but realizing Ellie had preserved the images as evidence had her moving the unfinished cinnamon roll aside to make room for the binder.

Really, though, what the hell was she supposed to do with a book full of Mrs. Butt's butts? Put them on the bulletin board with America's Most Wanted?

And fucking hell, Ellie could catch charges for possession of kiddie shots if some asshole climbing a political ladder like Blake or a younger deputy who wouldn't think twice about arresting a sweet, little old lady used her to make a name for himself.

Josh swiveled toward Harper, his head close to hers, his wrist dangling over the back of her chair again. "Wait, I have to check something."

As he flipped the binder open and quickly sifted through the images encased in plastic sleeves, he lifted her ponytail and twirled it through his fingers. Her tummy tumbled, and her nipples drew taut against the torn lace under her shirt.

She scooted to the opposite edge of her chair and pulled her hair from his fingers. He didn't seem to notice the effect his casual touches had on her. At least not since they'd entered Ellie's house.

Glancing up, she caught Ellie watching them with a knowing smile. Fuck, whatever fantasy the woman was concocting would be all over town by the end of the day.

Harper resigned herself to the "evidence" in front of her. "What are you looking for?"

"Ha!" He jabbed a brown mole on a pasty-white butt cheek. "That's my little brother Evan. I'd recognize that mole anywhere."

She rolled her eyes again and slapped the binder shut as she looked at Ellie. "I'll take this with me if you don't mind."

To destroy.

Ellie planted her hands on her hips. "Well, I was hoping to give it to the sheriff."

The twinkle in Josh's eyes died. "Ellie," he said softly, "I've told you—"

Harper laid a hand on his arm. In her experience, it was better to play along. "I'll make sure the sheriff gets it. I promise."

"Oh, is the sheriff's sink leaking, too." Ellie nodded. "All right, then."

Pushing back her chair, Harper stood and gathered the evidence. "I should be going. Thank you for the coffee and the cinnamon roll. It was delicious."

Josh stood, too, a little more slowly. He rounded the table and gathered Ellie in a hug.

Harper turned away to give him privacy. She hated that she'd been the one to open his eyes to what the beginnings of dementia looked like in someone he cared about.

"I love you, Ellie," he murmured in the crook of Ellie's neck. He lifted his head and kissed her cheek, his Adam's apple working in his throat. "I'll be back to check on you later."

"You must be blind, boy," she said teasingly, patting his cheek. "You're girlfriend's over there. She's the one you need to be huggin' on and whispering sweet nothin's to."

His chuckle didn't quite hold the levity it had earlier. "I'll take that under advisement."

"But you can come by if you want," Ellie insisted as he let her go. "My sink's leaking again."

Josh opened his mouth, then clamped it shut and motioned to the front door. "Yes ma'am. I'll take care of it."

Harper handed him his coat and hat, then put hers on.

As she crossed the threshold onto the porch, Ellie grabbed Harper's elbow and tapped the binder. "When you see the sheriff, you tell him to come see me. Somebody's got to do something about them aliens landing in my back field. They were here last night. I saw the lights."

"This *is* the sheriff," Josh tried one last time.

Ellie tilted her head to one side. "I could have sworn she was yer wife."

"No, ma'am." Harper patted the woman's wrinkled hand as she'd seen her do to Josh's.

Ellie wagged an accusing finger at Harper. "Well, you should be. The way you two were carrying on in my front yard."

Chapter Eight

The three-mile ride from Ellie's only took a few minutes. Her ranch sat along the same county road as Josh's and wrapped around the Mills' place. Josh and Evan and all their friends used to trek the woods that stretched between the three properties. They built forts and bridges over creeks, then hunted when they got older. They'd always ended up at Ellie's because she fed them cookies or cinnamon rolls with cold milk.

As Josh neared the south corner of the McNamara ranch, he pulled his truck to a stop behind Mealer's cruiser. In his rearview mirror, he watched Harper's SUV roll in behind him. She'd gone all business when they returned to their vehicles outside Ellie's, suggesting he lead the way to his place, and he'd been grateful. For that, and for showing him what he'd overlooked. Ellie wasn't well.

She'd been like a grandmother to him—he'd never known his—and he'd understood he would eventually lose her someday. Just as he'd lost his parents. But now... The thought of watching her mentally decline and her escalated exit from his world nearly gutted him.

He swallowed a lump in his throat and got out of his truck as Harper approached. Her strides were full of purpose, her sharp gaze already assessing the scene. The temperature had risen enough that her breath no longer turned to fog as it had when he'd kissed her, but it was still cold, forcing her to shove her hands into her coat pockets.

Josh did the same, though he could think of other ways to warm them.

Rusty climbed out of Cal's pickup parked in front of Mealer. Exhaustion carved deeper into the lines around his eyes.

"Boss," he greeted Josh and nodded at Harper. "Ma'am."

"Rusty Harris—my foreman," Josh said. "My other hand, Cal Jessup found the fence down and my livestock in the road. I sent him back to the house. If you need him, I can call him."

She shook hands with Rusty and turned to Josh. "I need to talk to my guy first, see what he's found."

His gaze followed her as she walked through the tall grass in the ditch, past the opening in the fence, and onto his property, careful to avoid the tracks Mealer had marked off with cones. From the corner of his eye, he became aware of Rusty watching her, too.

Josh's gut knotted. His foreman might be older, but he still chased skirt.

"Call Mark," he grumbled, "and have him bring what we need to fix the fence."

"Already did." Rusty hooked a thumb over his shoulder at the roll of barbed wires and tools in the back of Cal's truck.

"And that's why I pay you the big bucks," he said on a sigh, guilt crowding out petty jealousy. His guys were the best, and he was a possessive, self-centered asshole.

"Actually, it was Mark's idea."

"Maybe I should make him foreman."

Rusty barked out a laugh until a yawn interrupted.

Josh slapped him on the back. "As soon as they're done, we'll get the fence up and you can head on in."

"What took so long, anyhow?" Rusty asked.

Josh lifted his hat, ran his fingers through his hair, and settled his hat back in place, another wave of guilt threatening to pull him under. First, he'd failed to see Ellie's quirky comments for what they were, and now, for leaving Rusty to watch over the herd until they could get the fence repaired. He needed to get some sleep, or he'd be falling asleep in the saddle on tonight's watch.

I should just give him the night off and make the rounds myself.

But he couldn't put the blame entirely on Harper. He'd delayed them with his selfish need for answers…for her.

"The sheriff's had a busy first day," he said, "and I've been working on a possible new guy to help you out."

"Do you think they'll come back?"

Josh exhaled a long breath, trying to loosen some of the tension coiled like a boa constrictor around his chest. He should feel good that he'd only lost ten head, but something was off, and damn if he couldn't put his finger on it. "From what I've heard, they never hit the same outfit twice, but I think we should stay alert."

They talked about what needed to get done and what could wait until tomorrow, but inevitably, his gaze strayed to Harper, tracking her movement as she worked. Mealer showed her something on his phone, then he led her along the trail of flattened grass. He pointed here and there where he'd left little plastic markers with numbers and, finally, at a spot where mud tire tracks faded on the blacktop heading toward the highway.

She looked up several times to catch him watching her but didn't let him break her concentration.

Josh had seen her in action this morning with Leon, Radcliff, and Ellie. She'd been strong when she needed to, then compassionate as the situation called for it, but this was different. None of them posed a danger to her, and Josh had a hard time reconciling her to the woman taking control of an investigation that could put her in harm's way.

At the fence post where the cuts were made in the barbed wire, Harper glanced up once more. This time, she motioned with a slight nod for him to join her.

When he'd almost reached her, she said something to Mealer, and he moved to the big bag he'd been working from and began packing up.

"Walk with me," she said and spun on the heels of her boots. "This print—" She pointed to the muddy tire indentation. "—is deeper than the ones leading from the road. And there you can see a trail of hoofprints stops." She looked up at him, one brow raised in question.

He thought he knew where she was going. "I'm with you so far."

"So," she said, "the deeper tire print means the weight of the trailer changed. It's probable that it was parked here when the cows were loaded." She jerked a thumb over her shoulder. "Same with the tires of the truck used to pull it. The weight of the truck didn't change, but the tires dug deeper into the ground for traction to pull a heavier trailer."

He nodded.

"Judging from the distance between the rear axle of the trailer and back tires of the truck, and the fact there are no front tire marks of the trailer, we think we're looking for a gooseneck of approximately twenty-four feet."

"That's what Rusty figured."

She glanced at his foreman. "How many employees do you have?"

"Three, but I've been calling around for extra hands while this rustling threat is hot."

"Do any of them have a problem with you, any squabble over their pay or the work or anything else?

"No." Josh rubbed the back of his neck, not liking where this was going, but he understood she had to ask. "I trust them. They're all good guys. Rusty's been with the ranch for over thirty years. He worked for my grandfather and my father after him. He and Mark live in the bunkhouse. Mark's been with me a few years. Since he was seventeen. He's a good kid, always eager to learn and works where he's needed without complaint. Last night, that put him making rounds between herds with Rusty. And Cal signed on seven or eight years ago. He lives in town with his wife and daughter."

She nodded. "We'll have to check them out."

"You won't find anything."

"You'd be surprised what people are hiding, but if for no other reason, we'll run a history on each one to rule them out."

He didn't like it, but he wasn't going to argue.

"Deputy Mealer took your foreman's statement, but he'll need to come in to sign it. And we'll need to talk to the other two." She glanced at the herd keeping its distance out by the mesquite trees. "Mealer said they only took ten."

"That's a close guess. Only an inventory will tell us for sure."

"What kind are they? I've never seen that solid cinnamon color before." She shrugged. "You have to remember I grew up in the city. I don't know anything about cows. I've only seen the longhorns and the ones with white spots on their faces."

"Those are Herford. Mine are South Poll. I'm the only rancher in the county raising them." He took in the herd he'd helped his grandfather and father build. "They have high calving ease, an elevated fertility, a longer lifespan, and a calm disposition. Plus, when it comes to the beef market, they're known to yield a lean and tender meat."

She smiled. "You sound like a commercial for beef."

"Yeah, I guess I'm a bit proud, but you have to understand. Some of the ranches around here go back generations of families who've worked hard to keep the bloodlines clean and to create a legacy. We take our cattle raising just as seriously as any horse farm in Kentucky."

"I see." Her gaze swung the other direction, and his followed, landing on a rider coming down the hill from the Mills' house. Reed.

"Let's see if your neighbor saw anything." She struck off toward the fence line separating the two properties.

Josh kept pace with her, glad it wasn't Walter toting a shotgun.

Reed reined in his mount, his interest clearly on

Harper as he addressed Josh. "Just got back from the north end. Granddad wanted me to come find out what all the commotion was about."

Moving closer to Harper, Josh made the introductions. "We got hit last night. Rustlers."

Reed's eyes rounded, finally locking on Josh. "No shit?"

"Did you see anything last night, Mr. Mills?" Harper asked, her raspy tone curt, but Josh recognized the effect it had on Reed.

"Mr. Mills is my granddad." Reed leaned a forearm on the saddle horn and gave Harper the lazy grin he used when they were out hunting pussy. "I'm just Reed."

"Just answer the question," Josh barked, then tamped down the urge to smash his fist into Reed's face and added, "My cattle have been stolen. We just need to know if you saw anything."

"Right, sorry." Reed shook his head. "I didn't see or hear anything once my head hit the pillow, but all was quiet when I left around dawn."

"What about your grandfather?" Harper blew into her hands. "Would he be able to answer a few questions?"

Reed laughed. "He's perfectly capable. Whether he will or not, I can't say, but you're free to ask."

"Thanks, Reed." She returned his smile, and though it could have been out of professional courtesy, Josh's fingers curled into fists at the thought of her possibly falling for Reed's charm. "We'll be over as soon as we finish up here."

"When you say 'we', I hope you don't mean you and Josh." Brow creased, Reed glanced at Josh. "No offense, but you know how he is."

The only offense Josh took to Reed was the way his eyes roamed over Harper's body.

"I'm referring to myself and Chief Deputy Sheriff Mealer," Harper said before he could answer.

"All right, then." Reed sat up and turned his horse toward the house. "I'll see you soon, Sheriff."

As Josh followed Harper toward the road, he tried to unclench his jaw before he broke a few of his teeth—and possibly Reed's. Maybe there was something to be said for the rules of BDSM after all. If they'd been at The Arena, Josh would have made damn sure Reed knew Harper belonged to him. Reed wouldn't have crossed the line.

But they weren't at the club, and she wouldn't appreciate him going all caveman like he almost had with Radcliff. Harper was a beautiful woman. Men were going to stare and flirt with her as long as they thought they stood a chance.

Damn, but he didn't like it one fucking bit.

The closer they got to the road, the slower he walked. He didn't want his time alone with her to end.

"Hey." He stopped, forcing her to hang back as they neared the road. "What are you going to do with Leon?"

She glanced to where Mealer stood waiting for her and shrugged. "I guess I'll have to book him."

"But you don't want to."

"What makes you say that?" She blew into her cupped hands again, making him feel guilty for keeping her out in the cold longer than necessary.

"If you wanted to, you'd have done it this morning." He shoved his hands in his pockets. Not because they were cold, but because he wanted to drag her against him to warm her up…among other things. "Why can't you take him home?"

"His wife said not to bring him home."

That made sense. "Her dad was a drinker. I don't think I ever saw him sober. Died of liver disease."

"Leon needs a job."

"I offered him one."

Her gray eyes grew wide, then she laughed, and his dick stretched behind his fly. "I wondered what you said to get him all excited."

"So, what do you think?"

"I'll call Kelsey," she said with a quick nod, "and tell her you'll be picking him up."

Still unwilling to give her up, he said, "I'd go with you to talk to Walter, but Reed's right, my presence would only antagonize him."

Her eyes narrowed. "Thanks for your concern, but I don't need your help. Contrary to what you saw this morning, I know what I'm doing."

Shit. He'd stepped in it this time. He held up his hands. "I'm just saying be careful. Walter's been known to pull a shotgun on folks coming onto his land without invitation."

"I'll keep that in mind."

"Hey, I just want to keep you in one piece. You still owe me, remember?" Need coiled in his groin as a blush bloomed under her windburned cheeks, telling him where her thoughts had gone. He grinned. "Answers, you naughty girl. Answers."

The same strand of hair that came loose earlier whipped around her face. His fingers itched to feel the silk of it slide between them.

"But now that you mention it," he said, inching closer, "don't let Reed charm you out of your panties. You know, the ones soaked in the pleasure *I* gave you. They're mine."

Her lips parted as her tongue slipped out to wet her dry lips, and the pulse point in her throat fluttered faster.

So fucking beautiful. He cupped her jaw and ran a thumb across her lower lip. "*You're* mine."

She jerked her head back, and he tracked her deer-in-the-headlights gaze as it shot to Mealer again, then to Rusty, both watching them.

"Jesus fucking Christ, what the fuck are you doing." Any hint of desire in those big gray eyes vanished as they flashed with anger. "What the fuck am *I* doing?" She spun away and stomped two steps away before wheeling back around, her hands on her hips. "We're done here."

He snorted. "Not by a long shot."

"You can get your fence back up," she said as if he hadn't spoken. "I'll contact you if we have anything new to report."

This time, her steps were measured, deliberately calm, as she walked away, but Josh knew she was seething. He wasn't sorry, though, for touching her, for making her pulse race, for showing anyone who could see that she belonged to him.

And she'd better damn sure get used to it because he wasn't letting her go.

****

The Mills house was like most ranch-style homes—a single story built close to the ground, a low-pitched roofline with wide eaves, and a dedicated front porch. An elderly man—mid-eighties maybe—sat out front in a ladder-back rocking chair. A shotgun leaned against the wall beside him where Harper hoped it would remain.

She wasn't in the mood for threats from crusty old men. Or men in general.

You're mine.

Anger flared through her all over again, and right alongside it, lust burned almost as hot as it had when Josh whispered his claim and then touched her…in front of Mealer and his hired hand.

Weakness.

Fucking hell, she'd woken up in a nightmare of her own making, stuck in a web of sticky truths. She wanted him. There was no denying it. He made her feel soft, feminine, desired. Men had wanted her before, but never with a single-minded focus, as if she were the only woman in the world, his only desire.

As she jammed the gearshift into Park, she had the urge to beat her head against the steering wheel. Instead, she shoved thoughts of Josh aside and joined Mealer in front of his cruiser. She scanned the surroundings. No other vehicles. Maybe they parked around back. "Any insights you'd like to share?"

He scratched his bearded chin. "The Mills and McNamaras have a longstanding feud going back four generations, so he won't be helpful."

She'd gotten that much from Reed and Josh earlier. "Anything else."

"Walter's a hot head, but he hasn't shot anyone yet. Just don't piss him off?"

Harper glanced at Mealer, surprised to see him smiling. She nodded, for the first time feeling as if he might actually have her back. "I'll do my best."

With a casual, easy saunter and a wide smile, Reed met Harper and Mealer halfway between the house and their vehicles. He thrust a hand toward Mealer. "Curtis. How's Lori?"

Mealer shook Reed's hand. "She's doing better, thanks. Just finished her last treatment."

His brown eyes twinkling, Reed extended his hand to Harper. "Sheriff, welcome to Stone Creek. I hope this morning hasn't put you off our little town and you'll be sticking around."

"Thank you." Not really in the mood for pleasantries, she forced herself to shake his hand. His grip was firm and warm but stirred nothing more than a reminder to find her gloves. They were in one of the boxes she had yet to unpack. "Is that weapon loaded?"

"Always." His smile broadened, but he smoothed out the veiled innuendo by adding, "Coyotes, mountain lions... Out here, you have to be prepared for anything."

She schooled her features, barely resisting the urge to roll her eyes for the umpteenth time this morning. She didn't dare look at Mealer. If he was the type to spread rumors, he had an arsenal already.

Reed led the way up the meandering walkway and stepped onto the porch to stand beside his grandfather. She and Mealer remained on the sidewalk.

"This is my granddad," Reed said. "Walter Mills."

Except for the gray hair and weathered skin, Reed resembled his grandfather—brown eyes, square jaw, long slender frame.

"Mr. Mills, I'm Sheriff Harper Quinn."

On the older man's forward rock, a stream of

tobacco spewed from his pursed lips and landed on the lawn not far from her boots. He wiped his chin with the back of his sleeve. "Not for much longer."

"Granddad," Reed chided.

Harper didn't give him the satisfaction of a reaction. "Did you hear or see anything last night on the property next to yours?"

"You mean the property those McNamara's stole from my family?"

"Granddad." Reed's tone held more warning this time.

"No, I didn't see or hear anything." His lips turned up in a menacing smile, revealing a chipped tooth. "But I wouldn't tell you if I had. They're just getting what's coming to 'em."

He might just be a cantankerous old man, but the venom he spat tugged a thread Harper couldn't discount. "Do you own a gooseneck trailer, Mr. Mills."

Mealer groaned beside her.

"I own two." Walter leaned forward in his chair. "What of it?"

"Would you allow us to take a look at them?"

"Not without a warrant." He eyed the shotgun.

Harper braced her hands on her hips, her fingers resting on her Glock. "I can get one if I need to, Mr. Mills, but I'll be searching your entire property instead of just the two trailers."

"Whatever you gotta do. I ain't got nothing to hide."

"Grandad, just stop," Reed snapped. "You're wasting the sheriff's time. The sooner they figure out who took Josh's cattle, the better, 'cause we could be next."

Walter glared at her long and hard, waiting for her to break, but Harper stared back until he finally sat back dismissively. "They ain't gonna find anything by lookin' at my trailers but go on. Have yer look. Then get the hell off my land."

"Thank you, Mr. Mills," Harper said then followed Reed around the house and down to the barn.

One trailer sat off to the side, pretty much a bucket of rust. Grass grew tall around flat tires and the cinder block under the neck. The inside hadn't seen cattle in years. Instead, it contained several barrels and assorted junk.

The other trailer, sleek and black, was parked along the side of the barn and showed signs of fresh manure in the back. Dried mud crusted the edge of the tires, but that didn't prove anything. Not that she expected it to.

She wasn't quite sure why she'd pressed Walter Reed for a look at his trailers. Maybe just to see how he'd react or more likely because he'd pissed her off, but she didn't believe he was the leader of a state-wide rustling operation. Still… "When was the last time you used the trailer?"

"I took a couple of calves to the auction yesterday." He glanced at Mealer, his easy smile slipping. "You can check with Texas. She can verify I was there."

Mealer nodded. "We'll check it out."

"I know you're doing your job and all," Reed said, "and that my granddad can be a mean old bastard. He's bitter when it comes to the McNamaras. But he's no cattle thief, and neither am I."

"No one is saying you are," Harper said, "but we have to pursue and rule out all possibilities no matter how remote."

As they returned to their vehicles, Mealer got into his cruiser and Harper stood outside her car. "If you hear anything or have any trouble yourself, give us a call."

"I'm really not that worried about rustlers. The only access to the ranch is through here, and as you can see"—he motioned to his grandfather—"he's not letting anyone through." His lips curled into a smile. "How about I call you anyway? Invite you to dinner?"

"Thank you for the offer," she said, opening her car door, "but I'm afraid I'll have to decline."

"Rustlers to catch. I get it."

"Something like that."

Or someone.

Chapter Nine

Juggling four paper sacks of burgers and fries and a cardboard crate of drinks, Harper butted her way through the door to the sheriff's office at a little after one o'clock. Her stomach had been eating her backbone, so she'd stopped by Faye's Diner down the street and couldn't go back empty-handed. It gave her a minute to regroup.

Josh had been living rent free in her head since she met him at The Arena. He was a distraction she couldn't afford. He was making her stupid and careless. Hell, he should have been her number one suspect from the beginning. Insurance fraud was all too common in cases of theft.

But she liked to think she was a good judge of character, and her gut told her he wasn't the kind of man to commit fraud.

Still, it was time to serve Josh McNamara with an eviction notice.

The office was warm and, thank fuck, empty except for Kelsey and Mealer…and Leon.

She set the bags on the counter. "Anybody hungry?"

Phone glued to her ear, Kelsey mouthed "thank you" as Harper scooted a bag and a drink toward her.

Mealer strolled over. "Can't go wrong with Faye's. Best burgers in town."

"I didn't know what to get, so I went with the basics." She handed him a drink and a straw. "What are you working on?"

He stabbed the straw through the hole in the plastic lid, his expression sour. "Catching up on paperwork."

She nudged two sacks toward Mealer. "If you have a minute, I thought we could talk in my office over lunch."

Wariness stole across his face. "Sure."

Harper grabbed the remaining sack and the drinks, pushed through the gate, and crossed to the cell where Leon lay on his back staring at the ceiling.

Leon sat up slowly. "Sheriff?"

"Here. You need to eat." Through the bars, she handed him the burger. "The sooner you get food in your stomach, the better you'll feel. Mr. McNamara will be here soon to pick you up."

"Thanks," he said, accepting the food. "Not just for this. I mean for—"

She hadn't done anything really, but when he couldn't seem to get the words out, she said, "Everyone needs a little help now and then, Mr. Hargrove, but I don't want to see you on that side of the cell again."

"I don't want to be here either."

Turning around, she found Kelsey grinning at her and Mealer standing in the doorway to her office, stuffing fries in his face, his expression skeptical.

Weakness.

Her stomach growled, driving her feet forward. "Let's go over what we know."

Mealer moved farther into the room and plunked into an empty chair.

She hung up her coat and cap and turned to find a

basket of blueberry muffins next to her burger. An envelope that read *Welcome to Stone Creek* sat on top. "What's this?"

"From the president of the Ladies Auxiliary." Mealer grimaced. "I'd take a hard pass unless you want a clean colon. I'd swear Kitty puts castor oil in them."

"Thanks for the heads up." She relocated the basket to the top of a filing cabinet and settled behind her desk, glad to be off her feet for a minute.

Damn chair actually feels pretty good. Maybe I'll keep it.

Fifteen minutes later, she and Mealer had devoured lunch and slogged through the morning's events. She'd apprised him of the wellness visit with Ellie, omitting all the personal shit between her and Josh—he'd seen enough—and he'd gone into greater detail regarding the evidence collected at Josh's place.

Harper gathered the trash from her desk and stuffed it into the wastebasket. "I'll call TSCRA and fill them in."

"They'll take over the case," he grumbled.

She'd said as much to Josh. "Maybe. But I got the impression earlier you didn't like paperwork."

His face flushed red. "Uh, yeah, about that. I don't mind it." He glanced through the window at Leon. "Sheriff Jenkins didn't like paperwork, so I thought you might not either. Besides, Leon's a good guy. I hated to add a PI charge to his record when he's having a hard enough time finding a job."

"Leon has a job at the McNamara Ranch. Josh will be here to pick him up this afternoon." She leaned forward. "And for the record, I love paperwork, the more thorough the better."

"Good to know, Sheriff."

"What can I expect from the nightshift?"

"Both are good men, dependable, honest." He tilted his head to one side. "Dylan's young but smart. He's eager but not careless. Keith has some experience with Austin PD. He moved home to take care of an elderly mother. She's gone now, but he's not going anywhere. He has a thing for Faye. He's got a level head and keeps Dylan grounded. Not that anything ever happens in Stone County to cause concern."

"Except PIs and cattle rustling?"

He winced. "Yeah, this is the biggest thing to happen since Jody's mail truck got carried down river during a flood. Jody—he's our postmaster/mailman—was found up in a tree, safe and sound, but his truck didn't show up for a week, and it was a hundred miles downstream. Folks were more upset about their mail than poor Jody."

Harper sat back in her chair and folded her hands over her stomach. Seems all it took was a full belly to get Mealer to open up. "What's your assessment of the case so far?"

He seemed surprised that she'd ask. "Uh, what do you mean?"

"I mean, I have some thoughts, but I want to hear yours." She didn't want him to go through the motions. She wanted her people to think for themselves, to show intuition and initiative. From what she'd seen, Mealer had shown both.

And she'd missed having someone to bounce ideas around with. Mealer was her new partner, so to speak, since they'd be working days together. She needed to know his strengths and weaknesses and whether she could trust him.

He swallowed. "I've been following the investigation of the rustling ring, and the MO really doesn't fit with our case."

"Like the fact that they used a smaller trailer, only stole ten cows, and rounded them up on horseback."

"Exactly," he almost shouted his excitement. "The gang that hit Bastrop and Caldwell Counties used two semi-trailers and got away with over fifty head with each hit."

While she'd waited for the burgers, she'd done a little research on her own. "And they used mountain bikes to herd the animals into the trucks."

His brows furrowed. "You like Walter Mills for it, don't you? That's why you pressed him about the trailer."

"That and he pissed me off." She shrugged. "But I'm not ruling anyone out."

"I don't know. Reed's right. Walter's no thief, and to him, a man's cattle are sacred." He scratched his beard again. "And wouldn't he have done it years ago if this was about the land?"

"Maybe he's using the local theft as a way to cover up his own."

"Someone is, that's for sure." He sighed. "The rangers are still gonna take over."

"No doubt about it, but we'll work it until they do. In fact, put together a list of people in the county who own twenty-four-foot trailers." Harper liked that Mealer was disappointed. She was, too. She'd felt alive today, working the case.

And while Josh worked those magic fingers inside you.

"Why didn't you take the job?" she asked, suddenly hot. "I know they offered it to you."

"You heard me tell Reed that my wife, Lori, just finished her last treatment?"

"Yes," she said. "Cancer?"

"Breast cancer." He blew out a long breath. "They caught it early, though, and she had a double mastectomy a few months back. The chemo and radiation have been hell, but we're staying positive. But to answer your question... I couldn't take the job because I couldn't take on the added responsibility. My wife needed me. She still does, and I want to spend as much time with her as possible. She comes first."

The men in Harpers life—her father, her brothers, and Blake—wouldn't think twice about setting their loved ones aside for the job. Hell, she'd probably do the same. "Just let me know if you need time off. We'll work it out."

Nodding, he rubbed his beard, which he seemed to do when he was gauging his words. "It's where I was this morning, why I was late getting to the park. Lori called. She fell in the bathroom and couldn't get up." He swallowed, and his eyes glistened. "I was helping her back to bed."

Guilt wove its dark fingers into her chest and squeezed. She'd been cursing Mealer for not being there to back her up, and he'd been taking care of his sick wife. "Should she be alone? Do you need to go check on her now?"

"No, my daughter Jenny stays with her during the day, but she can't get there until after she takes my grandkids to school."

"Just call in next time."

He nodded again, then rubbed his beard some more. Clearly, he had more on his mind.

"What?"

Shaking his head, Mealer pushed himself out of the chair. "I should get back to work."

"If you have something to add…"

"It's none of my business."

"Spit it out, Mealer." She'd rather hear whatever he had to say than let her imagination fester, and she had a good idea what was on his mind.

He stood behind his chair, gripping the back. "My Lori, she was excited when she found out our new sheriff was going to be a woman, and she lectured me for days not to treat you any differently than I would a man…or her and Jenny."

Fucking hell, here it comes.

"That one," he continued, "Jenny? She took leave from her job to take care of her mama, but she's an ADA in Austin. She'd have my hide if I didn't treat you as an equal—rank withstanding. But she tells me how the men in her profession treat her. She was blessed with her mama's beauty, which she says—and I believe her—makes it difficult to be taken seriously."

Harper didn't say anything, but she knew all too well the obstacles Jenny faced in a field comprised predominantly of men.

"What I'm trying to say is, I know the attention you received today was unsolicited, but it's a small town and people like to talk."

"And because I'm a woman, my relationships are up for scrutiny while a man's aren't. Believe me, I'm fully aware of that."

"I hate to say it, but…yes. Unsolicited or not, and I

could see that Reed's wasn't."

In other words, Josh's was?

Fuck. This was exactly what she'd been afraid of.

"Thank you for your candor." *But it's none of your fucking business.* "Anything else?"

"Just one more thing, and then I'll go back to minding my own business." He stroked his beard. "Josh is hardworking, generous, and honest as the summer day is long, but when it comes to women, he's a player. He eats buckle bunnies for breakfast."

****

The gray clouds overhead had thinned out by mid-afternoon, allowing the sun through, but Josh and Rusty had fought the wind as they repaired the fence. Josh was tired and hungry…and frustrated.

He'd heard fuck all about his stolen cattle and the investigation, and his dick wouldn't stop grinding against his zipper every time he thought of Harper, which had been just about every second since he woke up this morning.

Rusty chucked the bale of barbed wire into the back of Cal's truck. It landed with a loud clang.

Josh slid the toolbox alongside the wire. "Go home. Get some sleep."

"Where're you goin'?"

"Back into town."

Rusty's bushy mustache lifted as a smirk pulled across his craggy face. "You sure you wanna stick your hand in that cookie jar? She didn't seem too interested."

She's interested. She's just stubborn…or still running scared. "I want to know what's going on with the investigation."

"Uh-huh."

"And I need to go get Leon Hargrove." A harmless lie. Leon could walk home to get his things and his truck, maybe even work things out with Ashley before he started work, but offering Leon a ride home gave Josh another excuse to see Harper. "He's the guy I told you about earlier. He's coming to work for us."

"He got any experience?"

"Not with livestock, but he knows how to ride, and he can learn." Josh closed the tailgate. "He's going through a rough patch and needs some help."

"You and your strays," Rusty said, referring to Cal and Mark.

Cal had come to him just out of high school. He'd gotten the preacher's daughter pregnant, and her family had kicked her out. The young couple had nowhere to go. Josh had taken Cal on and hired the boy's new wife, Brianna, to cook and clean. Since then, Brianna had finished college online and now worked at the bank, and last year, they'd bought a little house in town.

Mark was a true stray Josh had picked up on the interstate. The boy had no family and no destination in mind and was drifting from town to town, working for food.

They'd both worked out okay.

Josh shrugged. "Leon's available, and we need another pair of eyes."

"You're the boss," Rusty said and climbed into Cal's truck. As he made a Y-turn and headed back to the house, Josh called Cal.

"Hey, Josh," Cal answered.

"How's Star doing?"

"Regular as clockwork."

At least one thing was going right. "Good. Can you

stay a little longer than usual? I'm heading into town and won't be back 'til around five thirty."

"About that..." Cal said. "I talked to Bri, and she's bringing out some of my things after she picks up Aubry from school. I'm staying here tonight to help out. I hope that's all right."

A whoosh of relief exploded from Josh's chest in a broken laugh. This was why he loved living in a small town. "Of course, it is. I appreciate it. Thank Bri for me."

"Bri and Shayna are gonna fix supper," Cal rushed on, "and pack us something to tide us over during the night."

"Shayna's there?"

"Yeah, her and Evan got in about thirty minutes ago."

Damn it to hell. Evan never listened. He'd told him he had it under control. "Thanks, Cal, I'll see you later."

Josh put the truck in drive and pulled onto the road toward town. He pressed the command button on the steering wheel. "Call Evan."

The first ring had barely started when Shayna answered in a hushed whisper, "Hang on just a second."

The rustle of sheets made him roll his eyes. *Jesus.* They hadn't been in the house for more than an hour, and they were already in bed.

A moment later, her footsteps tapped along the second-floor hall and down the stairs. He could tell because he and Evan had memorized every squeak and groan in the treads and floorboards when they were young so they wouldn't be caught sneaking in or out of the house.

"Sorry, Evan just fell asleep."

"Did you wear him out?"

She snorted. "For your information, he's napping so he can take a turn watching your dumb cows."

"They aren't dumb," he quipped, falling into the comfortable and sometimes asinine banter he and Shayna shared.

"Where are you?" she asked. "Brianna and I are making supper for you guys. Well, breakfast really."

Saliva pooled in his mouth. "Homemade biscuits? With lots of butter?"

"Whole wheat muffins. No butter."

He groaned. Shayna was a great cook, but she made healthy choices in her diet and made sure those she loved did the same. Fuck that. He hadn't eaten all day and needed something that would stick to his ribs. "Please tell me it's not turkey bacon."

Her melodic laughter floated around him, but it didn't trigger the reaction Harper's did. Harper's laugh was sultry and seductive, like the whisper of silk sheets on a summer night.

"So…Evan told me you met someone, but she ditched you."

Thanks, Ev. "Sounds much worse coming from you, but yeah, that pretty much sums it up."

"Did you talk to her?"

"That's where I'm headed now."

"And where is that exactly? You never said."

"Stone Creek."

"Oh, my freakin' hell, that must have been awkward, walking into a club fifty miles away for anonymity only to find the woman you're meant to be with has been under your nose the whole time? Who is she? Do I know her?"

Shayna had grown up in Stone Creek but moved shortly after she and Evan had the falling out that split them up for nine years.

"I don't know about meant to be, but yeah, it was crazy finding her here. Actually, she's the new sheriff in town." He told her how they'd met at The Arena and planned to meet again, but she'd cancelled their session. And how, due to Leon's drunken fall, he'd found her under another man this morning in the park and that he'd tried to talk to her all day.

"Does this mean you're revolving door is jammed?" she quipped.

Shayna teased him often about his proverbial revolving door because while he'd been laid up and she'd been his nurse, he never lacked for female companionship. But would Harper be the one to stop it from spinning? "Maybe."

"Does she feel the same?"

"Fuck, I don't know, Shay. We just met, but...I think so. I hope so. There's something there."

"Then don't screw it up."

He chuckled. "Best advice ever."

"Seriously, though, whether she's the one or not, the fact that you're doing the chasing says a lot. You have to try. Don't worry about the ranch. We've got it. We've got *you*."

****

Josh parked in front of the sheriff's office, sat back, and closed his eyes. Shayna's suggestion that Harper might be the last woman he let through his revolving door pounded in his head. That she could be "the one," as Evan liked to call Shayna.

What the fuck does "the one" look like? And how am I supposed to know?

Evan had told Josh he knew the second he laid eyes on Shayna. Sure, Harper had fascinated Josh from the start, more than any woman ever had, and there'd been an instant and explosive connection he'd never felt before, but love? Nah. Probably just some banging chemistry.

He pictured her this morning at the park after Mealer hauled Leon away. Cornered, his little wildcat had been spitting mad that he'd found her. And then, a few hours later, she'd begged him to make her come. No, not begged. She'd hissed orders at him. And then he'd made her say his name.

His dick stirred, and the corners of his mouth drew upward. Love or great chemistry, he looked forward to figuring it out.

The sheriff's office was busier than it had been earlier. Deputies Dollins and Ackerman sat at their desks. Mealer was on the phone.

So was Harper. She focused on her computer monitor, her brows knitted in concentration. She flipped a pencil on its eraser, slid her forefinger and thumb down the cylinder, and flipped it to the pointy end, then repeated the rotation over and over as she spoke to whoever was on the other end of the call.

"I have your statement ready to sign," Kelsey said from behind the counter loaded with cakes, pies, kolaches, sandwiches, and casseroles.

"The welcome committee strikes again?" he asked.

"Yup. Help yourself."

"No thanks." His stomach growled again. The sandwiches did look pretty good, but he wanted to take

Harper out to dinner. And then eat her for dessert.

Kelsey rearranged a couple of plates to make room for a folder, laid it in front of him, and flipped it open to reveal the neatly typed copy of the form he'd filled out earlier. She handed him a pen. "Just sign at the bottom."

Josh read the words he'd penned, signed the paper, and slid the folder toward her. "Can you let the sheriff know I'd like a word with her before I take Leon home?"

"She sent Leon home a half hour ago. She offered to give him a ride, but he said he needed some fresh air. Dumbass probably froze to death before he got there."

He glanced at Harper through her office window. Was getting rid of Leon her way of avoiding him? Her gaze lifted to his, held, then shifted back to the screen, as if she hadn't really seen him.

He chuckled. *I'm not giving up that easily.*

"Did he say anything else?" he asked Kelsey. Like where the fuck he was going and whether he still planned to work tonight?

"He asked me to give you this?" She handed him a neon yellow sticky note with a phone number on it.

Stuffing the note in his pocket, he turned up the wattage on his smile. "I'd rather have the sheriff's number."

"I can't give you her personal phone number," she whispered, casting a quick glance around the office to make sure no one overheard, then leaning closer. "But hey, did you know Darlene finally took down the For Rent sign at the old Pickens' place?"

"You don't say?" Josh asked, playing along. "I'm really happy to hear that."

Kelsey straightened and winked at him. "I'll see if the sheriff can see you now."

Josh glanced at Harper again. She'd been watching his interactions with Kelsey, and her eyes, narrow with suspicion, locked with his. He cocked a brow in challenge, but she cut the connection between them as Kelsey entered her office.

Rising, Harper handed Kelsey a basket from the top of a filing cabinet, said something, and Kelsey shut the door on her way out.

"The sheriff's tied up right now, but she said she'll let you know when we have anything new to report and to give you these." Nose wrinkled, Kelsey offered him a basket of blueberry muffins. "Mrs. Kunkle made them."

Half the town had come down with the shits at one time or another after eating Kitty Kunkles' muffins, and no one had the heart to tell her. Harper couldn't possibly know that, though…or could she?

His gaze flew across the room to hers. Her full lips pulled up in an innocent smile, but her eyes shot fiery amusement.

A laugh erupted from somewhere deep inside him, and it felt damn good after the day he'd had. His little wildcat was playing dirty, and he loved it.

Josh shook his head at Kelsey. "Thanks, but you tell the sheriff, I'm not a blueberry kind of guy." He raised his voice to make sure she heard him. "I prefer *cherry*."

Chapter Ten

From his truck outside Pizza Palace, Josh punched Leon's number while he waited on his order. With a clear view of the sheriff's office, he'd know exactly when Harper headed home.

He'd become obsessed with her. Hell, he'd gone borderline stalker. Wanting to see her, talk to her, slide deep into her wet heat? But if he thought, for one minute, she didn't want him just as much, he'd walk away.

"Fuck." Who was he kidding? The thought of Harper ending whatever this was between them tied his gut in knots.

Still, he was a glass half full kind of guy, and from the way she'd bitten her lip when he said the word cherry…

Yeah, that got her.

His balls tightened, and his dick flexed as he imagined her behind that big desk, trying to work, her panties wet and her pale skin flushed. Was she imagining him bending her over the top and railing her until she coated his cock with cream?

Pre-cum seeped into his jeans.

Fuck. If he didn't stop fantasizing about her, she was going to get a call about some perv jacking off in a public parking lot.

He rolled down the window to suck in some cold

air and pressed the call button.

"I'm on my way," Leon said as he picked up.

"Just checking. I wasn't sure if you'd changed your mind."

"Nah, I needed to clear my head." He was quiet for a moment, then added, "Me and Ashley talked. We decided to take some time apart. Well, she decided. I don't think she trusts me, but I get it. Her dad always said he'd quit and never did."

"Give it time." What else was there to say to that? He didn't know if Leon's drinking was an addiction or if he could set it aside with ease. "Listen, I'm still in town. Just stop at the house, and someone will point you to the bunkhouse. Rusty's expecting you."

"Thanks, dude."

After they hung up, Josh checked the time—ten 'til five. He'd placed the order for a five o'clock pick up, but he knew fuck all about the hours a sheriff kept. There was no movement down the street. Her SUV still sat out front.

At five o'clock, Mealer and Kelsey exited together—no Harper. Josh went inside to pay for his pizza. Fifteen minutes later, he stepped outside. They'd been running behind, and damn, now, he was, too.

Her car was gone. What if she hadn't gone home? What if she was on her way to The Arena? What if she'd scheduled a scene with another Dom?

By the time he pulled onto Dutton Street, his jaw ached from grinding his teeth. All for nothing. Her car was parked in the driveway of a house he hadn't thought about in years. Back in the day, it was *the* place to party. While he'd had to sneak out to have fun, Noah Pickens' parents were divorced, and his mom supplied beer to her son's underage friends.

Noah still owned the craftsman, but he was a professor at the university in Austin. His mother had remarried and lived close to Noah to be near her grandkids. Seemed odd to think of his friends as married with children almost a decade old. Only he and Reed were left, clinging to bachelorhood.

Lost in his thoughts, Josh almost turned into the driveway but corrected and steered down the street. Harper wouldn't want the neighbors to see his truck parked in front of her house all night. Not that he'd stay all night. The ranch was his responsibility. He couldn't have others working to protect it while he was out fucking around.

No, it didn't feel like fucking around. For some reason, he couldn't put Harper in that category. Not now.

At the old mill, Josh parked behind the rundown office and backtracked down the alley. Sunset was still a good half hour away, but Evan and the guys would have had their turkey bacon and bran muffins and were probably getting ready to head out.

He lifted the box to his nose, took a deep whiff, and laughed as he knocked on the back door.

A minute later, he knocked again, harder, but not hard enough to alert the neighbors. Still no answer.

His mind rolled back to the fall she'd taken at the park. She'd hit the ground pretty hard, and she'd been favoring one hip all day. He peered through the window in the door, then tested the knob. Locked.

Of course, it is. She's from the city.

Just to be sure, though, he went around the house to check the front door.

Not getting in this way either.

He rang the doorbell. Nothing. Now, he was really worried. After the racket he'd made, she wouldn't just ignore him. If anything, she'd be hissing at him to go away.

Another thought struck him. What if whoever was behind the rustling had come to warn her off?

His strides quick, he retraced his path, checking each window as he looked for signs of Harper, and was just about to kick in the back door when he remembered the times he'd come here after football practice with Noah while his mom was still at work. She'd hidden a spare key outside because Noah kept losing his and she got tired of taking off work to let him in.

I couldn't be that lucky.

Leaving the pizza on a table by the door, he jogged down the back steps to the shed and ran his hand between the wall and the privacy fence. He trailed his fingers over the siding and found the hook and chain. He detached the key ring with a flick of his thumb, and it came away sticky with cobwebs.

"Harper," he called out as soon as he entered the kitchen. Silence and the stillness of the house fed his fears. The only movements were the dust particles dancing through the sunlight coming in through the window over the sink.

He laid the pizza on the island next to Ellie's binder of "evidence" and hurried through the dining room to the living area. More boxes were stacked throughout the space, some open and yet to be unpacked.

A muffled noise came from the second floor. "Harper?"

The twinge of pain streaking up his thigh as he took the stairs two at a time didn't slow him down. At the landing, he paused to listen. A splash and a soft hum drifted from the far end of the hall. Light flickered across the carpet from the doorway. The scent of cinnamon and vanilla tickled his nose. Another slosh of water.

A sigh of relief shuddered through him as he sagged against the wall behind him. A hit of foolishness followed. She was taking a damn bath. That didn't explain why she hadn't heard him, but from the sound of her slightly off-key hum, she wasn't hurt or in danger.

Josh started to turn away but stopped. Heading back the way he'd come and waiting on the back porch would be the gentlemanly thing to do. Plus, Harper was the sheriff and could arrest him for breaking and entering. But…

The splat of droplets hitting an unknown surface triggered images of water cascading over her breasts and dripping off the end of her nipples to reenter the water lapping against her body.

A smile pulled at his lips. He'd always been more scoundrel than gentleman, and his little wildcat couldn't arrest him if she was in the tub…naked.

****

Steam rose from the hot water soothing the trauma Harper's body had taken while sandwiched between Leon and the hard ground. Earbuds blaring, she hummed Taylor Swift's latest hit, the lyrics blocking out the world. She hardly ever had time to pamper herself with a long soak in a bubble bath, and it was the only time she allowed herself to let go of her job, her fucked-up life, and just be.

To bad it isn't working.

Today had been fucking chaos. Except for the afternoon, which had turned surprisingly quiet compared to the morning. A few people had come in and out of the office, bringing food as a welcome to their lazy little town. The concept was foreign after being spat on or having rocks thrown at her squad car in Houston.

But her theory on law enforcement in Stone Creek had proven true, and nothing eventful had occurred to call them out of the office. She'd been able to have a chat with a TSCRA ranger. He'd confirmed their suspicions that the theft at Josh's ranch didn't appear to be related to the rustlers who'd hit the other two counties. He'd promised he'd be out Wednesday to have a look at the information and evidence they'd collected. Just to be sure, Harper had called the sheriff's departments in the surrounding areas and got the same story.

When Dollins and Ackerman had come in early to introduce themselves, she hadn't had a reason to stay late. Instead, she'd assigned them to call as many auction barns and slaughterhouses as possible before the close of business. She and Mealer would take care of the rest tomorrow.

And she'd sent Leon home as one less reason to have to deal with Josh. She'd have to talk to him sooner or later to update him on the case.

With nothing left to do, she'd come home to start unpacking but ended up in the tub thinking about him.

"I prefer cherry."

The words had sounded like a threat, and her heart

had slammed to a halt. For a moment, she'd thought he was going to reveal their tenuous D/s relationship to her staff. Then she'd understood them for what they were. Not a threat of exposure but a playful reminder of how he'd eaten her pussy.

Her pulse had stuttered to a start, battering around in her chest before firing up full throttle, and just like that, the zombieflies had fluttered awake again, as if they'd been waiting for him to breathe life back into them.

Even now, her nipples hardened under the warm water, and her pussy contracted around itself. She couldn't even think of him without stirring a lustful craving for his touch, for his mouth…for his cock.

Trailing her fingers down one thigh to the bare lips of her pussy, Harper thought of how his tongue had dipped in to tease her clit. She mimicked his actions with her middle finger, rasping over the swollen knot.

The swish of fabric filtered through the noise cancelling buds just before the candlelight streaming through her eyelids shifted, as if something passed between her and the flame. She stilled, trying to keep her breathing even as she listened for sounds of an intruder, but Taylor sang about lost love too loudly to guess his location.

Her Glock was locked away, and the only weapon nearby was a fucking loofah brush on the windowsill to her left. Could she reach it in time?

"Don't stop on my account."

Harper's eyes shot open. As if she'd conjured him, fucking Josh McNamara loomed at the end of the clawfoot tub, his ass propped against the countertop, his long legs crossed at the ankle. Broad shoulders spanned the width of the vanity mirror behind him. His dirty-blond hair fell over dark blue eyes, the storm of lust in them unmistakable.

Talk about sex on a stick.

She resisted the urge to jerk her hand from between her legs and cover herself. A thick bank of bubbles did that, and movement would only dislodge them. Instead, she tapped her buds to turn off the noise cancelling option. "What the fuck are you doing here? How did you get in here?"

"Which question do you want me to answer first?" The drawl of his deep voice plucked the invisible string between her tits and her cunt.

Damn him. "How did you get in?"

He shrugged out of his coat and draped it on the counter beside him, then he laid his wallet, keys, and phone on top. "I knew where to find a hidden key."

"Let me guess," she spat out, jealousy flaring from a dark place inside her. "You fucked the woman who owns the house?"

His sensuous lips twisted into a frown as he grabbed the back of his flannel shirt, pulled it and his thermal undershirt over his head, and dropped them on the floor. "No, I went to school with her son Noah—the redhead from the picture at Ellie's. He showed me where the extra key was." He dangled it at her, then flung it on the counter. "Why do you keep doing that?"

"Doing what?" she asked, distracted by the delicious contours of his torso. She wanted to lick every hill and valley from his sculpted shoulders to the deep cut of his groin hidden by his jeans.

"Throwing my past in my face." He folded his arms across his chest. "Let's just get this out of the way. I've fucked a lot of women. Is that what you want to hear? Some I regret. A few I shouldn't have because I hurt them. They wanted more than I did. But you're the only one—"

She lifted a brow as he snapped his mouth shut. "The only one who said no?"

He chuckled as he bent to remove one boot, then the other. "Don't flatter yourself."

"Am I a challenge then?"

"You are definitely a challenge, but you know as well as I do there's something between us."

That *something* had been creeping up on her all day, and it scared the fuck out of her.

Chemistry. That's all it is.

"And for the record," he added, "I haven't asked how many men you've fucked. We met at a sex club, for Christ's sake."

She blanched. Not at the crudeness of his words but at the truth. She was no virgin, and she'd never been timid about taking men home with her. Why should she judge him for doing the same?

The thud of his boot hitting the tile jarred her from the haze of desire clouding her thoughts. She'd cataloged his actions but not their meaning. "What are you doing?"

He chuckled as if knowing exactly what his presence did to her. "Answering the question of why I'm here."

"You need a bath?" she snapped.

"Now that you mention it." He released his belt buckle and the snap of his jeans, then lowered his zipper.

Saliva pooled in her mouth, and she tried to shake

herself from his thrall. Why was she just sitting here, letting him control the situation? All she had to do was get up, dress, and ask him to leave. She was sure he would if she asked.

Hooking his thumbs in the waistband of his jeans, he shoved them down past his knees and straightened. She was barely aware of him shedding the rest of the denim and removing his socks after his dick sprang forward. Thick, ropy veins threaded the length of his shaft. Arousal drew his ball sac close to his body.

"You're why I'm here, Harper. You…and this." He gripped his dick and stroked from base to tip. "I've been hard for you all day." He stepped closer. "Scoot up."

Her gaze flew to his. If she let him in the tub, there was no going back.

Whether he was oblivious to her indecision or he already knew the outcome, he held out a hand. "Buds."

"Huh?"

"Wouldn't want them to get wet."

Like a good little sub she'd never been, she obeyed and handed them to him. As he turned to place them on the counter with his things, she drank in the sight of his rounded ass and the carved muscles of his back. The long white scar she'd seen the night they were at The Arena stirred her curiosity.

"How did you get that scar?" she asked.

Blue eyes twinkled as they connected with hers in the mirror over the sink. "Tangled with a wildcat."

"If you don't want me to know, all you have to do is say so."

"I'm serious."

"Are you sure it wasn't a bar fight?" *That* she

could imagine. Or was it from one of his buckle bunnies who'd gone psycho? "Never mind. I don't want to know."

"It's nothing as exciting as that." He turned to face her, cock in his hand and a sexy grin playing at his lips. "Evan and I were hunting and came across a cougar—the four-legged kind." He winked, and she fought the urge to roll her eyes. "I got too close."

Harper wanted to ask more, but he stalked toward the tub with all the stealth of the animal he described. She scooted forward, and he climbed in behind her. Water sloshed over the side as he curled his warm body around her, his cock prodding her back. Circling his arms at her waist, he filled his hands with her breasts.

"God, you feel good." He nuzzled the whisp of hair at her nape, then brushed his lips over the sensitive skin beneath her ear, making her shiver. "I like your hair like this, all piled on your head."

Despite her trepidation of letting him in, she melted into his honesty. She'd regret it in the morning, but she'd enjoy him tonight.

"How'd it go at the Millses'?" he muttered against her neck.

"I can't discuss the case with you, but I will say Walter Mills is a handful."

He snorted and sat back, taking her with him. "I'm sure Reed fell all over himself to help you."

She rested her hands on his forearms. "I thought he was your friend."

"He is, but I don't like the way he looked at you. Radcliff either. Like you're a piece of meat on a charcuterie board."

That Josh knew what a charcuterie board was and

that he could pronounce it made her smile. "That's how *you* look at me."

"No, I look at you like you're my cherry pie." He laughed. "Either way, I want to eat you." His cock flexed against her hip.

Her mouth watered again, and she shoved thoughts of the case from her mind. "I can't take care of you in this position."

He grunted and lifted her so that the head of his dick nudged her opening. "I beg to differ."

Eyes closed, she wiggled, savoring the delicious sensation but… "You said you preferred me on my knees, and…I want you in my mouth."

With a growl, he released her. "Let me wash off this shitty day, and I'll let you do anything you want."

"Let me do it." She whirled on her ass to face him and backed up, giving him room. "Go under. Get your head wet."

He slouched low and dunked under the water. When he surfaced, a grin covered his face, and Harper sighed at the sexual collage of darkly dangerous and mischievously naughty. Water streamed from the hair plastered to his face. Droplets clung to long, dark gold lashes.

Fucking gorgeous.

Rising on her knees, she lathered his hair with shampoo. His hands explored her body, finding the ticklish spot he'd discovered Saturday night. She swatted his chest, and bubbles splattered, dotting her tits, which he zoomed in on.

His grin faded, and his gaze shot to hers, then down to her hip. "Jesus, Harper. I knew you'd hurt yourself, but damn."

She glanced at the ugly bruise the size of a football and shrugged. "It looks worse than it feels."

"Liar. I watched you favoring it all day. It's not nothing." Josh pushed her away and plunged under the water to rinse. Already rising as he righted himself, he stepped out of the tub.

"Oh!" Harper yelped as he swooped her up and settled her on the rug.

"You need ice on that." He grabbed the towel she'd set out and dried her with gentle hands, avoiding the bruise. Dropping to his knees and still sopping wet, he patted down her legs.

She pushed a wet strand of hair from his eyes. "Seriously, I've had worse. And you know I like a little pain."

The towel froze mid-pat, and he peered at her from under his lashes, desire lurking behind concern.

She smiled. "I think we should reverse positions."

"Fuck." He rubbed the towel over his head vigorously as he stood, his blue eyes searching her face.

A shiver racked her body, and goosebumps peppered her breasts and arms.

It's not the man. Just the cold.
Liar.

He wrapped the towel around her, knotting it in the valley between her breasts. The pad of his thumb traced the scratch on her cheek. "Are you sure? We can just sleep if you want."

"No." Sleeping with him was the last thing she wanted. She cupped her hand around his. "I want you."

The battle in his eyes shifted, and that sexy smile of his returned. "I'm all yours."

Chapter Eleven

Josh wasn't sure why Harper changed her mind, but he wasn't about to spook her with an inquisition right now. The questions and concerns romping around in his head could wait for later.

Instead, he lowered his mouth, claiming her with his lips, tongue, and then his teeth as he nipped her bottom lip. She nipped back, making him laugh as he picked her up and carried her from the bathroom into the bedroom.

He passed a half dozen boxes that lined the wall and stopped beside the unmade bed.

"Let me down," she breathed against his lips.

The instant he set her on her feet, she pulled the knot on the towel and let it fall to the floor. Her nipples grazed his chest as her delicate fingers worked between their bodies and curled around his dick.

She looked up at him, her pale skin illuminated by the fading sunlight slicing through the blinds. "I thought I'd dreamed how big you are."

His smile grew to a grin as he pumped his hips, fucking her hand. "You dreamed about me?"

"Conceited fuck." Letting him go, she flattened both hands on his chest. "Lie down." She hooked an ankle around his and pushed.

Josh could have taken her with him, but he relaxed into the fall and landed on his back, his feet dangling over the edge of the mattress. She stood between them, an enticing silhouette in the window—legs spread wide, hands planted on hips that flared, the deep tuck of her waist, and the length of her slender neck.

Determined. Fearless. Unapologetic. Beautiful. Mine.

He tucked his hands behind his head. "If you wanted me on my back, all you had to do was ask."

Eyes rolling, she reached for the clip holding her hair.

"Leave it." As much as he'd love the feel of her silky mane draped over his thighs and hips, he'd be able to better see her mouth around his dick with it up. At her questioning lift of a brow, he added, "For now."

Arms falling to her sides, she placed a knee on the mattress. Her hands took a slow glide up his thighs, nails scraping lightly, as she crawled between his legs. He spread them wider to make room, and his dick stood up like a rocket ready to launch.

Crouched low, ass in the air, she wrapped a fist around the base of his cock and aimed the head toward her mouth. Her tongue slipped out to wet her lips, and a trickle of pre-cum dribbled over the ridge and down his shaft.

Gray eyes flickering up at him, she ran her scorching tongue up the length to catch the evidence of his arousal, then circled the crown as if lapping at melting ice cream around the top of a cone.

A groan wrested from his chest. He wanted to fist his hands in Harper's raven-black hair, guide her onto his dick, and bury himself to the back of her throat. Instead, he grasped a handful of cold sheet and let her take the reins.

She smiled around the next teasing lick up his cock. "I love watching you battle your need to take over."

"And I love watching you suck my dick. It's a win-win." He groaned again as she drove him over her velvety tongue to the back of her throat. Those lush cherry lips hit the band of her fingers, and her inner cheeks, hotter and softer than he'd imagined, clamped around the shaft. Fire sizzled down his spine.

"*Fuck*." The muscles of his ass clenched, shoving his dick a fraction deeper. "Suck it."

Her eyes dilated, and tears leaked from the corners, but she hummed and began to suck.

"That's it, baby, suck it hard," Josh rasped. He lifted his head higher and gently funneled his fingers into her hair, the clip barring his progress. "I dreamed about you, too. Just like this."

Backing off a bit, she gave herself room to swirl around his head and probe the slit before retreating to the tip. Her cheeks worked the sides of his dick on the next downstroke. Back and forth. Up and down. Her tits swayed, adding to the erotic image of his dick disappearing inside her mouth.

His heart pounded faster every time she took him deeper.

So fucking deep.

Another withdrawal and plunge of excruciating heaven nearly sent him over the edge. His head dropped to the bed, and he tried to slow his breathing. He was close. Too damn close. He wanted this moment with Harper to last longer.

But the familiar tightening in his sac began and the fast ride into oblivion was just over the next rise and fall of her sweet mouth.

"Coming," he warned through clenched teeth.

Harper angled her head, and Josh sank to the back of her throat. A white-hot current splintered from the base of his spine, streaking along his nervous system to engulf his entire body.

"*Fuck.*" He fisted his hands in her hair as ribbons of cum pulsed through his shaft and into her mouth. Her throat closed around each wave, drinking him down, adding to the pleasure. He rolled his head against the sheets, relishing every last draw of her cheeks and lap of her tongue.

When she released him with a pop, he untangled his fingers from her hair. His arms dropped heavily to his sides. "One down. One to go."

Laughter opened his eyes. Her hair was a mess. Mascara ran down flushed cheeks. Her breathing was shallow, and her skin glistened. She wiped her puffy lips with the back of her hand, then licked it.

Hunger gnawed at his gut, and blood surged into his cock. Bolting upright, he hauled her against him and slanted his mouth over hers. The taste of himself on her lips only made him crave her sweet essence on his tongue.

Josh broke the kiss intent on doing just that. Instead, he looked down at Harper, need parting her lips, so beautiful he couldn't draw his next breath for the ache in his chest. It didn't make sense. They'd just met. Yet, Shayna's words echoed in his heart, and he could no longer deny them. Or their meaning

Ah, my little wildcat, you broke my door.

Her eyes opened, and her brows dove inward. "You okay?"

She wouldn't want to hear the words crawling up his throat, fighting their way to be heard. They would only scare her off. Hell, they scared him.

He shook his head and pulled the clip from her hair. "Nothing. Just wanted to make sure you're comfortable."

"I'd be more comfortable with you inside me."

A smile pulled at his lips. "That can be arranged."

Twisting at the waist, he rolled her beneath him so that they lay lengthwise up the bed. He pinned her hands above her head. "But first"—He slid his lips along her jaw and began kissing his way down her beautiful body—"I'm going to eat some cherry pie."

****

Heat coiled in Harper's belly like the spring action of her Glock, eagerly waiting for Josh to squeeze the trigger. Her clit pulsed. Her breaths, when she could catch them, were quick and shallow.

As he made an unhurried journey over her body, he plied her with open-mouthed kisses, nipped at her skin, then laved it with his tongue. His fingers tenderly traced the bruise on her hip as well as those he'd left Saturday night. Every touch was like fuel to the flame of an already raging inferno, and she wanted him to fucking blow it up.

Yet when he sat back on his heels and rested his hands on her bent knees, he did nothing. His face, cast in shadow, was impossible to read, but he seemed lost in his head.

Or maybe he'd changed his mind.

She propped up on her elbows. "Is there a problem? Or are you just taking a coffee break?"

"Touch yourself," he said, his tone rough. "Like

the naughty girl you were in the bathtub."

The command stirred her inner sub. Unfortunately, Cherry was never one to give in too easily. "And if I don't? Will you spank me?"

A low chuckle rumbled in his chest, drawing him out of whatever thoughts held him prisoner. He pressed her knees out and down, exposing her pussy.

"Baby, you're getting a spanking either way." He trailed a finger along her inner thigh. "I owe you for your brattiness the other night, remember?"

"I remember how much you liked it."

His finger stopped mid-thigh. "I like everything about you, Harper."

The serious tone in his voice had her lying back, uncomfortable with his attempt to deepen their connection, but unable to deny the idea tempted her. *He* tempted her. "You don't know everything about me."

How could he? He'd only known her for two days. The only woman he really knew anything about was Cherry.

"I know enough." The bed rocked as he stretched out between her legs. His shoulders wedged against her thighs. Callused hands cupped her ass and tilted her hips toward his face. His warm breath whispered over her hungry pussy. "I want to know more if you'll let me."

Tears burned behind her eyelids. Getting caught up in the fantasy of what he suggested was just a shit show waiting to happen. She'd disappoint him as she had her family, as she had herself. Or he would her. And he'd change.

Like Blake did.

Or maybe she'd been blind to Blake's faults from

the beginning. At least Josh was honest about his.

"Touch yourself, Harper," he said again, spreading her folds with his thumbs. The flat of his tongue lapped at the juices slicking her thighs. "Show me how you'll pleasure yourself when I'm not here to do it for you."

Afraid of the emotions he evoked but desperately wanting him and the pleasure he offered, if not the connection, she skimmed trembling fingers over her breasts and down her ribs. At the dip of her belly, she hesitated.

"Come on, baby," he coaxed. "Give me more of your sweet juices."

Like a hot brand, his tongue swept from her center over her clit, searing her mind and burning away all thought but the decision she'd made earlier—to give in, to give him what he wanted, to be his.

If only for tonight.

With one hand, she clutched his hair. "I'm not doing all the work. That's what you're for."

He gave her that crooked grin that made her tummy flutter. "Don't worry, baby. I've got you."

Harper closed her eyes and slid her middle finger over the swollen knot, then made leisurely circles around it.

A groan vibrated from his chest and into her thighs and core. "Damn, that's hot."

He probed her entrance with two fingers, inching them deeper. The exquisite stretch created a frenzied need to get to the finish line, but she kept the pace slow. Then his tongue joined her finger, working her clit in places her finger missed.

"Oh god, yes, fuck…" She couldn't bite back the plea that rose in her throat. "Josh…"

Instead of holding her back as she thought he might, he beckoned her orgasm with the crook of his fingers over her G-spot. Once, twice... "Come for me, wildcat."

"*Yes!*" The tight coil in her core sprang loose in an explosion, and like shrapnel, shards of fire and ice ricocheted off every nerve, paralyzing her with the sweetest pleasure. Flashes of light streaked across the back of her eyelids, then faded to black as she spiraled through a vortex of bliss.

Harper wasn't sure how long she floated in the darkness until Josh's murmur drew her back.

"...good girl...love watching you come."

She opened her eyes and moaned as he licked between his fingers. Then he brought her hand to his mouth. "Can't let any go to waste."

His hot, wet mouth closed around her middle finger, and the first pull set off a mini-gasm that stole her breath.

Fucking hell, he's good.

Chuckling, he laid her hand on the bed beside her hip and began a slow journey across her abs, licking the grooves on one side. Her belly contracted, and she felt him smile against her skin.

She clutched his hair with both hands, meaning to end the delicious torture. Instead, she tugged, trying to guide him to her tits. Did he need a fucking map?

Another smile teased her ribs just before his tongue bathed the underside of one breast where he'd painted his brand Saturday night. Closing his mouth over it, he sucked, hard. Her hips jerked off the mattress. Her clit hit his breastbone. Another shock jolted through her, strong but fleeting.

A strangled cry tore her from the euphoric aftermath, and warmth spread across her cheeks. She sounded like a fucking cat in heat. Her brain tried to shut down the reactions to what he had done to her—was still doing to her—but her body wasn't having it.

Tears leaked from the corners of her eyes, yet she held him at her breast with both hands, relishing the pain.

Easing the pressure, he swiped his tongue up and across her nipple. "I like seeing my brand on you. Do you?"

"Yes, more," she choked out. "Suck it…hard."

Josh's mouth covered her nipple and took her deep, the suction so painfully sweet she cried out. Like lightning, delicious threads of pleasure streaked to her clit. Pressure built again, every stroke of his velvety tongue feeding a volatile storm.

"Fuck me." She undulated her hips, grinding against him. "Need you to fuck me."

Ignoring her, he lavished all his attention on her breasts, one then the other and back again. Another orgasm hovered like a hurricane in the Gulf.

"Josh…please…I—"

His teeth caught and tugged, slowly dragging their razor-sharp edges toward the beaded tip.

"Motherfu—" Her breath hung in her throat as her climax unfurled, washing over her in a tidal wave of fire. "Josh."

****

Need drove Josh to his knees. Harper had sucked him dry only moments ago. He shouldn't be this close to losing his shit again. He'd never made a woman come from breast play, but his wildcat continued to prove she wasn't like other women.

He licked the rosy nipple he'd bitten. "Please tell me you have a condom."

"Night...stand."

Stretching across her, he opened the drawer and groaned. Next to a bright pink dildo and an egg-shaped vibrator lay a single condom packet.

One? That's it?

Sighing, he straightened, rolled the latex down his shaft, and settled his hips into the cradle of her thighs. With one thrust, he slammed home and sucked in a breath through clenched teeth. The hot walls of her cunt fisted around him like a tailor-made glove. "Fuck."

Tight. So fucking tight. From the orgasms I gave her.

Heart banging against his chest, he pulled out and screwed his way in again. He cursed the condom in his head, wishing he was bare, that he could feel her juices on his cock and her velvety grip.

She whimpered but hooked her ankles over the back of his thighs and arched to meet his next thrust. Her hands slid down his back and smoothed over his ass, urging him deeper.

Burying his head into the crook of her neck, he pounded into her, hard, fast, unrelenting. His chest ached. He wanted more, to fuck her until he crushed all her doubts. To show her with his body what he couldn't say out loud.

A soft cry of pain slipped past his lust-fogged brain. Another tugged at a thread of concern.

He lifted his head and slowed the pace. It was dark now. He couldn't see her face. "What's wrong?"

"Noth-ing." Her voice cracked on the next roll of

his hips against hers. "Don't stop."

The bruise. He'd forgotten about it. "Christ, Harper, I'm hurting you."

"Pain is good."

"Not this kind of pain. I won't add to the damage."

Her legs locked around him, and her nails dug into his ass. "I need you to finish."

Josh captured her hands and held them above her head. "Don't worry, baby, I'm not done. Just changing things up." Her legs loosened as he pulled out then sat back on his heels. "Turn over."

As soon as she'd flipped onto her stomach, Josh hiked her ass in the air and rimmed her entrance with his dick.

Face pressed to the sheet, she moaned and rocked back. The mouth of her pussy opened wide and engulfed the head of his cock. A shudder rippled through him, and he fought the impulse to slide into her hot haven.

Clasping her uninjured hip with one hand to hold her still, he slapped her ass with the other. "Don't fucking move."

She squirmed, and he sank another inch. "Then you move."

"God dammit." He ached to give in to her demand, but he landed another swat and massaged the pink staining her creamy white flesh. "I've let you top from the bottom long enough. Too long."

She huffed a stray curl from her face and glared at him through narrowed eyes. "You love it."

"I'm amused by it." On a long inhale, he steeled himself for the battle of wills about to ensue. "But I think you need a reminder of who's in control."

Exhaling, he withdrew completely.

"Fu—"

Smack! "That's for hurting yourself."

"I'm not—"

Smack! "For not knowing your fucking limits."

Her fingers clutched the sheet.

"Do you want my dick?"

"You know I do," she whined, but her tone still held resistance.

Banding an arm around her, Josh bent over her and gathered a handful of her glorious mane. "I'm going to ride you hard, just like you like it, but only if you ask nicely."

The stubborn wildcat sank her teeth into her bottom lip.

He tightened his grip until a mewling cry parted her lips and her body relaxed into the sting.

"Please, Josh," she said, her words barely audible. "Please fuck me."

"That's a good girl." He kissed her cheek and straightened. With a hand on her hip and the other at her waist, taking care to avoid her bruise, he fed his cock into her welcoming heat until he hit bottom.

Immediately, he retreated and slammed home again.

"Oh god." She rose to her elbows, her head thrown back.

Faster, harder, Josh pounded into her, skin slapping skin. The rasp of her panting breaths mingled with his labored gulps of air. Those sexy noises that drove him wild barely filtered past the drum of his heartbeat.

Electrical impulses skittered along his spine.

Fuck, not yet.

Shifting, he changed the angle so that he bumped her G-spot. At the same time, his fingers stole around her hip to stroke her clit, her desire soaking his hand. Her body jerked, and her pussy convulsed around his cock. A high-pitched keening drowned out all other sounds as she came. The intoxicating scent of her climax filled his senses, making him dizzy with a need to join her.

Sweat beaded his brow and his muscles strained as he waited for her to finish.

The second her body sagged, he pulled out, ripped the condom off, and pumped his cock, his hand slick with her cream. Energy surged through him, stiffening his spine. Thick ropes of cum jetted from his dick to paint her porcelain ass and lower back until he emptied his balls.

Mine.

"I have...officially...iced your buns." He fell to the bed beside her, one arm slung over his eyes. He heaved in a deep breath and blew it out. "Been thinking about doing that all day."

A muffled giggle slipped past the rush of blood thundering in his ears.

"I like that sound."

Her leg snaked along his as she stretched out on her stomach. "So you've said."

"I like all your sounds." He grabbed the towel off the floor to clean her up. "The way you laugh. The way you shout at me in a hushed whisper so no one can hear but me."

"Josh." Her tone held a warning he didn't want to hear.

Tossing the towel to the floor, he lay next to her

and traced the seam of her lips with his thumb. "I love this vulgar little mouth of yours, and I especially love that purring sound you make when you come."

She pressed her face into the sheet and groaned. "We can't do this."

The knots in his gut tightened, but he wouldn't let her push him away again. "I'm pretty sure we just did."

"Why can't you just…"

"What? Leave you alone? Give up on something I believe could be good—special?" He shook his head though she couldn't see him. "If you think I'm going to make it easy for you to do the same, you picked the wrong guy."

"I didn't pick you," she muttered. "Wrangler did."

"Calling bullshit again, wildcat. We picked each other before Wrangler introduced us, and you know it." When she didn't answer, he swallowed, hard. "Is that really what you want?"

Please don't say yes.

"I—" Rising on her elbows, she twisted a look at him. "Look, the relationship we might have had at the club was based on anonymity. That was blown out of the water this morning."

"Bullshit." He shook his head again. "You bailed on me before the park."

With a growl, she flopped onto her back and stared at the ceiling. Her nipples grew taut and goosebumps skated over her ivory flesh. "I've told you I'm new here. I have a lot at stake, and I can't fuck this up."

Josh reached across Harper to pull the covers across them. "What exactly does that have to do with us?"

"I can't look weak in front of my people."

Harper weak? Ridiculous. And to hear her say he'd made her feel any different... "When have I made you feel weak?"

"Every time you look at me."

Chapter Twelve

Josh fought to suppress a smile. That was a huge admission from a stubborn woman, and it fed his determination to keep fighting for her. "I'm glad to know I have that effect on you, but Harper, you're one of the strongest women I've ever met. And as you keep pointing out, I've met a lot."

At the lift of her brow, he added, "I'm talking about my mom. She worked the ranch beside my dad until the day she died. And Shayna, my sister-in-law? She's had to be strong for her family. Her mom had cancer. And if you knew my brother. He's a fucking hard-ass, but Shayna's got him wrapped around her little finger. And she puts me in my place all the time."

The lines of obstinance around her eyes wavered so he pressed on. "And Ellie? The woman's had her fair share of heartache, but she just keeps marching on, helping others. She was my rock when my mom died. Evan's, too. I was twenty-four. We were grown-ass men, but it happened suddenly—brain aneurism—and we all fell apart. Ellie was there, picking up the pieces and making arrangements. Then again, three years ago, when my dad died."

"I'm so sorry." Her raspy voice was soft, drawing him from his sorrowful thoughts. "I haven't had time to make any calls to get her the help she needs."

"Don't worry. Shayna's in town. I'm going to ask

her to check on Ellie."

"Is your sister-in-law a doctor?"

"No. She's a nurse, and she's worked with patients with…dementia." He cleared the grief from his throat and blinked away the burn behind his eyelids. "Sorry to unload on you."

Turning on her side, she palmed his jaw. Soft gray eyes peered deep into his. "Don't ever be sorry for loving your family. You're one of the lucky ones."

Aching to draw her close, to accept the comfort she offered, he settled for a hand on her waist. "My point is, I see your strength and your spirit. I'm not trying to break either. I don't want to."

Doubt creased her brow.

Gently, he eased his hand over her hip and along her flank. "This morning, when I saw you at the park, I thought you were amazing."

She snorted. "Yeah, when was that? When I had my face in the dirt?

The scratch on her cheek beckoned his fingers. "No, I saw you before that when I nearly ran over Leon. I didn't know it was you at the time. I thought you might be a deputy. I don't know. But I looked in my rearview, and I saw you run through traffic to save his life. Harper, that was not weakness."

She shrugged. "I was just doing my job."

"Bravery can't be taught. It's instinct," he said, looking for another crack in the wall around her heart. For every stone he pulled down, she added another. "I watched you all day. How you handle people, how you listen and assess the situation then control the outcome. You have great insight in reading people."

"I used to think so."

Desperation clawing at him, Josh tried another tactic. "People have careers and still manage to have hot, monkey sex, you know. Some even have relationships."

"Been there, tried that. It didn't end well." Her sarcasm didn't hide the hurt in her voice, and it crushed his soul to think of her so in love with someone else that she still ached for him.

Driving his fingers through her hair to cup the back of her head, he tilted her face to his again. "I'm sorry you were hurt, but don't let that asshole's screwup get in the way of us."

Harper peered up at him from under her lashes, but there was no hurt in her eyes. Shame and anger burned in their depths. "He didn't screw up. I did."

****

Harper flattened her palms on Josh's chest and pushed. "Let me up."

Without hesitation, he untangled his fingers from her hair, and she ground her teeth against the disappointment streaming through her at the loss of his touch. She hated pushing him away when he was fighting for her, for them—or the possibility of them. As much as she battled against him, she'd be lying to herself if she didn't admit she wanted him to win the war.

Sitting up and pulling the sheet with her, she scooted back to lean against the headboard. She tucked her knees to her chest and wrapped her arms around her legs.

Josh lay still beside her, a hand around her ankle, as if afraid she'd bolt. "Talk to me."

She didn't want to talk about Blake, but maybe if

she told Josh the ugly truth of her humiliation, he would understand why she couldn't let her guard down for even a second. Or maybe he'd realize he didn't want her after all.

Probably for the best.

"You have to understand," she said, staring at unpolished nails, one broken to the quick. "I didn't grow up with loving, supporting parents. My mom ran off when I was born, and my father is a die-hard cop who bleeds blue and demands respect, sometimes with the back of his hand. He raised me like he did my brothers—rough and hard. He expected the best. Mediocre wasn't good enough."

His thumb circled the rise of her anklebone. "I'm sorry."

She shook her head and managed a smile she didn't feel. "Don't be. It made me tough. I've fought, sometimes literally, through life, first with my brothers, then at the academy to prove myself. I spent years chasing drug dealers and gang members through the streets of Houston until, finally, I earned my detective shield."

"Did that make your father happy?"

Harper shrugged. "For a while."

"You're pretty young for a sheriff, aren't you? Surely, that's a big deal."

"Interim sheriff. And it might have been if the circumstances behind me leaving the force were different." Her gaze cut to his, and the pity in his eyes curdled in her stomach. "Doesn't matter. I gave up trying to make him happy long ago. I loved being a cop, and I was damn good at it. I *am* good at it. *I* wanted that promotion." She thumped her chest with her fist. "Not for him. For *me*. And I earned it."

Pushing up to sit beside her, Josh patted his lap. "Come here, baby."

He reached for her, but she held out a hand. If he touched her, she'd fall apart, and she had to finish, to open wounds that had barely scabbed over but still brought pain. Maybe then they would finally heal.

"As a patrol officer, my first partner, Zeke, was the best. He treated me with respect, not because his mother taught him to respect women, but because I was a fellow officer and his partner. He mentored me through my first few years, and he was the one who encouraged me to make detective, not my father.

"Shortly after I joined the Gang and Narcotics Division, my new partner transferred to Sex Crimes and Blake moved into his spot as my partner. We clicked because we were both newly promoted and very competitive. We pushed each other, and it worked for a while. Until our relationship changed."

Harper rested her head against the headboard and stared at the ceiling, watching the light from the candle in the bathroom dance with the shadows. "We worked long hours. Our social life was nonexistent. I don't remember how it happened or who made the first move, but it just seemed easy to fall into a physical relationship."

She sighed. "My father always warned me not to fuck within the department, and he tried to warn me about Blake. At the time, I ignored him because I hated him getting into my business…and because I thought I loved Blake. Looking back, I know it was never that. I loved the adrenaline rush we shared working a case.

"After a while, Blake changed in little ways here

and there. He started taking the lead at every scene. Said he was protecting me. I called bullshit, and for a while, he was better. Then the paperwork began falling to me more and more while he went out after shift for a drink with the guys from the unit. Like I wasn't one of them.

"Then he began offering suggestions on cases that we'd talked about at home. We were living together by then. Stupidest fucking thing I've ever done. He made the ideas I'd come up with sound like his. I thought he'd forgotten it was mine, and when I mentioned it, he said, 'No, don't you remember…' and he'd fill in the blank with something I'd actually said. Or he'd get mad and say I was being ridiculous. That I must not have heard him give me credit. I know now he was gaslighting me and driving a wedge between me and the other detectives."

Her throat tightened and the bridge of her nose stung as the memories piled up, one on top of another, stirring old feelings of confusion, frustration, and humiliation. She swallowed them back as she continued. "I'd lay out a plan of action or a theory of possible suspects, and half the guys looked at me like I'd stolen the idea from Blake because, 'um, he just said that.'"

A bitter bark of laughter choked her. "One guy accused me of trying to sleep my way to the top when I actually had seniority over Blake. Stupid fuck."

"It's okay, baby. You don't have to do this. I get it now." Josh wiped at a tear she hadn't realized had fallen.

"No, wait, this is the best part." She slapped his hand away and shot out of bed to pace, a fierce need for

Josh to know the whole ugly truth driving her. "Blake and I were both up for lieutenant, and Blake got the promotion. I admit I was jealous, but I was happy for him. That night when I got home with a bottle of his favorite wine, expecting to celebrate, he ended our relationship and said he was putting me up for a transfer to another precinct. Said he was doing it for both of us. That it wouldn't look good for him to be fucking a subordinate and I'd never advance because it would be seen as him favoring me."

Harper sucked in a deep breath and exhaled, shuddering as the memories released her. She'd kept them bottled up for so long, never telling anyone the whole story, especially how it ended. She'd been too ashamed.

"I tried to make it work with my new unit, to prove myself to them, but word had spread, and they'd already formed their opinions about me. I got lip service and every shit detail that came along. My career was dead in the water, and I was dying inside. Then Zeke heard about the opening here and made a call; he knows Radcliff somehow. I jumped at the chance for a fresh start."

Wrapping her arms around her middle, she stared at the carpet under her feet. Josh had gone silent, and she was afraid to see the pity she'd seen earlier in his eyes. Or, worse, the disgust she'd seen in her family's.

"I just need five fucking minutes alone with that asshole out behind the barn."

Her gaze snapped to his. The hard line of his jaw and icy glint in his eyes matched the deadly edge in his voice. His fists clenched at his sides.

"What?" he snarled. "The guys' a dick and

deserves an ass-kicking for what he did to you."

Harper blinked. Josh had been angry with her throughout the day, but not like this. This was no-holds-barred fury. On her behalf. It felt good to have someone on her side, but that didn't change the past or her current situation.

With a weary sigh, she looked away. "Blake *is* a dick, but I was a fool for not seeing what was right in front of me. I can't be that fool again."

"You trusted him, Harper. That's what people who care about each other do." Bounding off the bed, he stood in front of her and gripped her chin, forcing her to look at him. "You did nothing wrong. *He* broke your trust. *He* betrayed *you*."

Another tear trailed unheeded down her cheek. "But I made it easy for him."

"And you're worried it'll be the same with us?"

"Just look at me," she waved a hand to encompass the bed. "I'm already breaking the rules. You're the victim of a crime. I'm handling your case."

"You said yourself the association will take over."

"But they're not here yet, and I shouldn't be involved with you."

"But you are," he whispered, the harshness in his voice fading. He slid a hand to the back of her neck and pulled her closer. "*I* am."

She whimpered at the heat of his skin against hers.

"I won't hurt you. I'm not him." His other arm snaked around her, and his eyes pleaded with her to listen. "Don't punish me for his sins. Don't punish yourself."

Harper wanted to believe him, to trust that he wouldn't betray her. That she wouldn't betray herself.

With every fiery touch, Josh had set fire to the walls she'd built around herself, scorched holes in her resolve, and burned a path to her soul.

"I can't. I—" A sob closed her throat. More tears flowed. She couldn't stop them.

Fucking weak.

With as much backbone she could muster, she jerked her chin from his grip and looked up at him. "You need to go."

He stared at her for a moment, his stark eyes searching hers. His Adam's apple bobbed as he swallowed. "Is that what you really want?"

No. Yes. I don't know. "I can't do this. I won't."

His lips thinned as he stepped back and turned away. "Then I guess we're done here."

Her heart sank, and the words to call him back bubbled up in her throat. Instead, she sat on the edge of the bed and watched him retreat to the bathroom. She covered herself with the sheet that smelled of sex and Josh's cologne. The back of her eyelids burned, and she blinked to hold back more fucking tears.

Silence rang like a death knell except for the sounds of her heart cracking and her commonsense crumbling. What if he was right? What if they could make it work?

Once the investigation was turned over to the TSCRA, she'd have no excuse to hold him off other than her own fear. He'd be busy ranching, with no reason to be in the office interfering with her work. What if they could just be a normal couple?

Not a couple. Lovers. No one had to know. They could keep it quiet. Maybe limit their time together to The Arena.

She shook her head. He already crowded every corner of her mind. Her fucking pussy wept for him. She couldn't let him into her heart.

Best to end it now before it's too late.

"God dammit." His angry curse burst from the bathroom a second before he did. Coat in hand, he finished buckling his belt as swift strides carried him across the room to the door. He paused, hand on the knob.

"Better get dressed, *Sheriff,*" he said, his tone bitter. "You've got work to do."

Before she could ask what the fuck he meant, her phone vibrated against her nightstand. She picked it up and read the screen. *Keith Dollins.*

"Quinn," she answered.

"Sheriff," Deputy Dollins said, "I'm out at the northwest corner of the McNamara ranch, up near the highway. Looks like rustlers hit 'em again."

"I'll be right there." Harper's gaze shot to the empty doorway.

Josh was gone.

****

Red and blue lights circled the black sky about a mile up the highway. Josh gunned the engine, anger boiling through his veins. He wasn't sure who he was angrier with—the damn rustlers who'd stolen more of his cattle tonight, Harper for stealing his heart, or himself for not guarding against either.

He hit the brakes hard, stirring dirt and gravel as he skidded to a stop on the shoulder behind Evan's tailgate.

Josh was out of the truck before the engine died.

"What the fuck happened?" he bellowed as Evan

left the deputy and headed in his direction.

"They hit before dark, in broad daylight," Evan said. "Before we got out here."

"God damn motherfucking—" Josh kicked the front fender of his truck. He wanted to smash something—someone—but the bastard who'd fucked with Harper's career, her confidence, and her ability to trust wasn't available, so he turned around and got back in his truck before he gave Evan a black eye.

He slammed the door and blew out a long breath, trying to rein in his anger.

The passenger door opened, and Evan climbed into the dark cab. "What the hell's wrong with you?"

"What do you mean 'what's wrong with me'?" he shouted. "More of my fucking cattle were stolen. That's what's wrong."

"I'm just as upset about *our* fucking cattle, but I'm not putting dents in expensive vehicles." The calm in his brother's voice grated like nails on a chalkboard, but that was Evan. Always the voice of reason and the calm in the storm. "Let's try that again. What's up your ass?"

"Nothing." Not a fucking thing he wanted to talk about. Not how he'd begged Harper to give them a chance. Or how she'd shut him down. Or how he'd snuck out the back fucking door and down the fucking alley, like what they had shared was somehow dirty, because even after she'd thrown him out, he still wanted to protect her.

And then there was the fact that once again, he'd failed to protect his fucking cattle from fucking rustlers. No, he'd left that up to his brother and the guys who always seemed to have his back.

I've fucking failed everyone.

Blowing out another breath, Josh lifted his hat, ran his fingers through his hair, and shoved it back on his head. God, he was tired, running on pure adrenaline. "Where is everybody?"

"I've got Rusty and Mark pushing both herds to the meadow down by the lake. They'll be away from roads and closer to home. I sent Leon home to sleep, so he and Cal can take over in the morning and set up a soft camp for tomorrow night, just in case these assholes are brave enough to come deeper onto the property."

"Good plan." He hadn't thought past getting here. Damn, he needed to get his priorities straight. Harper had hers etched in stone, and he wasn't one of them. It was time to take care of business at home before he had no cattle left to steal. "There won't be enough grass there for both herds. We'll need to supplement with hay. It'll cost a fortune but not as much as the loss we've taken the last two days."

"Who do you think is doing this?"

Josh rolled his eyes. "I know fuck all about cattle rustlers."

"Then you don't know?"

He shifted on his seat to face his brother. "Didn't I just fucking say that?"

"No," Evan said, "I mean you haven't heard our case is different? The MO is not the same as the group making their way through other area ranches? The deputy told me they're using two semi-trailers to load fifty head and motorcycles—not horses—to round them up.

"I haven't heard that." Josh slumped into his seat. Harper trusted him so little she'd keep something like that from him? He scrubbed a hand over his face. "I'll take it from here. You go home."

"I'll stay with you."

"Ev, I've got this." He was barely holding it together as it was. When Harper got here... Fuck.

"Are you sure? Shayna said it's the new sheriff—"

"Jesus Christ, can you just get the fuck out." Josh couldn't see Evan in the shadows of the cab, but he knew his brother well enough to know he wanted to push, to help fix the problem. Some things just couldn't be fixed. "Look, I wasn't here like I should have been, and I'm sorry for that. I need to do this."

The dome light filled the truck as Evan opened the door and stepped out. "I'm around if you want to talk."

The door shut again, leaving Josh alone in the blessed darkness. His brother's truck pulled onto the highway just as a familiar SUV rolled to a stop behind him, lights flashing.

Baseball cap pulled low, hands tucked in her pockets, Harper hurried past him on the passenger side without checking inside. She couldn't see through the tinted windows anyway. Not that she was looking for him.

The deputy stepped into the light to acknowledge her. Keith Dollins. A good guy. He'd have her back. Josh was glad for that.

Watching her do the job she loved, Josh expected the rage to build again. She'd chosen it over him. Instead, all he felt was numb. Fuck, if this was love, he didn't want it.

As Harper spoke with Keith, who pointed here and there—how the fuck they saw anything, Josh would never know—she searched the blank landscape on the other side of the downed fence, as if waiting for something to happen. Was the city girl worried about a stampede?

Then Keith pointed in his direction, and her head swiveled around, her gaze locking on his truck. Could she see his silhouette in the headlights of the passing car? Had she been looking for him out in the pasture? Was she worried he'd cause a scene? Or what if...

No. She's not looking for you. She hasn't changed her mind. Get that fucking notion out of your head.

After a few minutes more of talking to Keith, she walked along the ditch toward his truck. She knocked on the window, her face tinted blue, then red, then blue again.

Tipping his hat lower, Josh rolled down the window. "*Sheriff.*"

Her mouth twisted at the greeting. "Mind if I get in?"

Wind whipped around her, reminding him how cold it was. Funny, he hadn't felt it until now. He shrugged. "Be my guest."

He started the engine and cranked up the heater as she opened the door and used the handle to pull herself into the passenger seat. She stared straight ahead, her profile lit by the glow from the dash, which meant she could see his.

Fuck that. He dimmed the panel.

Enclosed in the darkness with Harper should have felt intimate, yet the tension between them was as thick as the ice forming in the water trough by the barn.

"It's too dark to see anything tonight," she said, her tone all business, "and unfortunately the department doesn't have the resources for LED light towers. We'll have to come back at first light. In the meantime, don't touch anything and don't walk around out there. Deputy Dollins will remain to preserve the scene."

"Got it." He waited for her to leave but she just sat there. "When were you going to tell me you think this is a local job?"

Her head snapped around, and he wished he could see the expression on her face. Surprise? Guilt? Mistrust? "I should have. I'm sorry."

"Why didn't you?"

"This is exactly what I was trying to tell you. I can't think straight around you."

"Are you saying it's my fault you forgot to tell me?" Sarcasm hid the *what if* scenario sparking to life again. Maybe he'd given up too soon.

"Can you think of anyone who has a vendetta against you?" she asked, ignoring his taunt. "What about your neighbor?"

"Walter?" He chuckled. "The old goat hates anyone with the name McNamara, but he's not a thief."

"Mealer says there's some sort of feud between your families. A land dispute?"

Josh rubbed the back of his neck. He didn't like the doubts Harper was planting in his head about his neighbors, but he was learning to trust her intuitive instincts. She hadn't been wrong about Ellie's need for medical attention. "It's a long story, but it comes down to three feet of land running the length of the property line. He's bitter that the land his father thought was his turned out to belong to my family."

"And his grandson?"

"Nah, Reed's a solid guy. A friend."

"I'm not ruling anyone out."

"You can rule out my guys and my family. They

were all together at the house having supper when this happened." He shifted to look at her again. "And I was with you except for when I stopped to get a pizza. I didn't get a receipt, but you can check with the kid who waited on me. I used my card."

"Will you stop."

"Just trying to cooperate, *Sheriff*. Wouldn't want to get in the way of you doing your job."

"Josh, I'm sorry." A shaky breath shuddered from her. "I never meant— I shouldn't have—"

Hearing the catch in her throat tightened his own. "No, I'm sorry. I'm just— Harper?"

"Yeah?"

"Would you consider meeting me at The Arena?" He sounded like a fucking pussy, begging for scraps, but he had to try one more time, and it was better than being an asshole and making her cry. "It's out of town. No one would see us, and you'd be off duty. It wouldn't interfere with your work."

"I already considered that option."

"And?"

"It's not a good idea, Josh."

"You're probably right." He swallowed down the disappointment making his stomach pitch, but the fact she'd thought about it already was something. Wasn't it?"

She reached for the door handle.

"Wait." He couldn't let her go. Not as things stood between them. "What about the other offer? The one where I take Blake What's His Name out behind the barn?"

She choked on a half laugh/half sniffle. "I always thought it would be a dark alley."

Josh ached to pull her onto his lap and hold her. He gripped the steering wheel instead. "You just say the word, wildcat."

"Careful, cowboy." A smile laced her words. "I might have to arrest you for conspiracy to."

To what? Love you?

He grunted. "Might be worth it."

Chapter Thirteen

The morning dew frosted the ground as the sun topped the trees, shedding light on the scene out at the McNamara ranch. Too bad it couldn't shed some on her fucking life.

Exhaustion weighed on Harper as she trudged through the ditch to join Mealer. She hadn't slept for shit. Every time she closed her eyes, the look on Josh's face when she'd kicked him out haunted her. She'd hurt him.

She wasn't feeling too great herself.

Mealer rose from a squat next to a set of tire tracks by the fence. "Sheriff."

"What do you have for me?" she asked, turning her focus to the job she had begun to question in the early morning hours. Not the job really but the control it had on her life, on her decision making. Why couldn't she have a life outside the badge?

"Barring a closer look," Mealer said, "I'd bet it's the same trailer as before."

"Did you let Mr. McNamara know?" She glanced at the red truck she'd seen parked along the road behind the deputy's cruiser, knowing it wasn't his and he wasn't there.

The window rolled down, and Leon's rugged face appeared. He waved, his smile reminding her that Josh had been essential in putting it there.

She smiled and waved back but couldn't make out the passenger.

"I talked to Josh just before Leon and Cal showed up to relieve him and to fix the fence as soon as I'm done processing the scene. He looked pretty beat." Mealer waited until she faced him again to add, "You only missed him by a few minutes."

Harper ignored his knowing gaze and the disappointment of not seeing Josh, but she was glad to know it was a matter of timing and he wasn't avoiding her. And that he was headed home to get some sleep. "Anything new?"

A grin creased Mealer's face below his mustache. "Yesterday, I couldn't get any good hoof prints." He pointed to one side of the tire marks. "But here, not only did I get a good set, but we hit the jackpot." He pulled up a picture on his phone and handed it to her. "Look at this."

The hoof print looked more like that of a man's sneaker minus the heal than a horseshoe. "What the hell is this?"

"I think they call it a hoof boot. It's used temporarily when a horse loses its shoe. I could be wrong about that." He pocketed his phone. "I'll call the local farrier to see what he can tell us."

"Good work." Her heart thudded at the sound of gravel, and both of them once again turned back to the road. A dark blue dually pulled in behind her SUV. "Who's that?"

"That'll be Sheriff Jenkins—uh, former sheriff. Name's Tom."

Harper didn't take offense at Mealer's slip. He'd worked for Jenkins a long time. She couldn't expect him to break a lifelong habit in one day. She was, however, concerned about why Jenkins was showing up at a crime scene when he had no jurisdiction.

What the fuck does he want?

"Introduce me?" she asked.

"Sure."

She and Mealer met Jenkins halfway. The man was tall, at least six-four, and lanky. His hair was snow-white under a black beanie. Silver-rimmed glasses sat on a hawkish nose and framed narrow eyes. Black coveralls and a red and black plaid coat finished off her assessment.

"Tom." Mealer shook hands with his former boss. "This is Sheriff Harper Quinn."

She extended her hand to Jenkins. "It's nice to meet you. I've heard a lot about you."

The man laughed as he grasped Harper's hand and gave it a firm shake. "Sheriff Quinn. I hope you don't believe everything."

Harper gave him her best good-ol'-boy smile. "Some would say where there's smoke…"

He let go of her hand and nodded at Mealer. "I like her."

Mealer looked relieved.

"What can I do for you?" Harper asked.

"I heard about Josh's bad luck, and thought I'd drop by to see if there was anything I could do. We never had this kind of thing in our county before, not for at least fifty years anyway." In other words, not while he was in charge. But if he'd never handled a rustling case, how could he help her?

And it was odd that this never-happened-before crime took place as soon as he retired. Coincidence? Or was that why he was here? To see what evidence they had? Or plant false evidence? She made a mental note to check into Jenkins. She'd met a lot of dirty cops, some thought to be as saintly as the good *former* sheriff.

"You left me with a top-notch deputy." Harper hooked a thumb at Mealer. "But I'll let you know if we need anything." She thought she heard Mealer groan, but her phone rang so she couldn't be sure. The caller ID read Kelsey Price. "Excuse me."

Punching the green button, she stepped away and put the phone to her ear. "Quinn."

"Mary Lou from the mayor's office called. He wants a meeting, like, now."

"I'm in the middle of something." Harper turned to watch Mealer and Jenkins. From their serious expressions, she figured they were talking about the case. Not good. Or maybe they were talking about Mealer's wife's condition. She needed to get back over there.

"I told her that, but she said it wasn't a request."

Motherfucker. As much as she wanted to tell both Jenkins and Radcliff to back the fuck off and let her do her job, she couldn't afford to alienate either. Radcliff could get her fired as easily as he'd hired her, and Jenkins had the hearts of her staff.

"Fine, tell her I'll meet him at—" She checked her watch. It was a little after eight. "—eight-thirty."

She hung up and rejoined Mealer and Jenkins.

Jenkins rocked back on his heels as she approached. "I was just telling Curtis that Josh might never recover his cattle. Best to just call it a loss and collect the insurance. A case like this is a drain on our recourses and near impossible to solve."

Sounded familiar. Probably been talking to his buddy Radcliff. And they weren't *our* resources.

"Something to consider." She turned to Mealer. "I have to get back to the office. Let's get this wrapped up so these guys can get the fence mended."

Hoping Mealer got the message not to stand around jawing with his ex-boss all day, she stalked through the weeds, teeth clenched, to her vehicle. If Jenkins expected her to go to Josh with his unwanted and unsolicited advice to call the cattle a loss and file an insurance claim so they could expedite the closing of the case, he could kiss her ass.

In spite of Jenkins' attempt to influence the handling of the investigation and Radcliff's demand that she drop everything to meet him on a whim, she damned well intended to solve this robbery if she had to spend every fucking night babysitting Josh's remaining cattle.

****

Josh drove to the back of the house and parked beside Evan's truck. He leaned against the headrest. His eyelids drifted shut. His body grew heavy. He'd had maybe five hours sleep in the last forty-eight hours, but there was so much to do.

Just a few minutes.

A knock on his window startled him out of the twilight of unconsciousness claiming him. He sat up and rubbed his hands over his face, then shifted to see who needed him.

Shayna scowled at him from beneath an oversized hoodie. An even bigger coat hung from her shoulders. "You coming in where it's warm, or are you going to sleep out here in the cold and catch pneumonia?"

Two days ago, he would have teased her about sharing body heat to stay warm, but now... Now, there was Harper.

Except there wasn't.

"It's warm in here," he grumbled.

She lifted a brow. "I have homemade biscuits just out of the oven."

"Thanks, but I'm not hungry."

"Liar." Not waiting for him to move, she opened the door and tugged on his arm. "I can hear your stomach growling all the way in the house."

Killing the engine, Josh didn't resist her efforts to drag him out of his truck and into the house. A wall of heat and the smell of freshly baked bread hit him as he crossed the threshold into the kitchen. His stomach yowled like a...wildcat.

"I just need some coffee." He couldn't remember the last cup he'd had.

"No coffee." She laid a hand on his shoulder. "You need to sleep."

He dropped into a chair as Shayna set a plate with real bacon and a heap of scrambled eggs in front of him. Two giant biscuits dripping with butter followed.

"Eat." The brisk command lured a smile. Forever the drill sergeant, his sister-in-law.

He picked up a biscuit and bit into it. His tastebuds came alive, waking up the rest of his body with every buttery bite.

A glass of orange juice appeared in front of him as Shayna sat down across the table.

"You look like shit."

"You sound like Evan," he said around a mouthful

of eggs.

"I'll take that as a compliment," she said, beaming. "Where is he, by the way?"

"Upstairs, sleeping."

Josh paused chewing and swallowed. "Isn't he going to relieve Rusty? Never mind, I'll do it."

He pushed back his chair, but she reached across the table and laid a hand on his. He stared at the fork he still held.

"Evan just came in from there," she said. "He relieved Rusty after you relieved him."

His foggy brain wouldn't compute the meaning behind her words. That wasn't the plan they'd discussed last night. "Why?"

"He knew you'd be done in when you got home, and Rusty would be the only one who knew how to properly go about setting up camp this morning." She patted his hand and sat back. "Everything is taken care of. Now eat."

Guilt swirled in his belly along with ineptitude. Evan had everything under control while he couldn't seem to get anything right. With the ranch. With Harper. Why had he pushed so hard? Why hadn't he just kept it light and fun? She'd seemed somewhat open to that.

Maybe if he'd been here, where he belonged, she wouldn't be running scared.

He shoved his plate back. "I need to check on Star."

"No, you don't." Shayna nudged his plate toward him. "She's fine."

Scratching the stubble on his chin, he tried to piece together exactly how she would know that. She was a nurse, not a veterinarian.

She laughed. "Cal came up earlier. He said you'd want to know."

Shaking his head, Josh scooped up another bite of egg. Of course, Cal checked on Star. He loved that horse almost as much as Josh did.

"I take it your talk with the sheriff didn't go well."

The eggs turned to sawdust in his mouth, and he laid the fork beside his plate. "Her name's Harper, and no, it didn't."

Her big brown eyes softened with an empathy that reminded him she recognized his pain. Evan had torn her heart to pieces when he left her. Not that his brother had fared too well during their nine years apart. "Do you want to talk about it?"

"Nope, nothing to talk about. I want her. She doesn't want me. End of story." Yet as the words left his mouth, he couldn't accept them. Harper did want him. She just didn't want to want him.

"Maybe give her some space."

"Maybe." He cleared his throat. "I need a favor."

"You want me to speak to her?"

That was the last thing he wanted. Harper would be mortified to know he'd been talking about her. And to have Shayna be the one to do it... *Fuck me.*

How would he ever explain the dynamics of his relationship with his sister-in-law? Not that he had anything but the love of a friend for her now, but brotherly might be pushing it. They were getting there though.

"Nah, but did you bring your nurse stuff with you, that bag you had when you were taking care of me?"

"Why?" Her brows furrowed. "I'm not looking at

your dick, so if you've got some disease, I'm not your girl."

Despite the ache in his chest, he huffed a laugh. "No, I'm good. Do you remember El—Mrs. Butts?"

"Sure," she dragged out the word, as if still suspicious.

"Would you go see her today? Check on her." Josh explained his visit to Ellie's, the concerns Harper had raised about her, and what he'd witnessed for himself. "Harper wants to call some agency that checks on the elderly, but I'd rather someone she knows take a look at her."

Shayna nodded. "Of course. I'll ask Evan to go with me when he wakes up."

"Thanks, Shay. I really appreciate it. And you and Evan for being here." Maybe it was the comfort of a good meal or sharing some of the burden of Ellie's care with his family, but he felt lighter.

Pushing out of his chair, he picked up his plate, but Shayna took it from him.

"I've got this," she insisted. "You go grab a nice hot shower and get some sleep."

He tucked the chair under the table but headed for the back door.

"Where are you going?" She inclined her head toward the hall. "The shower is that way."

Out of habit, he threaded his fingers through his hair and reached for his hat, but it wasn't there. He'd left it in the truck with his phone. "I'm going over to the auction barn to talk to Texas."

He couldn't do anything to fix things with Harper. Not right now, anyway. But he could sure as hell do something to find his fucking cattle.

****

Radcliff was waiting in Harper's office when she arrived at eight fifteen. He sat in her chair with his feet on her desk, flipping through a folder. It wasn't one of hers. She'd locked everything up last night. But she had no doubt if she hadn't, he'd have no problem reading through them.

She'd have liked a few minutes to prepare—freshen up, get a cup of coffee, check in with Kelsey—but he probably knew that. He struck her as the type to play head games.

Harper hung up her coat, pulled her Glock, and stood at the corner of her desk. "Excuse me."

Over his shoulder, he eyed her gun, then peered up at her, brow cocked. "Sheriff?"

She placed her hand on the drawer handle. "I need to secure my weapon."

"Of course." He shifted but only enough for her to get the drawer open, stow her gun, and lock it, then he settled deeper into her chair. "Tom wore his gun at all times."

Since he had no intention of budging, Harper rounded the desk to stand across from him, hands on hips. "What can I do for you, Mr. Mayor?"

One ankle crossed over the other, he set his folder aside and steepled his fingers. "I need to know where we are on the McNamara case."

"We're still following up on a few leads. The ranger from the association is supposed to be here tomorrow. I might have had more information for you if I hadn't been called away from the scene for this meeting. Mealer is still out there gathering evidence. It'll take a while to go through it all."

"That's it? That's all you've got for me?"

There was more, but she didn't trust him not to go shooting off his mouth to make himself look good. She couldn't risk information getting out and back to whoever was stealing Josh's cattle, like maybe the former sheriff. Fuck, for all she knew, the mayor could be in on this with Jenkins. "I thought you didn't want us wasting time on this."

Radcliff held up his hands. "I know, I know. But my phone blew up last night after word spread that Josh was hit again. Area ranchers are worried they'll be next. A few don't have the capital to insure their cattle or enough hands to keep an eye on their herds twenty-four/seven. A loss like Josh has taken will send some of those ranchers under."

"That's certainly a possibility." Though she didn't think so. The person behind this seemed to be targeting Josh.

"What can we do as a show of action to slow the grumbling?" He said *we*, but he really meant what could *she* do.

"I'll have Dollins and Ackerman patrolling more at night, and I'll do my best to get out more during the day since the latest theft happened in broad daylight. I can't spare Mealer. He's processing the evidence." She planted her hands on the desk and leaned forward. "Unless you want to fork over enough to hire another deputy."

He smiled. "Nice try, Harper."

She straightened and shrugged. "It was worth a shot."

"But you bring up another reason for this meeting." He pulled a folder from his briefcase. "We haven't gone over your budget."

Harper looked at her watch. She didn't have time for this today. "Can we do this another time?"

"I'm sure you're very busy, but you understand I, too, have a tight schedule with very little free time, and since I have this slot allocated to you…"

An hour later, after squeezing every penny out of the county she could get, Radcliff slithered out of her office and back under his rock.

Mealer had returned, and as soon as Radcliff vacated her office, he shot out of his chair, excitement sparking in his eyes.

Kelsey beat him to her door. "You have a call on line one."

"Who is it?"

"Zeke Mayfield from the governor's office."

Harper held up a finger to Mealer. "Ten minutes."

She shut the door and picked up the phone. "Sherrif Quinn."

"Well, doesn't that sound official." Zeke's gruff voice was a welcome interruption.

"No more than you," she said, sinking into her chair and shivering in revulsion when she found it still warm from Radcliff. *Fucker.* "The governor's office? Really?"

He coughed through a laugh. "I thought it would make you sound important to your people."

Stomach churning, she grabbed a tissue to wipe the dirt from Radcliff's shoes off her desk then tossed it in the wastebasket. "It'll take more than a phone call to wipe out my past mistakes, but I appreciate the gesture."

"You think they know?"

"I would have done my homework on my new boss, and I'll bet your buddy Radcliff did, too."

"He's not my buddy, Harper. He's the son of an old friend. I did the boy a favor once, and he owed me. That's it."

"Sorry, it's just... He's a real dick." She picked up a pencil and tapped the eraser on the desk.

"You can handle him." He sounded so sure. "And I wouldn't worry too much about the others. They'll get to know and see the real you."

If only I could be as certain. "I hope so."

"I know so," he said. "Now, tell me about your first day."

Harper gave Zeke a quick rundown of events from the day before—the staff, the townspeople bringing in food, the mayor. She talked about Mrs. Butts and ended with Josh's stolen cattle.

"Wow, rustling? Right out of the gate, huh?"

"Tell me you didn't do it to make me look good," she teased, aware of Mealer pacing through the front office.

A gravelly chuckle crackled over the line. "It would only work if you caught me."

"You're too smart for that."

"You'll get 'em, Harper." He paused, no doubt shifting through the facts she'd given him. "I'm sure the first thing you did was check out the owner. A lot of insurance money is paid out for rustled cattle."

A cold sweat coated her skin. She'd considered and dismissed any possibility that Josh could be responsible, but officially ruling him out should have been the first thing she'd done. Instead, she'd been blinded by his pretty face and the memory of a big dick.

"Harper?"

"Yeah, sorry. I was thinking of something else."

"You did rule him out, right?"

"Of course." *Just not officially.* "Hey, I gotta run."

"Keep me posted," he said. "I'm a bored old man, living vicariously through you now."

"Will do." Harper hung up. She hated brushing Zeke off, but Mealer was wearing a hole in the floor, and she had an error to correct.

If Josh didn't already hate her, he would by the end of the day.

And she wouldn't blame him one fucking bit.

Chapter Fourteen

After seeing her senior deputy cozied up to Jenkins, suspicion whispered loud and long in Harper's ear. Mealer's wife was ill, and cancer treatments could financially cripple a family. Insurance didn't cover a lot of things, certainly not everything. Plus, Mealer was in the perfect position to tamper with evidence and misdirect the investigation.

Fuck, she was tired. Seeing ghosts everywhere. But that was the job.

She grabbed a cup of coffee and waved Mealer into her office.

As he sat across from her, she stalled him with a hand before he could launch into his findings. "I know you have a lot of respect for the former sheriff, but I should remind you he's retired, a civilian now, and shouldn't be read into the case."

Mealer's head snapped back. "You think I shared case information with him?"

"I'm just reminding you that you shouldn't."

"I'm not a rookie, Sheriff. I know procedure." He sat back and looked her square in the eye. "He asked if he could help, and like you, I told him you would bring him in if you needed to, then we talked about Lori's treatment."

It could have gone one way or the other, the case or his wife's condition, but Harper wouldn't apologize for doing her job. She pushed a little harder. "I'm wondering why he'd want to help work the case when he thinks it's a waste of time."

It wasn't a question, but she could see the wheels turning.

His brow furrowed. "No way. Not Tom. I've known him for years. He's a good man. My daughter's godfather."

"I've seen good men do things they wouldn't otherwise when pushed into a corner." That seed planted, she went another direction. "Do you agree with him? Do you think we should sideline the investigation? Let the ranger deal with it?"

The lines on his forehead eased, and some of his excitement returned. "I told my Lori what's going on. Not the details. Just what everyone else knows, and that, for the first time in I don't know when, I was excited to come to work this morning. Don't get me wrong, I wouldn't wish harm to anyone, but the last few years have been hard, and this"—he slapped the papers in his hand on his thigh—"is giving me something else to think about besides losing my wife."

The need to follow leads, work clues, and solve a case was at the heart of every good cop, but Mealer could also be disguising his desire to control the case and manipulate evidence with enthusiasm for the job.

"So no," he continued, his voice animated. "I don't think we should give up. This is what we do, what I took all those forensic classes for. I'd rather figure it out before the ranger gets here."

"I agree." She indicated the papers in his hand. "What do you have to show me?"

Mealer handed her a list of trailers with columns

organized by license number, trailer type, and registered owner. Three rows were highlighted in green. He pointed to the one in the middle of the page. "Walter has a third trailer."

Adrenaline zipped through her as she launched out of her chair and rounded her desk. They were going to nail that fucker if he was responsible.

"Kelsey?" she hollered and turned back to Mealer. "The old coot lied."

"Appears so."

Kelsey skidded to a stop inside the door. "Sheriff?"

"I need you to type up warrants and get them in front of the judge asap. One to search Walter Mills' place for three twenty-four-foot gooseneck trailers and a look at his financials."

"And hoof boots." Mealer handed her another sheet of paper with the specs on a horse's boot. "I talked to the farrier and sent him a picture of the print. He told me we're looking for a fetlock boot. I matched our print to this brand."

"Fuck, Mealer, you're a genius." She studied the boot. "Get with Kelsey on this so there's no problem with the warrants. And call in one of the guys—Ackerman since Dollins was out at the scene all night. We have a lot of ground to cover."

Both of them stared at her.

"Sorry, guys. I have a gutter mouth when I'm excited or angry"—*or horny*—"and fuck, this is good."

Mealer shook his head.

Kelsey grinned. "Who's the other warrant for and what do you want on it?"

"Same as the above for the McNamara ranch." She handed the information about the boot back to Mealer without looking at him or Kelsey. Harper could practically feel Kelsey's smile wither, and shock radiated off them both. For that reason, she'd write up the warrant herself for Tom Jenkins' financials just to be sure, though she had no probable cause other than he was a nosy motherfucker. "Anything else in that stack of papers you want to share? Who else owns the type of trailer we're looking for?"

As soon as Kelsey was out of earshot, Mealer asked, "You really think Josh stole his own cattle?"

"No, I don't," Harper said without hesitation. "But everyone's a suspect until they're not. The sooner we rule him out the better. We should have done it yesterday."

But I was too busy avoiding him or screwing him.

Curious, she couldn't stop herself from asking, "Do *you* think he could have done it?"

His expression turned sheepish. "I have to admit it crossed my mind, but only for a second because it's Suspect 101. But Josh committing fraud? No. That guy doesn't have a dishonest bone in his body. In fact—"

Eyes scrunched closed, he groaned and rubbed a hand over his beard.

"What?"

Mealer opened his eyes, but they rolled upward. "I can't believe what's about to come out of my mouth, but I love my wife and she threw a fit last night when I told her I warned you off Josh. She didn't talk to me all night and was still busting my, er, hide this morning. She made me promise to retract my statement. She has a soft spot for Josh. He's done her a kindness or two over the years."

He stood.

"Anyway, she said to tell you, and I quote," he made air quotes and spoke faster as he edged toward the door, "'Josh is a great guy, and if that man's chasing you, he thinks you're special, so let him catch you 'cause Josh doesn't do the chasing. Women stumble over their own two feet and fall all over him. You must be special.'"

The deputy hightailed it straight back to his desk and ducked behind his monitor. Was this spiel just another attempt to distract her from seeing what was right in front of her? Was he using his sick wife and Josh to throw suspicion off him?

Every instinct said he wasn't, but if she was wrong about Mealer, he was one hell of an actor because his plan was working.

You must be special.

Harper swiveled her chair to face the back wall and swallowed the zombieflies trying to escape from her throat. The burning sensation at the back of her eyelids had her breathing deep and pinching the bridge of her nose. Yearning tightened her chest. Was she special? Josh had said as much before she dumped him.

It didn't matter now. Once she served the warrant, she wouldn't be special anymore.

Maybe she could— No, warning him went against every rule in the book. Still…

She kicked the floor to twirl her chair around and opened the case file to find his number then hesitated. Not for the reasons she should. What if he was asleep? She hated to wake him.

But her day was about to get jammed. She might not have another chance, and she couldn't blindside him or let him believe she suspected him.

Fingers trembling, she punched in his number and hit the connect button. With every ring, tattered wings began to stir in her belly. Her mouth pooled with saliva, and for a moment, she thought she'd vomit.

The rich baritone of Josh's voice startled her, but she'd gone to voicemail.

What if he didn't listen to voicemail? Not everyone did. Besides, she'd risked enough just leaving a record of her call to his phone. Leaving a voicemail or text was career suicide.

She sighed and searched for his brother's number.

One ring. Two.

"You've reached Evan McNamara's phone," a feminine voice answered in a professional tone.

Another voicemail. "Fuck."

She was about to hang up when she heard a giggle.

"Hello?" the woman prompted.

Mortified that she'd cursed at the woman, Harper said, "This is Sheriff Harper Quinn. May I speak to Evan McNamara?"

"Hi, Sheriff," the woman's tone changed from professional to interested. "Evan's not available. I'm his wife Shayna. Can I help you?"

"I'm looking for Josh."

"Josh isn't here right now. Would you like me to take a message?"

"No." *Shit.* This was getting complicated. "I need to get in touch with him. Can you tell me where he is?"

"He mentioned going to the auction barn to talk to Texas."

"Thanks."

"No problem."

Harper hung up without saying goodbye as she

recalled where she'd heard the name Texas. She slowly lowered the phone to her desk. A haze of red blurred her vision. Her fingers curled into fists.

A multitude of reasons for Josh to go to the auction barn swam through her fury-driven brain—three topping the list and pissing her the fuck off.

He was there to sell stolen cattle.

He was investigating on his own.

Or he was there to see his childhood crush Texas Tallulah Taylor.

****

"Come on back," Texas said, relocking the front door of the auction barn after letting Josh in. "I'm sorry to hear about your trouble."

"Thanks." He followed her through the quiet building and up a set of stairs to the back offices. The lot had been empty when he drove up since there was no auction today. He'd scoured his contacts and, with just enough charge in his phone to call her, asked for a meeting. "I appreciate you seeing me this early in the morning."

"That's okay," she said over her shoulder, her blonde ponytail swinging with her hips. "Will's picking me up for a late breakfast before Jarod and I head into Austin. I'm meeting his parents tonight."

Josh tried to keep his eyes on the treads and not her ass, but her athletic build reminded him of Harper. Texas wasn't a girly-girl. She fit in with the ranch hands more than the Women's Jr. League. She was feminine, with plenty of lithe curves, but she was tall and sinewy, almost six feet. Harper was smaller, five-seven, a hundred and fifteen pounds wet, all sculpted muscles, but with a petite sleekness that allowed her to easily transition from one of Houston's finest to a mystery sub on stilettos.

"You don't sound too happy about going. You not ready to meet the parents?" He'd never understand why she was with Jarod when she loved Will. Or why Will continued his relationship with Krystal when she made him miserable.

Texas shrugged as she unlocked her office. "I just hate being away from the barn."

"I get it." He'd been away too much since he started going to the club, but that wouldn't be a problem anymore. "So, is it serious with you and Jarod?"

"I don't know." Her nose scrunched as if the thought didn't sit well. "Have a seat."

"I should have just called. You could have answered all my questions on the phone." He took the chair opposite Texas and rested his hat on his knee. "I'm not thinking clearly these days."

She waved off his concern. "I told you. It's not a problem. But like I also told the deputy who called yesterday, we haven't had any South Poll on the docket. With all the rustling going on, I've been keeping a closer eye on what's coming in, which is another reason I'm hesitant about leaving the barn. But if it will ease your mind, we'll go out to the pens and make sure your cattle aren't here."

It would, but he couldn't visit every auction barn in the state just to ease his mind. His other livestock, including Star and the foal she'd deliver in the spring, not to mention the hands, depended on him. The ranch was his home, but more than that, it was a part of him. Being without it would be like losing an arm or leg.

Josh stilled as realization washed over him. Was that the way Harper felt about being a cop?

Of course, it is, dumbass. "Shit."

"Something I said?" Texas asked, one golden brow lifting.

"No, something *I* said…and did." He just didn't know if it was too late to make it right.

"I know what that's like." She averted her gaze to the monitor on her desk. "I don't really know what else I can offer, other than a website for auction barns in Texas. There aren't as many as you'd think, but I'm sure the sheriff's department has already called most if not all of them. Come take a look."

Josh rounded the desk to crowd in behind her as she clicked on a bookmark. The site for the Texas Department of Agriculture popped up. One hand on the desk, his other on the back of her chair, he leaned closer to read some of the smaller print. "I must be losing it. I didn't even think about the TDA. I'm sorry I wasted your time."

"Don't worry about it." She clicked on a drop-down menu. "Here's where you find a listing of Texas livestock auctions."

The top of her head brushed his shirt as she peeked around the monitor at the door. "You're early."

Josh glanced up from the screen to find Will Sanderson standing in the hall. His narrowed gaze zeroed in on their proximity. Josh started to back away. Nah, he'd stay right where he was and give Will the needed push to get his head out of his ass.

"It's a good thing I did since the sheriff was knocking at your door." Will ducked under the doorframe and off to one side, revealing said sheriff.

Air stalled in Josh's lungs. His whole body tensed as he took in the woman who had him tied in knots. She wore the standard brown sheriff's shirt under her coat, and jeans that hugged her hips. Except for a few loose strands, her hair was pulled into a ponytail and held in place by a cap again. Under the shadow of the brim, gray eyes he'd seen soften with desire might as well have been green as they flickered from Texas to him.

He'd never been one to play games—never had a reason to—but jealousy looked good on Harper and fanned the flame of hope. Besides, being on the end of that burning anger felt a hell of a lot better than the emotionless void he'd witnessed last night.

Let her think what she wants. She's going to anyway.

He met her gaze. "Sheriff."

"I'm sorry," Texas said, "I didn't hear you knock."

"Obviously," Will coughed behind a fisted hand, then added, "I used my key."

"Like you said, it's a good thing you were here early." Texas seemed oblivious to Will's sarcasm as she sat up and pushed her chair back, giving Josh no choice but to back up. But hell if he couldn't take his eyes off Harper.

The sheriff's mask she wore so well slipped into place, and the fire in her eyes banked as she turned her attention to Texas. "I'm sorry to intrude. I was looking for Mr. McNamara, and I was told he'd come here."

"Oh, you're not intruding. This rustling is bad business, and I'll do what I can to help."

Josh leaned against the credenza behind him and folded his arms. "Texas was just showing me a list of auction barns I can call."

"I'd like to talk to you about that." Harper pivoted in the door and gestured to the hall. Clearly, she wanted him to talk privately.

"Have you found my cattle?" If she had found them, she'd have already said, but he couldn't resist pushing her buttons.

Her lush lips thinned. She knew what he was doing. "Not yet, Mr. McNamara."

"Well, then," he said, straightening, "whatever you have to say can wait. Texas was just about to show me the pens." He tilted his head to one side in challenge. "You're welcome to join us."

She smiled tightly. "I'd love to."

"Right, then." Texas stood and circled the desk. "Follow me."

Will stepped in behind her as she passed him, cutting Josh off.

Josh chuckled as he picked up his hat and joined Harper in the hall. The fact that she'd waited half worried, half pleased him. On one hand, she wasn't ignoring him. On the other, she was probably going to give him hell.

"What's so fucking funny?" she hissed under her breath.

"Will." He jutted his chin at the couple down the hall. "He's jealous."

"Does he have reason to be?" Her jaw tightened, and pink stained her cheeks.

Josh's heart swelled in his chest. He was sure she hadn't meant to reveal so much with that simple question. He'd pushed far enough. Time to ease up and go gently. As gently as he would a yearling ready for the saddle.

"No, wildcat," he said softly, "he has nothing to fear from me, and neither do you."

****

Before Harper could lie and tell Josh to go fuck himself, that she wasn't jealous, and that he was an ass, he clasped her hand with his and tugged. "We'd better catch up."

And for some fucking insane reason, she didn't pull away. Her hand felt good in his...so right, as if it belonged there. As if she belonged with him, to him.

Heat sizzled up her arm. Her nipples beaded. Her clit hummed. Her inner sub wanted to submit. To give him what he wanted. To let him possess her mind, body, and soul.

Fuck, fuck, fuck. She had to shut that bitch down.

She dug in her heels, only to realize he had let go of her hand as they exited the building and stood on a catwalk overlooking the pens.

"Watch how they look at each other when the other isn't watching," he whispered then left her to join Texas at the rail.

She'd have to be blind to miss how they snuck glances at each other. Harper caught herself doing the same thing and moved to stand on the other side of Will to block out the man who was making her crazy. Sanderson was at least six-foot-five, the perfect height for the Amazon blonde on his other side, and he had the body of a Viking god. But all that sinew and grace did nothing for her.

Harper leaned forward to catch another glimpse of the man who did.

Texas laid a hand on Josh's forearm. "I'm sorry they're not here. I wish they were."

Jealousy sparked again, and Harper fought the urge to toss Texas over the rail and into the pen with the other heifers.

Fuck. Possessive was not something she'd ever felt.

She lowered her gaze and caught a glimpse of Sanderson's white-knuckled grip on the rail.

"Would have made things easier if they were." Josh pivoted toward Will, and Texas followed his gaze to the giant man, her big blue eyes drinking him in. "How are things out at your place?"

Will's grip on the rail loosened. "We're taking precautions."

Josh nodded. "We've moved the herd away from the perimeters and set up a soft camp."

"Same," Will said. "I've been out there all week."

"Well, I'd better let you two get on with your breakfast." Josh's gaze flickered to Harper's for an instant of conspiratorial mischief as he reached around Texas to extend a handshake to Will. Then he looked at Will, his expression sincere. "Good luck and tell Krystal I said hello."

Harper rolled her eyes at his wicked behavior but didn't miss the pinched look on Texas' face at the mention of the other woman. Josh was right. Poor girl. She was a goner and probably didn't even know it. Or didn't want to admit it.

Like you.

Josh gestured toward the outer stairs leading to the side parking lot. "After you, sheriff."

Harper hurried down the steps to stay ahead of him, worried he'd do something stupid like settle his hand at her spine or lower like he had Saturday night.

Yet part of her ached for his touch.

Fuck, she had to stop thinking about Josh and the things he did to make her body come alive.

Gravel crunched under their boots as they walked in silence to the front of the building. At her car, she faced him, ready to put this conversation behind her. "Are you done playing matchmaker? Can we get on with the business of why I'm here?"

"Hey, I'm pretty good at it. I got Evan and Shayna back together, and they're married now." He stood too close. "Sometimes, people just need a little push."

She retreated a step. "And sometimes, they just need to be left alone."

He edged closer. "*You* came looking for me, wildcat."

"Don't call me that." Another step and her back hit the passenger door. The same door he'd fingerfucked her against yesterday. A tremor of lust shimmied through her. She pressed a hand to his chest. "And back the fuck up. Someone might get the wrong idea."

"You can't have it both ways, Harper." He trailed a finger over her cheek, his gaze following his movement. "You can't push me away, and then pull out the claws because you're jealous." His mouth tilted into a lazy grin. "Not that I mind the claws, but I'd rather have them scoring my back as I fu—"

"Don't." Desire ricocheted through her and laced her voice. Against her will, her gaze fell to his lips. "Please."

"Please kiss you or please stop?" He sounded as breathless as she was. "You're going to have to say it 'cause I can't tell?"

Fuck, she wanted him to kiss her so bad she could

taste it. Taste him. Instead, she increased the pressure of her hand on his chest. "Stop."

As if it were the hardest thing he'd ever done, Josh backed away and shoved his hands in his pockets. "Why are you here, Harper?"

Disappointment and defeat etched fine lines in the corner of his eyes and exhaustion dragged his speech. Dark circles smudged beneath bloodshot eyes. He looked tired. He should be home sleeping.

But no, he was here, forcing her to go out of her way to track him down, investigating on his own, and possibly putting himself in danger.

"Stop interfering in my case," she snapped, then tempered her voice. "We've already called all the auctions in Texas and the surrounding states. They're on alert. And it's dangerous. If the perpetrators get wind of you searching for them, they might come after you."

"Glad to know you care," he grumbled, "but they're my fucking cows, and I'll do whatever it takes to find them."

Anger and fear clashed inside her. How dare he disregard his own safety? The thought of him hurt or killed…

"Fine," she spat. "Then you'll understand when I serve you with a warrant to search your property."

Chapter Fifteen

"What the hell is this?" From his rocker on the front porch, Walter Mills waved the warrant Harper had handed him.

Harper had told him twice already. She sure as fuck wasn't in the mood for a crotchety old man's rant. Not after the way things had ended earlier with Josh. Her heart rose in her throat, but she shoved it down and drew on her last thread of patience.

She moved another step up the walk toward him and repeated, "It's a warrant, Mr. Mills, that allows us to search your residence, all outbuildings, and vehicles."

"You already been out here looking at my trailers." He turned to Reed. "Get these people off my property."

Reed shook his head. "I can't do that, Granddad."

Just to her left, Mealer shifted from one foot to the other, CSI bag in hand. He handed her two pairs of latex gloves. She passed one to Ackerman as he closed ranks on her right.

"A man shouldn't have his word questioned." Walter pushed out of his chair and headed for the front door.

"Please remain where you are, Mr. Mills." The old man probably had a shotgun in every corner, and Harper wasn't taking any chances. She glanced at Reed. "While Deputy Mealer and I search the premises,

Deputy Ackerman will keep you and your grandfather company."

Walter spat a stream of tobacco into the bushes next to Mealer. "You ain't gonna find no trailer in my house. What the hell kind of operation are—"

Reed held up a hand to quiet his grandfather. "If you needed anything else, all you had to do is ask. This warrant business is upsetting him."

"He shouldn't have lied to us, Reed," Mealer said. "A search of the county tax office records shows your grandfather owns three—not two—trailers."

"I ain't no liar, Curtis Mealer, and I'll fight any man who calls me one." There was nothing wrong with the old man's hearing.

With a sigh, Reed trotted down the porch steps and stopped directly in front of Harper. "Look, we did have three," he said, his voice low, "but we sold one last month. Maybe the new owner hasn't had time to change the title over, but we have the bill of sale."

Fuck. Having the trailer and boot together was key to making a case for another warrant to search for the cattle, which would be much more extensive. One piece of evidence without the other was circumstantial at best.

"We'll need to see that bill of sale." She looked at Walter then back at Reed. Something felt off. "You could have mentioned the sale of the trailer yesterday. Why didn't you?"

"I don't know. It never occurred to me." Reed ran his fingers through his hair. "You asked to see *our* trailers. I showed you the two we own. I didn't know I was responsible for ruling out the whole damn town."

Mealer shifted so that Reed couldn't hear him

mumble, "What do you want to do?"

"Execute the search," Harper said, holding Reed's defensive stare, unable to put her thumb on what was bothering her. "We'll start with the house."

"What else are you looking for, Sheriff?" Reed folded his arms across his chest. "Maybe I can help you."

"It's in the warrant." Eyes still locked with Reed, she gave Ackerman a go ahead nod. "Deputy."

Ackerman gestured for Reed to precede him. "Come on, Mr. Mills. Let us do our job."

Reed held her gaze a moment longer, then spun around and stomped up the steps to usher his grandfather inside the house, Ackerman on their heels.

"I hate this part," Mealer grumbled as he bent to collect his bag. "I've known these men all my life."

"I know." She'd served search warrants on complete strangers to clear them so that her team could move on to the next suspect. Those people were left feeling violated, their lives disrupted, their private matters aired. Some never trusted law enforcement again. And older folks like Walter carried resentment to the grave. Having to serve a search warrant sucked, but it was a necessary part of an investigation.

If she was wrong about Mills, it would be a long time before Mealer and Ackerman regained his trust. While she could live without it, she was quickly making enemies in a town of few people. "Come on."

When they entered, Walter scowled at her from an old brown recliner. Reed sat on a matching sofa, his elbows on his knees. Ackerman stood sentinel inside the door, feet spread, hands clasped.

Mealer set up his kit on the dining room table as

Harper approached Reed. "You want to get that bill of sale?"

"It's in the study."

She nodded. "Lead the way."

He wove around a coffee table and led her down a hall.

The study was small, consisting of a desk, chair, a couple of filing cabinets, and a wall of shelves. Harper took up a position at the door as Reed crossed to the desk. He opened a side drawer, and caution kicked in, sending her palm to rest on the Glock at her hip.

The bruise beneath protested the weight of her hand and stirred a reaction from her pussy. Her nipples grew taut. The memory of Josh's concern and his gentle touch the night before tugged at her heart.

With a mental sigh, she refocused on Reed as he sifted through hanging folders. Walter's angry rant reached her from the living room, pushing her farther into the study.

He looked up at her. "I can't believe this is happening just because my grandfather harbors some bitterness against Josh's family."

"Someone's targeting his ranch. Your grandfather's grudge goes to motive." She shrugged. "If you and your grandfather are not responsible, we'll find nothing and continue our investigation elsewhere."

"Have you looked at Josh?" He resumed his search. "I love him like a brother, but he's trying to start a horse breeding program. He's itching to move faster and could do that with the insurance proceeds."

The horse farm wasn't something she'd heard about, bringing home the fact she still knew so little about Josh. But Reed's attempt to redirect suspicion off his grandfather and onto Josh severed the thread of patience she'd been grasping.

"It's funny that you're throwing Josh under the bus. When I asked him about you, he said you're a solid guy. A friend."

Shame distorted Reed's face, and his shoulders slumped. "A shitty one, I guess."

Disloyal motherfucker.

Bile churned in her belly as she remembered the look of utter betrayal on Josh's face when she'd told him about the warrant to search his property. An immediate need to take back her words—if not the warning, then, at least, the spiteful delivery—had hung on the tip of her tongue. But then he'd tipped his hat and, without a word, turned on his heel to leave her drowning in regret.

It was for the best. If Josh hated her, he wouldn't want her. And she wouldn't have to fight so hard not to wish for what she couldn't have.

If that's what you really want, then why the fuck does it hurt this much?

"Got it." Reed pulled out a piece of paper and handed it to her.

Sure enough, the bill of sale for a twenty-four-foot Gooseneck was dated almost a month ago. The buyer was listed as Aaron Peterson. The name triggered a memory, but she couldn't quite grasp it. Too many thoughts of Josh crowded her brain.

She shook her head. It would come to her.

After finding no sign of a hoof boot in the house, she and Mealer left Ackerman with Walter and Reed and moved their search out back to the Mills' vehicles—one ancient, beat-up pickup, a white single-cab truck, and a maroon 4-door dually. Nothing there, but they hit the jackpot in the barn with a half dozen boots. Unfortunately, none matched the one they sought.

Mealer checked each horse for a boot or a missing shoe. Still nothing. Further searches of the other outbuildings were a bust.

She'd been certain they'd find something here. Maybe she was wrong about Mills.

What else are you wrong about?

Crossing the threshold into the house, she gave Walter and Reed the usual spiel. "Thank you for your cooperation. We'll be out of your way momentarily."

"Didn't find anything, did ya?" Walter snarled. "If this is how you treat the good folks of Stone Creek, you won't last long, Sheriff."

Reed rolled his eyes and scrubbed a hand over his face. He blew out a long breath. Was he relieved they didn't find evidence or that the whole ordeal was over, and he could get away from Walter?

Ackerman fell into step beside her as she crossed the yard to their vehicles. "Thank god that's over. Mr. Mills was giving me a headache."

"Let's help Mealer load his gear and get back to the office." She'd grab a couple of pizzas for lunch on her way into town. And get a copy of the receipt proving Josh's whereabouts while she was at it. Not for herself, but for the case file, for him, so that any question of his involvement would be put to rest.

Harper's stomach roiled again. Josh wouldn't see it that way, though. He might have suggested it, but he'd see it as her doubt. Just another betrayal.

Fuck me now.

****

"What do you think, sweetheart?" Josh nuzzled Star's velvety nose, then looked around the barn, wishing he could afford to build a proper stable for her. "Am I an ass or what?"

"Definitely an ass."

Josh glanced over his shoulder as Evan closed the side door. He rubbed his hands together to ward off the cold.

"About time your sorry ass woke up," Josh muttered in the tone their dad used on the mornings after Josh and Evan stayed out all night drinking and chasing tail. Only his dad hadn't used the words *sorry* or *ass*. God, he missed his old man.

"Shayna threatened me with a bucket of ice water if I didn't get up. Otherwise, I'd still be in bed."

"Actually, a nap sounds really good right now." He'd been too angry to sleep after Harper dropped the warrant bomb on him, and work around here wasn't going to get itself done. It fell to him, as it should, with everyone else out at camp watching over the herd. He'd head out there as soon as Evan and Shayna returned from Ellie's. With all that had happened, he'd be crazy not to make sure someone was here to watch the house and barn.

"We're taking off," Evan said, "but I can stay if you need help."

"Nah, I got it." Josh exited the stall and swiped a sleeve over his forehead. It might be freezing outside, but he'd worked up a sweat. "You haven't been by Ellie's in a while. She'll be happy to see you."

Evan frowned. "You look like shit."

"Shay said as much this morning," Josh grumbled.

"Are you two finishing each other's sentences now, too?"

"I see the sheriff's still got you tied in knots?"

"Her name is Harper, and she'll be out here sometime today to serve us with a warrant to search the property." Josh jabbed a finger at his brother. "How's that for tied in knots?"

"You can't hold that against her. She has a job to do."

"I know that." At least, deep down he did. "I just wish she trusted me."

"It's not about her trusting you, right now. It's about you trusting her. Frankly, I expected her sooner." Evan reached out to scratch Star's forehead. "Maybe you're the reason for her delay."

Maybe. Probably. Hell, he'd been in her business all day yesterday. Pushing, prodding, trying to get her attention like a buck in rut.

"Besides," Evan continued, "we have nothing to hide. Let her come, the sooner the better because the insurance company won't pay unless we're cleared. Plus, it'll put a stop to any gossip."

"What gossip?"

Evan shrugged. "People assuming we're looking for a quick score from the insurance company."

Josh didn't give a shit about that, but that wasn't why he didn't want to file a claim. He wanted to find his fucking cattle and the asshole responsible for making his life miserable and for forcing Harper to keep him at arm's length. Or was that just another excuse because she just didn't really want him?

"What's the issue between you two, anyway?" Evan asked, leaning against the stall. "Having performance issues?"

"Fuck you."

"Seriously, what's her trigger?"

Josh snorted. "Which one?"

"The one standing in your way, dumbass."

"I shouldn't have said that." Josh scrubbed a hand over his face. "Look, you might have dragged me into your relationship with Shayna, but I'm not discussing mine with Harper, and I'm sure as hell not sharing her."

Regret slammed into Josh as Evan's eyes rounded in surprise and hurt, then turned as cold as the wind outside.

Evan advanced on Josh. "I know you're frustrated right now, but you leave Shayna out of this. And we both know I didn't drag you into anything. You walked right into it with open eyes."

On a long exhale, Josh stared up at the rafters. They'd never let that time in their lives get between them. It hadn't lasted long. They both knew it wouldn't. Fuck, it had been too complicated.

He leveled his gaze on his brother. "I'm sorry. That was a shit thing to say, and I'm a shit brother."

"Not arguing with that." Evan's shoulders relaxed. "I shouldn't pry. I just don't like to see you hurting."

"I know." Josh rubbed the back of his neck. Maybe talking to Evan was the way to go. He wasn't getting anywhere on his own. "She...she's afraid I'll make her weak."

"Hmm. I can see how she'd feel that way. She's in a position of authority. She can't be seen as submissive."

"It's not just the power exchange." That was the easy part. "It's emotion in general. Someone she trusted betrayed her. She's got this tough exterior she hides behind."

"Then you have to find a way around it," Evan said as his phone pinged.

"Hmph, easier said than done."

"No one ever said love was easy"—Evan turned his phone to reveal a picture of Shayna and a text that said she was ready—"but I can tell you it's worth the work." He started walking backward. "You'll figure it out."

Josh wasn't so sure. He questioned every move he made, every word. Should he fight harder? Should he back off? Let her lead outside the bedroom? Or just…let her go?

"Hey." Evan paused at the door. "I'll try to be back before they get here."

As a tax attorney, Evan knew fuck all about criminal law, but having him here during the search would make Josh feel a lot better. But Ellie needed Evan more than he did. "Just take care of Ellie."

Josh got back to work as Evan's truck rumbled down the drive toward the road. The barn grew quiet except for an occasional soft whiny and the clang of the fork dinging the wheelbarrow. Every time he heard a noise outside, he checked for Harper's SUV. And every time, disappointment settled over him.

The circumstances could have been better, but truth be told, he wanted her here. He wanted her to see his home. To understand the things that were important to him, his life on the ranch, his family. And fuck, he wanted her in his bed. To wake up with her body curled against his.

Josh groaned as his dick stretched behind his fly.

He adjusted the straining bulge and closed his eyes, letting the fantasy of Harper in his bed fill his mind.

While the wind whipped outside his window, he would tease her awake, trailing his fingers over the curve of her hip. He'd take his time mapping out the dip of her waist and the rise and fall of her breasts as her breath quickened into shallow pants. Then he'd roll her onto her back, tuck her legs around his waist, and slowly bury himself in her hot, wet pussy.

Her lips would taste sweet, her little cries sweeter, when he fucked her mouth with his tongue and her tight, little cunt with his cock until she came. And then he'd whisper all the things he ached to do to her and start all over again.

Star nuzzled the back of his head, cutting into his daydream.

Josh chuckled as he turned and patted her neck. "You're right, sweetheart. I'm not giving up on her."

****

Harper set the pizza boxes on Deputy Dollins' empty desk. Ackerman dove into one and shoveled a piece into his mouth. Grease dripped down his chin.

"That was a crap search, Sher'ff," Ackerman said around the doughy crust.

Kelsey handed him a napkin. "Disgusting *and* disrespectful. Way to go, Dylan."

"No, I agree," Harper said. "But for every negative discovery, we get that much closer to a positive one."

"Uh, I hate to tell you," Ackerman said, scratching his head, "but I failed math. Never did get all that moving up and down the number line."

Mealer looked up from his desk. "She means we ruled out the Millses, Einstein, and now, we can move on."

Harper hadn't said it that way because she didn't want to admit her hunch about Walter Mills was wrong, but she smiled at their banter and looked at her watch. It was almost one. She turned to Mealer. "I hate to wake Dollins up, but let's call him in for the search at the McNamara ranch. There's a storm coming in, and we'll need all hands on deck to get done before it hits."

"What time are we heading out?" Mealer asked.

"Around two."

"On it," he said, stretching across the aisle for a slice of pepperoni.

"Ackerman, follow up on that bill of sale," she added.

"Yes, Sheriff."

Harper poured a mug of coffee and closed herself in her office. A couple of messages from the mayor wanting an update lined the edge of her desk. She ignored them and sank into her chair. She needed to think about where to go next in the case.

Kelsey knocked and opened the door, not waiting for an answer. "Do you have a minute?"

So much for a closed door.

"Sure." She sipped, hoping the steaming brew would warm her insides and burn away the thoughts of Josh clogging her brain. "What's up?"

Perched on the edge of the chair opposite Harper, Kelsey asked, "Are you really going to go through with the search at Josh's place?"

"Why wouldn't I?" Harper set the mug on her desk and wrapped her hands around it.

The girl's mouth twisted into a frown. "I thought you and Josh were…"

"All the more reason to—" *Motherfucker.*

"I knew it!" Kelsey whisper-shouted. "Oh my gosh, you lucky girl."

Harper held up a hand, trying to backpedal. "Kelsey, I should have said '*if* that were the case'."

"Uh-huh, I know exactly what you meant." Kelsey beamed. "Don't worry, Sheriff. Your secret is safe with me."

Harper held out about as much faith in Kelsey keeping a secret as she had with Ellie. Was this going to be her life in Stone Creek? Everyone insinuating themselves into her business, giving her unsolicited advice?

I'm so screwed.

Kelsey shook her head. "I don't understand why you'd want to hide your relationship with him."

"There is no relationship." *Not anymore. Not after this morning.* Harper ignored the pang in her chest and scrubbed a hand over her face. "Kelsey, Josh is a victim of theft. I'm working his case."

Waving aside Harper's concerns, Kelsey scoffed, "I know all the rules, but you can't throw away love for a few cows."

Love? Who said anything about love? Hell to the fucking no. "Listen, Josh and I only met two days ago." *Actually, four*, her heart corrected. "Love doesn't happen like that."

Kelsey's hand flew to her chest. "Ever heard of love at first sight?"

Harper rolled her eyes to the ceiling and tried not to scream. "This conversation is over. Whether I pursue a relationship with Josh or anyone else is not up for discussion."

"Exactly, so why fight it?"

"Dispatcher Price," Harper warned, "please shut the door on your way out."

"Um, I did have one more question." She winced and rose to her feet. "Can I help with the search?"

Harper sat back in her chair. The request had come out of nowhere. "Have you performed a search before?"

"No. I asked Sheriff J the few times when there was cause for one, but he said I was where he needed me." A spark of fire flashed in her young eyes. "I never complained because he'd been kind to me, but I want to learn." She took a deep breath and released her next words in the rush of an exhale. "I want to become a deputy."

Damn, the girl had ambition, after all. Now, if she could just curb her romantic delusions, she might actually have a shot at achieving her goals.

When Harper took too long to answer, Kelsey added, "You said you needed all hands on deck. I can have calls transferred to my phone. I don't have to be here. Nothing ever happens anyway, and it's not like we've never left a note on the door before."

Having Jenkins keep Kelsey sidelined because it would be inconvenient for him to find a new dispatcher pissed Harper off. Add to that, her belief that a man like Jenkins preferred to keep Kelsey out of the good ol' boys club, and Harper saw red. *Fucking asshole.*

Still, she couldn't rush into a decision, not on the heels of Kelsey's promise of secrecy. It felt like a bribe. "I'll get back to you before we leave."

Kelsey nodded vigorously. "Thanks, Sheriff."

Once the girl left her office, Harper planted her face in her hands.

Love? No fucking way. Lust? Absolutely. Josh had a body made for sin, and she'd happily burn in hell with him.

Beyond that...

She couldn't think about that right now. Right now, she had to suck it up and do her fucking job.

Like figuring out how to avoid Josh altogether and remove herself from the search with as little notice as possible in case their relationship came into question later. Ackerman didn't have enough experience to be on his own. She'd pair him with her most experienced officer—Mealer. They could take the house. She sure as hell wasn't going there, seeing Josh's things...

Uh-uh, too intimate.

That left Dollins on his own with all the outbuildings...and her standing watch over Josh. How was that going to look?

Harper groaned.

Maybe Kelsey *should* come with them. She could remain with Josh, and Harper could...what? Linger on the perimeter doing nothing.

"Fuck." *Is it too late to call in sick?*

With no idea what she was going to do and no clue what to expect from Josh, Harper rose to her feet and stood at her door. *I'm a professional. I can do this.*

"Kelsey," she called out so that the others would hear, "make a sign for the door and work your magic on the phone. You'll ride with me."

****

At the slamming of car doors, Josh's head snapped up, and he strained to listen. Another slam.

Harper.

Heart stumbling, he propped the fork against a

stall, shrugged into his coat, and stuffed his hat on his head. He stepped out of the barn into the biting north wind and counted four Stone County vehicles. Mealer, Dollins, Ackerman—the whole gang including Kelsey—milled about his barnyard, but Josh headed straight for Harper.

Dark clouds had rolled in, and the temperature had dropped. His weather app called for snow later in the afternoon. Stone Creek saw snow once in a blue moon, so Josh didn't worry too much about a white landscape, which meant ice and slush. Either way, Harper and her team would need to work fast to beat the storm.

Harper advanced toward him with a singular purpose, like a warrior ready for battle. A black beanie replaced her usual baseball cap. She held out the warrant. "We'll make this as quick and painless as possible."

Professional to the core, not a hint of emotion in those steel gray eyes. She was still mad at him, though. He could tell. Anger he could deal with. He was holding on to some anger himself.

He folded the warrant and stuck it in his back pocket for later. "You do what you gotta do."

"Is anyone else here?"

"Everyone's gone, so you have the run of the place."

Mealer approached, drawing her lethal gaze from his. The deputy held out a pair of blue latex gloves. "Where do you want to start?

"There's a lot of ground to cover. We'll get the vehicles and trailer out of the way before the storm breaks." She stuffed her hands into thin gloves that would offer no protection from the cold. Her fingers would be frozen before they were done. "Then you and Ackerman will take the house. Dollins and I will work the outbuildings."

"Do you need me to show you around?" Josh asked.

"Thank you, Mr. McNamara"—she shook her head—"but unless you have structures other than the ones we can see on the satellite map, I just need you to point me in the direction of your trailer."

"It's on the other side of the equipment shed," he said. "I'll be in the barn, finishing chores. I'll do my best to stay out of your way." He tipped his hat and started to turn away.

"Jo—Mr. McNamara?"

The slip of his name painted her cheeks pinker than the wind ever could. His palms itched to warm the icy sting out of them and pull her in close for a kiss.

He shoved his hands into his coat pockets. "Sheriff?"

"I'm afraid you'll need to find a comfortable spot and sit tight." Her tone was steady, but her gaze slipped to his chest. She didn't like this any more than he did.

He fisted a hand. "Look, Sheriff, I've got animals to care for before the weather gets bad. I can't wait around for you to play detective."

Her eyes snapped up to his, and if looks were daggers, he'd be a dead man. Good. She deserved it after this morning. He was going to enjoy punishing her...*if* he ever got another chance.

"Fine," she said between clenched teeth, then smoothed out her frown and slipped her sheriff's mask back on. "To prevent damage to property, I'll need keys to everything that's locked."

Josh pulled out his keys and handed them to her. "The key to the bucket of bolts is hanging on a hook in the kitchen. Everything else should be unlocked except the toolbox on the back of my truck and the equipment shed."

"What about your brother's?"

"He and Shayna went to check on Ellie."

At Ellie's name, her stern features softened. "Good." She squinted against a strong gust of wind. "Will you keep me posted on Shayna's findings?"

"Of course." Josh hunched his shoulders up around his ears.

Mealer cleared his throat. "What about the other vehicles?"

Josh shot him a glare. "The guys are out guarding the herd, and I don't have keys to their vehicles. Are they included in the warrant?"

"They are," Mealer stated, "but we'll take care of them."

Shit. Josh had told Evan about the search because, as co-owner, Evan had a right to know everything he did about the investigation, but Harper had risked a lot warning Josh, so he'd kept his mouth shut and hadn't told his guys. He really hadn't considered they'd be included.

Wrong. So fucking wrong.

"Anything else?" he asked.

Harper handed the keys to Mealer, who headed back to his car. "Dispatcher Price will be your shadow while we're here."

Irritation bubbled up again. "You mean my guard."

"It's for your protection," she offered as Kelsey bounced up beside her.

He grunted. "Come on, Kelsey. I've got work to do."

As he held the barn door open for his prison guard, he glanced back at Harper. She stood in the middle of her deputies, no doubt barking orders. No, that wasn't fair. Josh had watched her with her people, and she wasn't one to flaunt her power over them.

Mealer handed her a backpack. She nodded and pulled her hood up. The group dispersed amongst the vehicles. Mealer took his. She went for Rusty's.

Kelsey's teeth chattered beside him as Josh shut the door and shrugged out of his coat.

"She's just doing her job, you know," Kelsey said, wandering to Star's stall.

The adrenaline rush he'd felt while talking to Harper quickly evaporated, leaving him drained as he hung up his coat and hat. If he heard that phrase one more fucking time... "I do know."

"She won't admit it," she singsonged, "but she has feelings for you."

I know that, too. Josh glanced at her over his shoulder. "I don't think she'd like you telling me that."

"No, she wouldn't like it at all," she said as Star nibbled at her empty palm. "She told me to stay off my phone unless I received a call transferred from the sheriff's department and not to talk to you."

He chuckled and pulled the warrant from his pocket. "You don't obey orders very well."

"Sorry, did you say something?" Kelsey glanced at him in mock innocence. "I was talking to this sweet girl."

Josh shook his head. Harper was going to have her hands full with this one, but right now, her sly little minx was working in his favor. "Her name is Star."

"Star," she repeated. "A pretty name for a pretty girl."

She chattered away to Star as Josh sat on a bale of hay against the wall and read through the warrant. He skimmed all the mumbo jumbo but caught the highlights. He pulled out his phone.

"They're trying to match the trailer used by the rustlers with ours," Josh said when Evan answered his call.

"It won't," Evan said, his voice calm and confident, "so no need for concern."

Josh flipped a page. "And a hoof boot."

"They must have found a print, which is good. But we don't use them, so they won't find anything…unless whoever did this planted something."

"Fuck me, I never thought of that." Josh's stomach sank. "But I don't see how—"

"I'm just saying that's the only way they'll find anything."

Josh rubbed the back of his neck. "How long before you're headed back?"

"It shouldn't be much longer. Take a deep breath and sit tight," Evan said. "Was there anything else listed in the warrant other than trailer and hoof boot?"

"That's all I can see—" Josh read the bottom of the page. "—other than they'll be combing through our financials."

"That's standard for any theft investigation, and again, no worries."

"Right." This was just a formality. Nothing to fear. "How's Ellie?"

"Damn, Josh, I don't know. She was hysterical

when we got here. Kept rambling about aliens and Jody the mailman. Shay finally got her calmed down, and right now, they're making fucking cinnamon rolls."

Josh slumped against the wall. "What does Shayna think?"

"Alzheimer is only one possibility, but she's trying to get Ellie to trust her enough to let her check her vitals."

"Did she recognize you?"

"Yeah, after a minute. She thought I was you, at first." Evan snorted. "What the fuck? I'm much better looking, and I do not have crow's feet. Anyway, right now, she thinks I'm the plumber. I was fixing her damn sink when you called."

Josh blew out a sigh, glad Evan was there. And Shayna. She'd know what they needed to do. "Thanks, Ev."

"Don't worry. It'll be okay," Evan assured him. "Hey, Shayna's calling me to come ice the rolls. I'll keep you posted."

Josh scrubbed a hand over his face again then drove his fingers through his hair. How the hell was he supposed to not worry? He needed to think about something else.

Cinnamon rolls. He smiled as he thought of last night and how he'd iced Harper's buns, how she'd giggled at his teasing. After that, playing inmate to Harper's warden wasn't his idea of fun.

Unless…

Hmm. Maybe he could ditch the guard, take the warden hostage, and have his way with her. She had handcuffs. He could shackle her to his bed.

Yeah, I can get on board for that.

Blood flooded his cock, driving him to his feet. He snatched up the fork. Maybe he was safer worrying about Ellie and the search warrant. The last thing he needed was for Harper to walk in and assume he had a boner for her dispatch officer. Not if he wanted to convince her to give him another chance.

Chapter Sixteen

Harper blew into her hands as she entered the barn, Dollins behind her. The smell of fresh shavings cut the underlying odor of manure. And thank fuck, it was warm. Her body felt like sculpted ice, her muscles stiff.

"I'll get started in the tack room," Dollins said as Harper scanned the large galley-style space running through the middle of the barn.

Kelsey stood with her back to the wall, surprisingly quiet and attentive. She must have run out of things to say. *And pigs fly.*

Josh rested against the doorframe of a small lavatory, drying his hands. His gaze danced up and down her body then connected with hers.

Saliva pooled in her mouth, and her zombieflies took flight. She swallowed them down, along with the urge to return the sexy grin he wore. Instead, she cleared her throat. "Please take a seat out of the way while we conduct a search of the barn."

"I'm done, anyway." He sauntered toward her, his hand reaching for her.

She froze. *He wouldn't. Not again. Not in front of Kelsey and Dollins.*

But he stepped back with the coat she hadn't noticed hanging behind her, and relief rushed out of her on the breath she'd held. Another part of her burned with need as he ran his fingers through his sun-kissed hair and covered it with his Stetson.

Even the dark circles around his eyes wreaked havoc with her heart. She ached to wrap her arms around him, to offer comfort.

She had to find the bastards making his life hell.

"Any chance you're done with my house?" he asked. "I really need a shower."

As if on cue, Mealer poked his head in the door. "Need some help?"

"Looks like it's your lucky day, Mr. McNamara," she said to Josh as Ackerman filed in behind Mealer. "Kelsey will take you back to the house."

He arched a brow. "She gonna scrub my back for me, too."

Harper ignored the parting jab as he swept past her, but that didn't prevent the images of him in the shower with Kelsey from scorching her concentration throughout the entire search of the barn.

Thank fuck it didn't take long with all four of them working together. It helped that Josh kept his barn clean and neat, everything in its place. And thank fuck, *everything* didn't include a hoof boot.

Granted, they still had to process Evan's truck to complete the search, but she was certain enough they wouldn't find anything that she would let Dollins and Ackerman handle it before heading back to the office. The mayor would no doubt be waiting for a report.

As the guys loaded their equipment bags, Harper waited outside Josh's house for Kelsey, nerves jittering. Perspiration beaded her brow, despite the cold. Actually, she didn't have to see Josh again or give him the department spiel she'd given Walter and Reed after searching their property. She could just get in her car and drive away.

The screen door at the back of the house banged shut.

"Hey, Sheriff." Kelsey jogged toward Harper. "I'm catching a ride with Dylan back to the office. He wants me to hear a song he wrote."

A song my ass. If Ackerman had his way, they'd be sharing more than lyrics.

Harper lifted her face toward the sky and felt the light sting of sleet. "Be careful," she said, then leveled a warning glance at Kelsey. "And I'm not just talking about the weather."

"You, too." Grinning ear to ear, Kelsey angled her head toward the house. "He's in the kitchen."

Shaking her head, Harper checked her watch. A quarter after five. With all the cloud cover, she'd thought it much later.

Hunting for Mealer, she found him closing the trunk of his cruiser.

"I'm glad nothing came of this," he said, pulling keys from his pocket.

"Me, too," she said. "Get home to Lori before it gets any worse out here. I'll get Dollins and Ackerman to finish up with Evan McNamara's vehicle over at Ellie's. It shouldn't take long. They can get started on the financials tonight as well, and we'll see where we're at in the morning."

Kelsey waved as she and Ackerman drove past.

"That gonna be a problem?" Mealer asked.

Harper sighed. "I hope not."

"What time is the ranger supposed to be here?"

"Around lunch, but with the weather, who knows?" She'd wanted more to offer the ranger. Fuck, she'd wanted a suspect in custody before he arrived.

"See you in the morning, then."

She nodded. "Yep."

After she doled out instructions to Dollins, he pulled out behind Mealer, and Harper walked to her car as if the ground was on fire. Fuck the official apology. He wouldn't want to hear it. And fuck the update. She'd call him tomorrow.

Harper climbed behind the wheel of her SUV but stopped short of starting the engine as a tingle of awareness skittered along the back of her neck. Closing her eyes, she struggled to ignore it along with the need to make her own apology. She owed him that much.

Unable to stop herself, she looked back at the house. Air froze in her lungs, and her pulse jumped.

With a shoulder against the doorframe, Josh stood in silhouette of the light behind him. She resisted the impulse to bang her head on the steering wheel. Why? Why couldn't he have just gone about his business of eating supper or watching TV or whatever the fuck he did at night?

Compelled by some invisible magnet, she pulled up the hood of her coat and got out of the car. Tiny spheres of ice crunched under her boots as she trekked across his backyard. She hesitated when he stepped back and opened the door.

"Don't be stubborn," he said, his tone coaxing. "It's too cold for that."

He was right, but crossing the threshold into his domain scared the fuck out of her. So far, she'd only met him on her own turf or neutral territory at The Arena.

Once inside, Harper pushed back her hood and

shivered as the warmth of the cozy kitchen enveloped her. She frowned at the mess her deputies had made of his home.

Every cabinet door was open, along with a few drawers. Canned and boxed food piled on the counter and floor. The pantry door was open, the trash can pulled out, a broom and mop leaning against it. A bench with a storage compartment was left open, and several items—a rubber boot, a coil of rope, and a pair of spurs—lay on the floor next to it.

Had to be Ackerman. This was not Mealer's MO. "Sorry about the mess."

"Don't worry about it." Josh closed the door and sauntered to the sink, his jeans molding to his ass. Another flannel shirt of black and white checks stretched across broad shoulders, sleeves rolled up to reveal a black thermal shirt. His hair was still damp from his shower.

She swallowed back a moan but could do nothing about the cream coating her panties. Fuck him for making her want him.

He grabbed a mug from the drying rack and held it up. "Coffee?"

"No, thanks. I only came up to say thank you for your cooperation today."

"I didn't really have a choice, did I?" he asked as he settled against the counter, one ankle crossed over the other. Wool socks covered his feet, but his boots sat by the table. Where was he headed in this weather?

She tried to get a read on him. He'd waffled back and forth between resenting and taunting her in the last few hours. Now, his tone was flat. Not angry. Just…done?

Did it matter?

Just say what you came in here to say and get the fuck out.

Harper cleared her throat. "For the record, I didn't enjoy doing this. I know you aren't stealing your own cattle. This was a colossal waste of my time and yours, but because we didn't find anything, we can move forward with other lines of investigation. It also proves we did our jobs, and no one can say I've given you special treatment."

"That was a mouthful of humble pie." He lifted a skeptical brow. "Or should I say a crock of shit?"

"Yeah, well, take it however you want." She turned to go.

"Why did you warn me?" he asked, stalling her exit. "About the search."

Staring through the window in the door, she barely saw her car for the sleet coming down. "I don't know."

"Bullshit."

Her gaze snapped to his. Determination stared back at her over the rim of his mug. They'd been over this. "I told you because I didn't want to blindside you."

"And?"

"And I didn't want you to think I actually believed you were capable of insurance fraud."

With her admission, his body visibly relaxed. Did her opinion of him mean that much?

"You were going to leave." The change of subject jumbled her brain, and he must have read the confusion on her face because he added, "Just now. You were going to leave without a word. No update, no explanation, no pretty apology."

Harper blanched at the hint of hurt in the

accusation. What could she say that wouldn't be a lie or reveal the fact that she was fucking terrified of how he made her feel.

"Why did you?" Pushing away from the counter, he set his coffee on the table. "Why did you change your mind?"

"It's my job and—

"Fuck your job." He stalked slowly toward her, anger burning in the depths of his turbulent blue eyes. "If it were your job, you never would have gotten in your car. You'd have come straight to my door. I want to know why you didn't."

She reached for the doorknob, not out of fear of Josh but from the truth of his words.

"Don't even think about it."

"Fuck you." Harper pulled open the door and pushed the screen door back.

He reached for her, but she bolted into the dimly lit backyard.

"God dammit, Harper," he called after her.

Shoving her hands into her coat pockets, she let the wind hurry her steps. She'd be in her car before he got his boots on. If he touched her, she'd lose everything she'd worked so hard for.

Fuck your job? Had he understood anything she'd said? *And you thought he got you.*

Harper was halfway to her car when something whirred above her head, dropped, and made a zipping sound as it cinched around her middle, trapping her arms to her sides from the elbows up.

What the fuck? She looked down and barely made out the rope at her waist. *Oh hell no. He did not just lasso me.*

"Are you fucking—umph." A hard tug of the rope hauled her backward.

Several more yanks as he gathered the rope kept her off balance and stumbling until he spun her around. His hands splayed on her cheeks, tilting her head back. Icy rain pelted her face, forcing her to blink.

Harper struggled against him, but she couldn't get her hands free from her pockets. "Are you insane?"

He snaked an arm behind her back and hauled her flush with his hard body.

She gasped. Even through her coat, she could feel his massive erection.

"Not until you answer me," he bit out.

"Fuck you," she spat as her traitorous body softened. Against her will, her hips tilted.

"Is that an admission?" His breath feathered her lips. "You came for a hard fuck? Is that what you need?"

Yes. No. She shook her head, her need for Josh overpowering the fear that constantly whispered in her ear. She clung to that fear. It kept her heart safe. "I don't know."

"Yes, you do." He slipped the hand on her cheek to her nape and drew her closer. "You feel something for me. I know you do."

No. Yes. "I—" Harper's throat constricted as stupid, fucking tears lodged there. She swallowed. "I don't know what I feel."

His mouth slid across hers, his tongue probing then disappearing. She chased it with her own, tasting mint, coffee, and man—Josh. He moaned and deepened the kiss, slowly exploring. Her knees weakened, and she whimpered as her body handed him control.

Josh eased away. "Say the word, wildcat. Say your safeword, and I'll let you go." He nipped at her lips, the bite of his teeth sharp and stinging. "Or stay with me, and I'll give you everything you need."

Every last shred of denial screamed at her to run, but the lure of his promise and the subtle message behind it held her tighter than the rope digging into her arms. Need swirled deep in her core and seeped into the cracked shell around her heart. She ached to let him all the way in, but...

Don't do it. Say your safeword. He'll crush you.

Harper blinked up at Josh, his eyes unreadable in the dark. "Make me. Make me...stay."

He shook his head. "I won't force you."

"I need— I *want* you to make me stay with you. I—" She swallowed again, hard. "I'm scared."

****

The stark terror in Harper's voice pierced Josh's heart. For a moment, he couldn't move. Then her words took root.

Harper wanted to stay with him. That was the reason she'd come back to the house. She ached for him as much as he did for her. She just needed him to help her get past her fear.

With a growl, he scooped her up and over his shoulder. Her yelp teased his balls as her slight weight settled against his back. His blood thickened with lust.

Carefully maneuvering her through the door so he didn't hit her head, he turned to close it.

"What the fuck, Josh? You're not wearing shoes...or a damn coat. What were you thinking?"

"Only of you, wildcat." He wove around the kitchen table and toward the front stairs.

"Your feet must be freezing."

He'd been oblivious to the cold, his sole focus on her...on not letting her get away this time. He grunted as he took the steps two at a time. "Don't know. Can't feel 'em. Don't care."

"You'll care when your toes fall off."

"As long as it's not my dick, we'll be okay." He skirted the second-floor banister and threw his door wide. It banged against the wall. Harper flinched. He kicked it shut, engulfing them in darkness.

All he could think about was having her beneath him. He had to slow down. He didn't want the hard fuck he'd accused her of craving. He wanted to take his time, to worship her body with his hands and mouth, to show her how much he...loved her?

His feet stalled just shy of the bed. Emotion swelled in his chest. He loved Harper. He fucking loved her.

Dizzy with the realization, he lowered her to the floor and turned on the bedside lamp. She'd lost the beanie somewhere between the backyard and his bedroom. Wet shanks of hair clung to her wind-chapped cheeks. He brushed them away, searching her eyes for any hint that she might feel the same.

"Josh?" she murmured, uncertain and still holding on to fear.

"Shh, I've got you." He bent his head to drink from her lips. They parted on a sigh, and he invaded with his tongue. Sweet, warm, submissive to his sedate exploration. Her tongue swirled around his, then retreated, hesitant, which wasn't like the Harper he'd come to know. She was holding back. Still stuck in her head. He'd never seen her this vulnerable.

If he was ever going to get past her fear, he had to draw on her strength. He rested his forehead on hers. "Come on, wildcat. Give me all you've got."

Give me everything.

"I'm a little bit tied up, right now," she quipped with only a slight quaver in her voice, making him smile.

"There's my girl." The urgency in his gut lessened. He tugged the rope around her middle. "I was going to use your handcuffs tonight, but this works just as well. I have you right where I want you."

Josh led her to the foot of the bed, nudged her backward until her spine lined up with the corner post, then wrapped the rope around her and the post a few times and tied it off.

Dropping to his knees, he sat back on his heels and patted his thigh.

"Not until you take off your wet socks."

He tilted his head to one side. "Why are you so damn worried about my toes?"

"Because they're yours."

It was as close to admitting she cared about him as he'd come so far.

I'll take it.

He happily thumbed off the muddy socks and shucked two layers of shirts while he was at it.

When Harper's boot landed on his thigh, he palmed the back of her heel and pulled her foot free. He repeated the process with the other boot and tossed both aside, leaving her thick socks on to keep her feet warm.

"I want you to keep your toes, too." He glanced up at her and winked. "Besides, you'll look hot with only socks on."

She wiggled her toes the same as she'd done the night he removed her stilettos. He thought it was from wearing those ridiculously sexy shoes, but maybe she'd been on her feet all day like she was today. Or maybe she just didn't like wearing shoes. He had a lot to learn about her.

One at a time, he lifted each foot and rubbed her toes through the wool. She moaned, and his dick ate metal. When he couldn't stand any more, he placed her feet shoulder width apart.

Slipping his hands under Harper's coat, he felt around for the buckle of her gun belt and slipped the prongs from the notches. The waistband of her jeans sagged with the weight of her gun. The button and zipper gave way, and her jeans slid halfway down her thighs.

He smiled up at her. "Well, isn't that convenient."

That got him an eye roll as he peeled her pants down to her feet. She stepped out of them, and he moved them aside so he could get closer. He nuzzled her pussy, inhaling the sweet essence of her juices. A tremor of raw need shuddered through him. His dick throbbed, aching for a taste.

Hands splayed on her hips, he opened his mouth over the pale blue panties hiding her treasure. Slowly, he dragged his teeth together in a bite that grazed her clit.

She jerked and wrestled with her bindings. "Let me at least have my hands."

"You've pulled out enough of my hair." He licked the drenched silk, her tangy cream zinging over his tastebuds. *So good.*

Her fists punched at her coat pockets. "Josh, I

need—"

"Punishing." He nipped at her mound.

She shivered. "For what?"

"For not taking better care of yourself." Josh trailed a finger over the bottom of the bruise on her hip, bigger and darker than it was yesterday. "I'm sure I could come up with several more transgressions if I could think past the taste of your pussy, but Harper—" He glanced up at her. "I don't need a reason. You're mine. I'll punish you whenever I want."

Challenge sparked in her eyes, but another shiver closed them as he bathed the bruise with his tongue. Using his teeth, he snagged the lace trimming her panties and yanked. The sound of lace and silk ripping rivaled her moan. He fisted the fabric decorating her other hip and tore it from her, then sat back and raised the shredded garment to his nose.

"This—" He inhaled again, her feminine perfume an intoxicating aphrodisiac. "—is mine."

"Josh?"

"Hmm?"

"Stop sniffing my panties and eat my pussy."

Josh barked out a laugh. Damn, he loved it when she tried to boss him around. He shouldn't give her what she wanted, but denying her meant denying himself, and she knew it. "Brat."

He tucked the mangled silk into his front jeans pocket and leaned forward to spear his tongue between her petal-soft folds. Her legs parted. Satiny skin taunted his fingers as he slid one hand to the back of her thigh. He anchored it over his shoulder and dove in for another lick.

The mouth of her cunt was slick with her desire.

"Is this all for me, wildcat?"

"Yes."

Smiling, he lubed two fingers with her wetness and crammed them deep into her velvety heat. Her whimper stoked the fire in his groin, the flames licking his balls. He retreated and plunged again, deeper. He worked her clit with the flat of his tongue.

"More," she demanded, straining against the rope. "I'm close."

"Thanks for the heads up, wildcat." He withdrew and plunged half the depth as before, keeping her on the edge. No need to give in to her demands so soon.

"More, Josh. I said more." Her inner muscles sucked at his fingers.

"I heard you, but I think you're confusing reward with punishment." He stroked in short bursts as he teased her clit with his tongue until it was hard and swollen. Like his god damn dick.

"Josh," she begged. "Please."

Her plea nearly had him shooting his load.

Fuck it. Punishment's overrated.

Sliding his fingers deep, he curled them over her G-spot and sucked hard. The muscles in her pussy contracted. A strangled cry tore from her throat, and the flavor of Harper exploded on his tongue. Sweet. Tangy. *His.*

Drunk on her cum, he consumed all she had to give until her body went limp, then he licked more from his fingers. It wasn't enough.

Rising, Josh cradled the back of her head and captured her mouth, sharing her essence in a slow invasion of lips, tongue, and teeth that threatened to suffocate him with the emotion expanding his chest.

He broke away and swallowed the words trying to escape. Too much. Too soon. Harper wasn't ready. Might never be.

Never was a long fucking time.

Fuck that. He had to change never into forever.

****

Trapped in the haze of euphoria, Harper stared up at Josh as he untied the rope securing her to his bed. He was so fucking good at eating pussy. No doubt from lots of practice.

Maybe, but he likes how I suck his dick, and that talent hasn't come without experience.

The rope fell away, and the zipper of her coat glided down her torso with a whir. He guided the jacket over her shoulders, and it joined the rope on the floor. His callused fingers slipped under the hem of her shirt, grazing her stomach. Her abdominals jerked. Her uniform and undershirt whipped over her head. Where it landed, she didn't care. Her bra was gone in the blink of an eye.

Cool air skated over her bare flesh and cleared the fog in her head. Relinquishing control to Josh—tied up or not—had brought incredible pleasure, but it was time to get back in the game and return the favor.

Skimming one hand over his pecs to his collarbone, she cupped the bulge in his jeans with the other. Her pussy clenched at the thought of him hitting the back of her throat. "Your turn."

Strong hands gripped her wrists and twisted them behind her back. "No."

"You know you want it," Harper taunted, straining forward and molding her breasts to his hard chest. "Maybe this time, you can ice my tits."

The growl she'd come to love skated along her nerve endings. Jaw clenched, he seemed to battle with indecision. Then his gaze met hers, and his hands stilled. One corner of his mouth twisted in a sexy grin, and the storm in his eyes abated. "Tempting, but no."

"Are you sure?" She licked her lips. "Don't you like me on my knees?"

What the fuck? I'm back to begging?

He grunted and walked her backward until her legs hit the bed, then he spun her around and guided her onto the mattress.

"I love your ass." His fingers kneaded her buttocks, giving rise to a cascade of goosebumps. "Get under the covers where it's warm."

"I'm not cold." A shiver called her a liar.

The smack of his hand landing on her ass cheek was loud and stung like a— "Motherfucker."

"I won't tell you again," he warned.

Damn, that hurt…so fucking good.

If she told him now that she wasn't cold, she wouldn't be lying. Heat flooded her body with need. But he didn't need to know that.

Glaring at him over one shoulder and rubbing the fiery handprint he'd left, Harper crawled up the bed and pulled the covers down. Sliding between the sheets, she drew them to her waist then reclined on her elbows. She shook her hair around her shoulders and thrust out her breasts, giving him a reason to hurry.

Josh stood at the edge of the bed, his hungry gaze roaming over her tits. She could almost feel his mouth on them. Sliding a hand under one, she cupped and lifted it in invitation. She pinched her nipple and sank her teeth into her bottom lip to keep from moaning.

"Keep it up, brat." He yanked at the button and zipper of his jeans and pushed his boxers down. His monster cock sprang forward and arrowed toward her lips.

He was big, and she loved every fucking inch. She bit her lip harder, wanting him inside her mouth, wanting him to thrust to the back of her throat so deep she gagged.

She reached for him again, but he retreated a step and shoved his jeans and underwear down long, lean legs, then he kicked out of them. He palmed the shaft and pumped from base to tip, milking a bead of clear fluid from the slit.

On its own accord, her tongue snaked out to wet her lips again. "Josh?"

"No," he rasped as he retrieved a condom from his nightstand, tore it open, and rolled it down his dick. "I'll explode."

The mattress dipped as he climbed in beside her, his weight on his elbow, one sculpted arm gathering her close. Warm breath feathered the swell of her breast just before his mouth enveloped her nipple. He drew on it, gently, slowly, unceasingly.

Each tug plucked at the string bound to her center. Need built higher. "Oh god, Josh. That feels...ahhhhh."

Harper skimmed a hand over his rock-hard biceps to his shoulders then onward until her fingers found their grip in the silky hair at the base of his skull.

More.

With the slightest effort, he rolled her to her back and loomed over her as he shifted his attention to her other nipple. She spread her legs, ready for him, but rather than settle into the cradle of her hips, he threw a leg over both of hers to pin her to the bed.

The strength of the suction on her breast increased. Her clit pulsed in time with each pull. She writhed, aching for relief. "Touch me."

When he ignored her, she sought to relieve the pressure with her own hand.

He clasped her wrist. "No."

"Then you do it," she snapped. "I—"

"I said no." He pinned her hand above her head.

"You liked it last night."

"I did," he said, his lips trailing higher. His tongue dipped into the hollow of her throat. "But tonight is different, and I want it to last."

Harper's breath caught at the raw emotion in his voice, but before she could analyze it or ask what made tonight different, he took possession of her lips and sliced a knee between her thighs. She welcomed his weight as he finally positioned between them. His thick shaft glided over her swollen clit.

Then the head of his cock nudged her entrance and, with excruciating leisure, breached her slit. She rocked her hips forward to take more, but he withdrew.

Her pussy spasmed with the loss, and she twisted her head to the side, sucking in a lungful of air. "Fucking fuck." She pulled at his hair. "Just fuck me."

"No," he growled but screwed his way back inside, penetrating deeper, inch by slow inch, stretching her.

"Yes." She nipped at his stubbled jaw. "More. I want it all."

"So…do I." His fingers flexed and slid from her wrist to flatten her hand against the bed. He laced his fingers with hers. "I want everything."

Harper closed her eyes to ward off the panic, afraid

to acknowledge the contrast between her words and his. She wasn't ready to hear them or return the sentiment.

Four fucking days. It's insane.

Still, somehow, he'd scaled the walls of her defenses and worked his way into her heart. How deep was yet to be determined.

She loosened her fingers in his hair and trailed them over his back to his fine as hell ass. Digging her nails into the firm rounded flesh, she urged him to move. "Take it, Josh. Take what you want."

He shook his head, but his hips jerked. The crown of his cock bumped her cervix. "Fuck me."

"Any time you're ready."

A chuckle tickled along her neck just before his tongue flicked the sensitive spot beneath her ear and lightly sucked.

"Mmm." Looked like she'd be wearing turtlenecks for another couple of weeks. She didn't care. She rolled her head to give him a broader canvas to work with, but he tracked kisses over her cheek.

"Shh, baby, let me make you feel good," he whispered against her lips, then slanted his mouth over hers and began a languid rotation of his hips as he pulled out, just enough to frustrate her, then slowly glided back in.

Shifting his weight to one side, he skimmed a hand along the back of her thigh and under her knee to urge her leg higher. She complied with his silent demand and hooked her knee over his hip. He slid deeper.

Heat flared from her center, firing off little pulses of pleasure. Sweat dotted her skin and trickled between her breasts, yet she burned for his touch. Any hotter and the sheets would go up in flames.

Harper arched into the searing pleasure, meeting his next stroke. He deepened the kiss, lazily fucking her mouth with his tongue in rhythm with his cock. With every thrust and heaving breath, the world around them evaporated. Nothing mattered. Only Josh.

As pressure built in her pussy, so did the tightness in her chest. The back of her eyes stung, and her nose prickled. A traitorous tear slipped free and trailed into the hair at her temple. A sob squeezed her throat. Too much. Not ready.

His grip on her thigh turned vise-like, shooting delicious tendrils of pain to her core. Pleasure and pain collided in an explosion that hurled her head-over-ass off the cliff of ecstasy.

A scream severed her lips from his as she fell.

"That's it, baby. Let go," Josh rasped as he continued to gently fuck her through a slow and glorious descent.

Just when reality rose up to meet her, he shifted to center his hips. His pubic bone grazed her clit.

"Josh." She panted around the rising need and raked her nails over the rippling muscles of his back.

Air hissed between his teeth, and his hips jerked. His dick flexed. He grasped her hand and imprisoned it above her head with the other.

"Look at me." He rolled his hips.

She thrashed her head from side to side. *Too much*.

"Harper, look at me," Josh demanded, his tone harsher, more urgent. "I want you to see me as I make you come again."

Struggling to obey, Harper opened her eyes. Shadows played across his face, but the soft light of the lamp illuminated the angle of his jaw and the full bottom lip, both clenched tight from the control he wielded. Golden waves fell over his brow, and her fingers itched to brush them back, then trace the veins forming under the smooth, sun-kissed skin at his temple.

But then Josh's slumberous eyelids lifted, and she was lost, drowning in a sea of deep blue.

****

The tether on Josh's control slipped as Harper shattered beneath him. He wanted to give her more, but the next slow grind into her spasming pussy broke him.

"Harper." He moaned her name through the orgasm ripping along his spine and spearing into his groin. Hot cum splashed in violent jets against the only barrier separating them.

Except for the wall around her heart.

The thought was sobering in the aftermath of his release.

Lowering his head, he buried his face in the crook of her shoulder and breathed in the flowery scent of her shampoo as air sawed in and out of his lungs. She felt so good beneath him. He didn't want to move. Couldn't if he wanted to.

His beautiful wildcat hadn't even tried, and she'd fucking ruined him.

When her legs slid from around his waist to the back of his thighs, he eased from her body and rolled to one side and off the bed to dispose of the condom. In the bathroom, he took care of business, washed up, and returned to find Harper exactly where he'd left her—small hands beside her head, creamy legs splayed, hair spilling like black ink on the white sheet.

Bare, exposed, a beautiful picture of satisfaction.

His.

Josh shook his head. Not completely, but she would be soon. That wall around her heart was starting to crumble. He'd seen it in her eyes.

Crawling onto the bed, he pulled the sheet and blanket over them. He gathered her against his side, tucking her close, her head on his chest.

"I can't stay," she murmured as she snuggled closer, sliding a leg over his.

A smile pulled at his lips as his gut twisted. "I know."

Her fingers skated over his ribs. "I have to go."

"I know." He glanced out the window. The storm had passed. The sky was clear. Nothing prevented her from leaving.

And she will once she hears what I have to say.

With the revelation that had just crashed down on his head, he needed her to know where he stood. He didn't want this to be the last time or one of many stolen moments. "I want you, Harper."

She palmed his semi erection. "I think you need another minute. Fuck knows I do."

"No, Harper. I want all of you. Not just this." He tipped her face to his. "Not just tonight. I want it all. You and me, working out a way to be together. I want to hold your hand in public and buy you popcorn at the movies. I want you and me to be an *us*. I can't be your dirty little secret."

A frown creased her brow, and panic chased away the lingering effects of afterglow. "I—"

Holding his breath, Josh braced for rejection.

"I'm here. I'm trying," she said, her tone pleading. "Can't we take it slow for a while?"

Saying no wasn't an option, but... "What's a while?"

"I—I don't know. I just got here, and elections aren't until May."

He ground his teeth at the possibility of hiding their relationship for months. If they even had one. But she said she'd try. That would have to be good enough. For now. "We'll figure it out."

From somewhere in the house, a door banged shut. Sounded like the back screen door. Muffled voices floated up the stairs.

Harper rose on one elbow. "Someone's here."

"Evan and Shayna."

Harper groaned and dropped her forehead to his chest. "I should have left when I had the chance."

Josh rolled away to sit on the edge of the bed. "You wanna sneak out the back door? I'm pretty sure I can distract them."

"That's not what I meant, and you know it." Her fingers ghosted over the scar on his back, soothing his pride and reminding him once again of the cougar in the canyon, boxed in and pacing the wall behind him until instinct forced him to fight for his life. Harper was like that cougar, cornered and afraid and fighting to protect herself. "I don't regret being here with you. It's just..."

Twisting to face her, Josh captured her hand and brought her fingers to his lips. "I know." And he did. At least, he was trying to. "Look, you don't have to worry. They won't say anything. They have secrets of their own." At her silence, he tugged at her hand. "Come on. I want you to meet them."

"You think meeting family is taking it slow?" Delicate fingers slipped from his as she flopped onto her back and flung an arm over her eyes. "Fuck me."

This time, her caginess didn't hurt as much. Maybe it was the way the sheet rode low on her hips. Or that her milky tits tempted him.

He trailed a finger over one peak. Her cherry nipples instantly hardened. Just like his dick. "Ah, wildcat. That sounds an awful lot like an invitation?"

A smile played at her lips and her back arched as she caught his hand and pressed it flat to her breast. Her eyes flashed with hunger and something else he couldn't quite make out. "Maybe later."

Later. The promise gave him the strength to give her the room she asked for. "I know you have Sheriff things to do. I should head out to help with the herd, and I want to see if there's any news about Ellie."

Josh pulled on a pair of jeans and a flannel shirt over long johns, aware of Harper lying in his bed, quiet, no doubt sifting through all the scenarios of how to sneak out of the house undetected. He was surprised she wasn't up and getting dressed. Part of him hoped her delay had less to do with hiding and more to do with wanting to stay with him.

As he sat on the edge of the bed next to her to put on a pair of thick wool socks, the shower in the bathroom down the hall turned on and Shayna began to sing.

"Sounds like Shayna's in the shower. She'll be in there a while, so now's your chance. Or you could stay." Bracing one hand above her head, he traced the healing scratch on her cheek with his thumb and dove in for a lingering taste of her lips. "But I'll understand if you don't."

Another quick kiss and he pushed off the bed

before she tempted him to get naked and fuck her into submission again.

"Josh?" Her choked whisper halted him at the door with his hand on the knob, but he didn't trust himself to turn around. This had to be her decision.

When she didn't say anything, he opened the door. "It's okay, wildcat. I'll call you tomorrow."

Forcing his feet to move, he shut the door behind him and headed down the stairs.

Nothing good ever comes easy.

His dad had said those words a lot, sometimes in reference to a task he wanted done. Most of the time, though, he'd followed up with a smile and a loving look at Josh's mom.

Fuck, old man, you never said love would be so hard or hurt so much.

Chapter Seventeen

Evan handed Josh a cup of coffee. "I made some for the ride out to camp."

"Thanks." Propped against the sink, Josh sipped at the strong, hot brew and took in the grease on his brother's forehead. "Did you fix Ellie's sink?"

"I put in a washer, but she needs a new faucet."

Josh nodded. He should have done that right off. "Did she let Shayna work her up?"

"It took a while, but yes," Evan said as he poured coffee from the pot into a thermos. "I'll let Shay explain. I don't know the medical terms." He looked at Josh. "The sheriff came by when we were leaving."

"The sheriff's upstairs." A creak from the floorboards above confirmed she hadn't snuck out yet.

Evan looked at him over the rim of his cup. "Figured as much since her car is still here. I meant the former sheriff, Tom Jenkins. He wanted to know why we were there."

"Hmph. What was *he* doing there is the better question?" Probably heard Harper'd been there and wanted to know why. Nosey bastard.

"He said the mayor told him about Ellie's calls to his office and the good *former* sheriff thought he'd check on her."

Fucking Radcliff. Didn't he trust Harper to take care of Ellie like he asked her to?

"Shayna had just finished her exam, and he left after she explained her findings."

So god damn Jenkins knew, but he didn't. "Can't you just give me the rundown? Is it Alzheimer's?"

Evan shook his head and shrugged at the same time as he turned away to start another pot of coffee. "Shay doesn't think so."

Josh lowered the cup, his mind whirling in all directions. A brain tumor? Stroke? Or maybe dehydration?

Nah, it couldn't be that simple.

"What does she think it is?" he asked.

Evan picked up his mug and faced him again. "Ellie's oxygen level was really low. Shay thinks maybe her CO_2 levels could be high, but we can't know for sure without a blood test."

"What does that mean?"

"From what I understand, high carbon dioxide levels can mimic dementia. It causes disorientation, confusion, even paranoia. We saw all those symptoms."

Josh had seen them, too, but only because of Harper.

"Shayna hooked Ellie up to a small tank of oxygen she carries in her bag. Ellie seemed more coherent after her oxygen level went up. But the tank ran out, and she declined again."

"Will she be fine with oxygen?"

"I don't know. The doctors will have to find out what's causing it."

Frustration rising, Josh scrubbed a hand over his face and scratched at the stubble on his jaw. "At the risk of repeating myself, what does Shayna think it is?"

"You'll have to wait and ask her. She rattled off a

lot of things, mostly medical jargon I didn't understand and couldn't repeat if I tried."

Josh poured out his coffee and rinsed his mug. *Wait. Wait. Wait.*

All he did anymore was fucking wait. He was waiting for Shayna to explain about Ellie. Waiting for the rustling investigation to yield results.

And waiting for Harper to love him…or not.

****

Harper stared at the ceiling above Josh's bed, confused as hell. Once again, he'd given her exactly what she asked for. Domination in the bedroom with a little bit of freedom to be herself. Support and encouragement with regard to her career. And space enough to decide what she wanted.

Yet she couldn't make up her fucking mind.

She was stuck. Stay or go? Wanting to do both, but the instinct she'd relied on for years to guide her became a fucking jumbled mess.

All her life, Harper fought men who tried to dominate her. Her father barked orders, expecting her to follow. Her brothers were the same. Blake manipulated her every move, making her think she'd made decisions and that they coincided with his. Her superiors told her what decision to make.

Josh was…different. He told her what he wanted, yes, but then he asked what *she* needed.

Her fingers traced the scratch on her cheek but felt only the echo of his gentle touch. In the last two days alone, he'd shown how kind and caring he could be—with Ellie, with Leon…

With me.

In contrast, he was also strong and determined,

calling her on her bullshit, demanding she take care of herself, and searching for his cattle on his own because he was giving her the space she'd requested.

Ugh, fucking vicious cycle.

She'd been a fool with Blake because she hadn't seen him for who he really was. And she was being a fool with Josh because she had repeatedly seen who and what he truly was, yet she was afraid of... What?

Of losing a job that wouldn't keep her warm at night or give a fuck about her?

Of losing out on a promotion? She couldn't reach any higher than sheriff here unless she wanted to run for a political office, and kissing ass wasn't her thing.

Of losing the respect of her family and fellow officers? Harper snorted. She'd done that before she got here. Funny thing was, the staff here seemed to genuinely like her, and both Mealer and Kelsey had given her a green light with Josh.

A laugh bubbled up inside her, and tears burned the backs of her eyes. The only thing she really feared losing now was the possibility of something more with Josh. *Something special.*

She swung her legs over the side of the bed and looked out the window. The weather had cleared. Stars glittered in the indigo sky. She could and should leave now in case that changed.

Laughter escaped again. She had *sheriff stuff* to do.

Harper stretched for her coat on the floor and dug in the pocket for her phone. Her fingers wrapped around it and stilled.

Since entering Josh's house, she hadn't, not once, thought about the investigation. Granted, it was only an hour or so, but it scared her a little. What if she lost herself in him?

She shook her head. Josh wouldn't let her do that.

No, he wouldn't.

Just like she wouldn't ask him to ignore his family or livestock.

Her decision really came down to the question of whether or not she wanted to be with Josh, and the answer was clear.

Fuck, yes!

Swallowing that bit of information and the sudden fluttering in her stomach, she pulled out her phone. No calls or messages. Good.

Harper dressed quickly, sans panties and suffering the damp cold of her jeans. As the weight of her badge settled on her chest, her weapon on her hip, she felt the same as she always had. Just as strong. Just as confident. She didn't feel weak like she'd been afraid she would by letting Josh into her life…maybe into her heart.

Only time would reveal that, but she suspected it was true.

With sure steps, she left his room and smiled as she passed the bathroom door next to the stairs. Shayna still sang…off key.

A few of the treads squeaked on her way down. Josh must have heard them because as she paused at the newel post, she caught a glimpse of him crossing the threshold from the kitchen into the hall. He stopped and stared at her, his expression uncertain, his jaw tight, as if preparing himself to watch her tiptoe out the front door.

With sure strides, she walked straight toward him. He opened his arms, and she melted into his solid warmth. He felt so fucking good. Like home. No, that wasn't right. Every home she'd ever had was cold, hard and competitive, a struggle to survive, like living in a war zone—every man for himself, dog eat dog, or a stab in the back.

Josh was...a warm, soothing bath on a winter's night, like the one she'd shared with him last night.

He crushed her in an embrace that stole her breath and made her eyes burn. "Are you going out the front or the back?"

"I...want to meet your family. I want—" Her throat closed around the emotion she wasn't ready to analyze. "—you."

His chest rose and fell on a long sigh, but rather than press her for more, he stepped back, his grin wide and sexy, stirring a need low in her belly. He took her hand in one of his and pointed up the stairs with the other. "As you can hear, Shayna is still in the shower, but Evan's got another pot of coffee brewing."

"I could use a cup," she said, a little edgy from nerves but letting him lead her to the kitchen.

The man at the sink was a smidge taller than Josh, a little leaner, too. His hair was lighter, shorter on the sides. Nice ass, but Josh's was tighter, probably from spending so much time in the saddle.

"Harper this is my brother Evan," Josh said as the man turned around.

Air stalled in her lungs. The smile on her lips died.

Oh god no, it can't be.

Gabriel. The name whispered from a memory of her time at Silver House, and the room spun at the flare of recognition in his—Evan's—icy blue eyes.

Willing the floor to open up and swallow her, she

blinked back tears, afraid to look at Josh.

"I have to go." She started for the door, but Josh wouldn't let go of her hand. She pulled harder. "Let go."

Josh looked from Harper to Evan, who looked as sick as she felt. "What's going on?"

No way in hell was she telling Josh she'd fucked his brother and another cowboy at a BDSM club in Houston. She couldn't hurt him like that.

Oh. My. God.

She wrenched free and backed away. "Doesn't matter. I changed my mind. I can't do this."

"No." Like a vice, Josh's hand closed around her upper arm and spun her around. Stormy blue eyes bore into hers, shredding her soul, searching for answers she couldn't give. "Tell me."

The command—half plea-half demand—closed her eyes. She swallowed but couldn't hold back the fucking tears spilling down her cheeks.

He hauled her flush against his body, both hands clutching her arms in a grip that would leave souvenirs of her last moments with him. "One of you tell me what's going on."

"Harper and I already know each other." Evan's deep voice weighed heavy with remorse.

"What does that mean? From where?" Josh asked her, and she heard his Adam's apple bob as he swallowed hard. He already knew.

Again, she tried to gain her freedom. "Just let me go."

"Where, Evan?" he asked his brother but shook her.

Evan's sigh of resignation swirled around her.

Oh god, please don't.

Her stomach pitched. She opened her eyes, silently begging him not to say the words that would cause Josh pain. Better for him to hate her for leaving him than to come between him and his family.

But Evan's apologetic gaze was fixed on Josh. "I know Harper from Silver House."

Motherfucker. Why?

Harper sagged as Josh stared down at her, the anguish on his face shattering her heart. "He knows you as Cherry?"

Lower lip quivering, she nodded. "I'm sorry."

His grip loosened, and his hands fell away to fist at his sides. "When?"

"It was before you fell off the ladder, before Shayna," Evan answered for her though she had no concept of time pertaining to the references he made. "Hell, it was before Clay and Lindsey."

"Over a year ago. Before Blake," Harper whispered as she backed toward the door. She couldn't watch the tender feelings he had for her die as hatred materialized in its place.

"I'm sorry," Evan said.

"Guess we're even." Josh's words floated after her as she fled the hall, but his growl caught up with her just before he did. Arms banded around her arms and waist, and her feet left the floor as he swung her into the living room. "Not so fast, wildcat. This conversation is far from over, and neither are we."

"Are you fucking kidding me?" As soon as her feet hit the floor, she put half the room's distance and a sofa between them. He stood blocking the door, loose hipped, hands at his sides, as if waiting for her to bolt.

Fuck but she wanted to. "How can you think we can work after this?"

"We both have a past, Harper. We already established we've been with other people. We met at a sex club, and for fuck's sake, I watched you with Buck." He took a step toward her. "We'll get through this, but you have to want it. You have to want *me*."

All the fight drained out of her. She did want him, but… "I fucked your brother, Josh. There's no changing that."

Despite his calm, he blanched. "It was a long time ago, before we met. Before he and Shayna got back together."

"Oh god…Shayna." The complications kept piling on. Harper wagged a finger back and forth between them. "This can never work. It's fucking crazy."

He picked up one of several picture frames lying face down on a sofa table, the aftermath of the search, and closed the distance between them. "About as crazy as this."

Confused, she looked up from the frame. "I don't understand."

"Take it, and you will."

With a trembling hand, Harper took the photo from Josh. It was one of him with Evan and Shayna, a banner behind them placing them at a rodeo last fall.

Josh captured her attention first, his easy smile. Blue eyes twinkled as if he'd just heard something funny. So happy. So carefree. The man she'd met at The Arena. A man without the stress of a stolen cattle and a fucked-up sheriff who'd had sex with his brother.

Shayna sat between Josh and Evan. Evan's face was turned in profile toward Shayna. He smiled like only a man in love can, no resemblance to the brooding man she'd met at Silver House. It was easy now to see why she'd thought Josh looked familiar when they met at The Arena.

The physical distinctions were subtle—the shade of their hair, the blue of their eyes, and the sharp cut of their cheekbones. So much alike, yet the differences in their demeanor set them miles apart. Evan was the Gabriel from her past, a golden angel lurking on the edge of darkness and danger. Josh's easy smile spoke of fun and mischief, disguising a generous soul and his love for family and friends and...for Shayna?

Harper shifted her focus to the woman between them. Shayna laughed into the camera, one arm behind Evan, her fingers in his hair. Her other hand rested on Josh's thigh, casual...intimate. They were lovers. At the time? Or before Shayna got back together with Evan?

Harper's chest tightened as jealousy sliced through her like jagged glass. She lifted her gaze to Josh's. "You and Shayna?"

He nodded.

She looked at the photo again, taking in the intimacy between all three of them. "You were their third."

"Yes."

"How? Why?" She couldn't look away, yet every nuance of their relationship hurt a little more. Was this how Josh felt now because of her and Evan? And still, he wasn't giving up. He wanted to fight for what they had. Was he strong enough to do that? Was she?

"It's complicated," he said, "but I'll tell you everything if you'll just give me a chance."

She'd fought all her life for what she wanted. Was

she willing to fight for Josh?

A squeak from the stairs in the hall was the only warning before Shayna bounced into the room. Her dark hair was wet from her shower, her face clean and shining, natural, but still as beautiful as the woman in the photo. The woman who'd taken Josh into her body, felt his touch…and touched him.

Bile rose in Harper's throat. She had to get out of here. She had to think.

"Oh Jo-osh," Shayna singsonged his name as she entered the living room. "Guess you can't brag about being the only rancher raising South Poll anymore." She elbowed Josh in the side and winked, but he remained focused on Harper. "Ellie said Aaron Peterson's raising them now?"

"Harper?" Josh said, her name a hushed plea.

Evan swept in behind Shayna—had he been listening?—and grabbed her hand. "Now's not a good time, darlin'."

"What's going on? What did I miss?" Big brown eyes darted between Harper and Josh and finally landed on the picture frame in Harper's hand. Her smile slipped. "Oh."

A frown etched on his face, Evan guided her toward the stairs. "We need to talk."

Something stirred in the back of Harper's mind, clawing its way past the shock, anger, hurt, and jealousy. She stalked toward the couple making their exit. "Wait. What did you say?"

Josh stepped into her path. "Harper?"

Evan blocked his wife with his body. "Now's not the time."

She ignored both men. "Shayna, did you say

Peterson?"

Shayna nodded.

Everything fell into place as Harper placed the photo on the sofa table. She looked up at Josh. She didn't know if they could work things out, but she could sure as fuck do her job. "I know where your cows are."

Chapter Eighteen

"What?" Josh blinked at the sudden change of subject. One minute, he'd watched the woman he loved suffering the truth of both their pasts, hurt, jealousy, anger flitting across her face in wild abandon. Then suddenly, she stood before him rock-solid, determined, her sheriff's mask securely in place...except for the mascara smudged around her eyes and the tears running down her cheeks.

"I'm pretty sure I know where your cows are," Harper repeated and brushed past him. She stopped at the casing separating the hall from the den. "Are you coming? I'll need you to identify them."

"Now?" He couldn't think of anything but surviving the shitstorm they were in, and she wanted him to identify his cattle? "You wanna do this *now*?"

She shot a glance over her shoulder at Evan and Shayna, who'd stopped at the foot of the stairs, then back at him. "I need time to think," she said, her voice low, "but I promise, we *will* talk about us and this...fucked-up situation. Right now, though, we need to go before Peterson moves your cattle. If he hasn't already."

Josh bristled. Fucked-up? Yeah, okay. It was pretty fucked-up. But if she needed to focus on something else to help her process the shit they'd just stepped in, he'd roll with it...for now. "You think Aaron took them?"

"I don't know for sure, but we need to go. I'll explain in the car." She disappeared down the hall.

Josh followed her to the kitchen and sat down at the table to shove his feet into his boots.

She scooped her beanie off the floor where it had dropped earlier and pulled gloves out of her pocket. Why the hell hadn't she been wearing them all day?

"I'll be in the car warming it up." Frigid air whooshed around him as Harper opened and closed the door softly, though the screen door banged shut behind her. It sounded final, like a knife to the heart. He didn't want this to be the last time she left his house.

Shrugging into his coat, he grabbed his gloves and hat and hightailed it across the backyard toward her SUV. Clouds of white billowed from the exhaust pipe. Ice clung to the fenders. The roads would be dangerous. Black ice. He wanted his cattle back, but not at the expense of her safety.

As he climbed into the passenger seat, she slammed the mirror on the visor shut, sniffled, and stuffed a tissue in her pocket.

Heaving a sigh, he didn't bother trying to talk her into waiting for the morning sun to melt away the ice. Instead, he asked, "Why Aaron?"

She put the car in four-wheel drive and pulled away from the house. "We thought we'd ruled out Walter Mills yesterday. Neither of his trailers had tires that fit with the tracks we found at the scene of the first incident. This morning, Mealer discovered Mills owned a third trailer, so we went back with a warrant after I saw you at the auction barn."

"You served Walter with a warrant?" He let out a whistle.

"Turns out they sold the trailer." She stopped at the end of the long drive. The highway was clear, but she looked left and right, then left again. "I'm all turned around. Which way to Ellie's?"

"Why are we going to Ellie's?"

"I'm getting to that."

"Take a left, and another left at the next county road."

"It turns out," she went on as they crossed over the northbound lanes and made the turn heading south, "they sold the trailer. I knew when I looked at the bill of sale that the name of the buyer, Peterson, sounded familiar, but I couldn't place it." She cut her eyes at him, then back at the road. "When Shayna mentioned Peterson, it clicked."

Josh shook his head. "I'm not following."

"You said you were the only rancher in the area raising South Poll, right?"

"Yeah?"

"Ellie mentioned Peterson yesterday, that he was keeping his cattle on her property?" She glanced at him again, then away, but the fire of excitement in her eyes warmed him. "Shayna said Ellie told her Peterson is raising South Poll now."

Had she? He hadn't heard a word Shayna said.

"I think Peterson's camouflaging the stolen cattle by hiding them in plain sight, right in the middle of his own herd where we'd never think to look."

"At Ellie's place." Josh stared at Harper both in awe of her power of deduction and attention to detail…and at the size of Aaron's balls. If she was right, he'd sorely underestimated the size of Aaron's brain, too, to come up with something like this.

"And the alien's lights?" She sounded almost giddy. "Probably the headlights of his truck when he moved the cattle onto her property."

"Son of a bitch." Josh pounded a fist against his thigh. When he thought about the fear Ellie had gone through and the fact, they'd all dismissed her alien story...

Harper eased into the turn onto the county road.

"In a couple of miles," he said, "we'll come to a T. Take another left."

The cab was quiet for a few minutes until they passed the scene of the first rustling job and then the Millses' house.

"Were you ever going to tell me about Shayna?" Harper asked out of the blue. "Or were you just going to leave me in the dark forever?"

He swiveled to face her. Would he have? "Honestly, it crossed my mind today for about a half a second."

"Hmph."

"A lot's been going on, Harper." At her skeptical frown, he said, "Look, I don't think of her like that anymore. She's my sister-in-law." For all his teasing of Shayna, which he mostly did to get a rise out of Evan, he hadn't thought of Shayna in a sexual way in a long time.

She seemed to digest that for a minute or two before darting a glance at him. "H-how?"

"How did it happen?" He scrubbed a hand over his face. "Fuck, that's a complicated story."

"So you said," she snapped, her tone pissy and rife with jealousy. "But I'm pretty sure I'm intelligent enough to understand."

Pissy and jealous. He could handle them better than tears, and it meant she was sorting through her feelings. At least, he hoped so. "You're right. I'm just trying to figure out where to start."

"The beginning usually works best."

Hiding a smile at her sarcasm behind another swipe of his hand over his chin, Josh launched into an abridged version. "Shayna and I became good friends ten years ago, after Evan left her. She needed a shoulder to cry on, and I wanted to know why Evan skipped out in the middle of the night. Then her family moved, and we lost track until I fell off a ladder and ended up in the emergency room at the hospital she worked at. From there, I devised a plan to get them back together by claiming to need a nurse and Evan's help to run the ranch.

"They were working their way through their issues, but Evan, as you know—" He fought the rising bitterness in his gut. "—is a hardcore Dom who likes to share his subs. He needed to know Shayna could accept his need to share. I was handy."

"It can't be that simple."

"Yeah, well, I guess it wasn't as complicated as I thought, but I won't lie to you. She was hot, and I was into it. But Harper, Shayna was always Evan's. I knew that going in, and as soon as she was comfortable with a new Dom from Silver House, I bailed and found The Arena because I'd tasted enough of the lifestyle to want to know more. I could say I regret what happened, but it led me to you."

She stared at the road ahead. "Thank you for telling me."

Josh smoothed a hand over his jaw. "Where does

all this leave us?"

"I don't know." She cut a glance at him and then away. "Let's just get through tonight."

They rode the rest of the way to Ellie's in silence, and Josh wasn't sure if that was a good thing or bad.

Harper killed the lights as they pulled off the road and headed up the winding driveway. The house was dark as they approached. She stopped along the hedges. "We'll be seen here if he shows up again tonight."

"Go on around to the back. We can park between the tool shed and the barn."

The SUV rolled quietly past the house and slid into the shadows.

"Should we let Ellie know we're here?" Josh asked. "I don't want to scare her."

Harper reached in the back floorboard and came up with a huge LED flashlight. "We need to let her know we're here and get her permission to search the property."

Together, they sloshed through the mud to the back porch, the beam from Harper's flashlight showing the way. The porch light came on and the back door opened.

"Who's there?" Ellie asked, clutching her blue robe at her throat and wielding a rolling pin.

"It's me, Ellie. Josh." He grasped Harper's wrist and shined the flashlight on his face until they stepped out of the shadows onto the porch.

"Honey, what are you doing here so late?" She glanced at Harper. "Why'd you bring the plumber. You fixed my sink this afternoon, and it's working just fine."

Josh didn't bother to correct her that it was Evan

who fixed her sink, and she'd only be upset if he explained that they thought Aaron was hiding stolen cattle on her property. "I wanted to show Harper how pretty the stars are from the meadow behind your house."

Her thin gray brows furrowed. "It's a little cold."

"What can I say? I'm a hopeless romantic."

Harper shook her head, letting him know it wasn't enough, and stepped closer to Ellie. "Mrs. Butts, may we search your property?"

Ellie squinted at Harper for a minute. "Sorry, Sheriff, I didn't see you there."

"That's okay," Harper smiled. "It's dark."

"You want to search my land?" Ellie shrugged. "Sure, though I can't imagine what you're looking for."

"Thank you. We'll let you know when we're done."

Ellie looked at Josh. "Are you a deputy now?"

"No, ma'am. Just helping out."

"Well, you be careful out there. Those aliens might come back."

Josh forced a smile. "We will. You go get warm."

As soon as the door was shut, Harper laid a hand on his arm. "I'm sorry I had to be so abrupt, but I had to be clear and straightforward in what we were asking."

"I know. I was just trying to keep from upsetting her."

"As it is, we're walking a fine line with Ellie's skewed mental state, and if Peterson was leasing the land, her permission wouldn't be enough. We'd need a warrant. We'll get one anyway once we ascertain whether or not your cattle are here."

"I get it."

She handed him the flashlight. "You lead the way. I don't know where we're going."

Yesterday, he'd seen Aaron's cattle up by Ellie's house, but they were nowhere in sight. The weather had probably sent them farther back toward the woods where they could stay warm in the thickness of the brush.

At the back paddock, Josh opened the gate. "What's the plan, besides the warrant if they're here. Should I call Evan and have him get the guys and a trailer ready?"

Harper shut the gate behind her. "No, I need you to leave them here. Peterson will be back for them sooner or later, and I need to catch him either unloading more stolen cattle or with yours in his possession, in his trailer. Otherwise, he could say he's only here to tend his own herd, and he doesn't know how yours got here."

The closer he got to the herd, the faster his heart pumped, adrenaline spiking his blood. He hated the thought of Aaron stealing from him, but he wanted this shit over with, so life could go back to normal. So that Harper didn't have to worry about the professional line they'd trampled all over.

And so he could work on repairing the damage done by the secrets tonight had revealed.

As he and Harper neared the U-shaped cove in the trees, a few white-faced Herefords lifted their heads.

"Stay close and don't make sudden movements. We don't want to spook them." He skirted the perimeter of the herd, searching for solid cinnamon faces, but couldn't see past the outer edges. "Over here."

He climbed onto a large boulder to get some height

and held out his hand. Harper took it, and he pulled her up beside him then fanned the light across the herd.

"There," she whispered, excitement lacing her voice. "Close to the trees. Come on."

Before he could offer help her down, she jumped, landing on the balls of her feet with the grace of a wildcat. He joined her on the ground and grabbed her hand to keep her from running off. She didn't pull away, but he couldn't be sure she was even aware of his fingers twined with hers.

As they breached the tree line, they found several more South Poll huddled in clusters. He ran his hand over the ice stuck to the forehead of a small heifer and aimed the light on her ear. No tag. "It's been removed."

Harper sidled up next to him. "What about the brand?"

The bluish white beam traveled along the animal's backbone to her hip. There it was. The McNamara brand.

"It's mine." Energy raged through his veins. "You found 'em. Just like you said you would."

Josh wanted to scoop her into his arms for a celebratory kiss, but she held a finger to her lips and cocked a head toward a set of headlights bouncing over the horizon.

Harper pulled out her phone. "We've got company."

****

Motioning for Josh to follow her deeper into the trees and the cover of the shadows, Harper dialed Keith Dollins' number. Voicemail. She hung up and called Ackerman.

"Hey, Sheriff, I was just about to call you," the

deputy answered. "We got nothing from Evan McNamara's truck."

She hadn't expected they would.

"And I got hold of Mr. Peterson," he rushed on. "He's in Lubbock. Been there all weekend. His daughter was in the hospital with alcohol poisoning after a sorority party. She's fine, but that means it's not him."

Fuck. She'd been sure it was Peterson.

Josh pulled her behind two tree trunks growing together as the beams of light sliced over them. Several cows protested the intrusion of the bright halogen lights, and the herd shifted noisily.

"Did you confirm that?" she whispered to Ackerman.

"I talked to the hospital security, and they confirmed his presence, along with Mrs. Peterson's, on their cameras going back to Saturday morning."

"Where's Dollins?" she asked.

"He's, er, indisposed."

"Okay, listen. I'm out in Eleanor Butts' back pasture. We've found the McNamara cattle, and we have an unknown suspect approaching the scene. I need you on a warrant asap. Tell Dollins to get his ass here now and to come in cold. Call Mealer, too. He'll want in on this. You follow as soon as you have the warrant."

She hung up. "It's not Peterson."

Josh peered between the trunks. "Who is it?"

"I don't know." She wedged in between his hard body and the trees to have a look. The truck was still too far away to make out a license plate.

"This might be a longshot," he said, his voice hesitant, one hand settling on her shoulder, "but Tom

Jenkins was here today. He came by when Evan and Shayna were here. Said Radcliff told him Ellie'd been calling him, and he came out to check on her. Do you think it's him, and he came out to see if Ellie had witnessed anything? Or maybe he and Radcliff are both in on it?"

Harper rolled the possibility around in her head. "Jenkins came out to the scene this morning, asking questions. I figured Radcliff had him checking on me, but maybe you're right and they're working together."

"Jesus, I can't believe this is happening," he growled. "If either of them touches one hair on Ellie's head…"

"We can't make assumptions," she warned. "Do you recognize the truck? Can you make out the color, make, or model?"

"I can't see anything but headlights."

"We need a better vantage point." She stepped away, headed for higher ground.

The hand on her shoulder slid down her arm and caught her hand. "Wait. He's turning."

Bark bit into the back of her skull through the beanie as Josh flattened her against the thickest trunk seconds before headlights splintered through the trees, leaving them in a tiny sliver of shadow. One wrong move would reveal their position.

Time slowed as she waited for some sign of movement from the truck. The scent of soap and Josh's familiar cologne swirled around her. Heat and tension radiated from his hard body, tempting her to relax against him, but she had to keep a clear head. "Can you tell how many there are?"

One arm braced above her head, he peeked around

the trunk. "No."

"There was only one set of hoof prints at the scenes, but I can't let my guys walk in blind." One side of the path offered the cover of thick brush. "If I crouch low, I can make it to that cluster of trees."

His grip tightened. "Harper?"

She tilted her head to look up at him, but the brim of his hat cast a shadow across his eyes. "What is it? Did you see something?"

His mouth twisted with worry. "You don't have to do this."

"What are you talking about?" she asked. "We're right here. We've got him. I can do this."

"I know you can, but not knowing how many there are…" He lowered his forehead to hers. "Just let them take the damn cows. I don't care. I'd give up my entire herd to keep you safe." His breath warmed her lips. "I know it sounds crazy because we just met, and we have a lot to figure out, but…I love you, wildcat."

Heat bloomed in her chest, and her racing heart stumbled. More than crazy, it sounded absolutely insane and a little too scary, but also wonderful…and right.

She shook her head. This was hardly the right time for declarations of love.

Was it ever the right time? Especially when she couldn't be sure what she felt.

Harper opened her mouth, snapped it shut, then shook her head again. "Josh—"

His finger landed on her lips. "It's okay. You don't have to say it. I just want you to know."

Why? In case something goes wrong?

She eased his hand away and stood tentatively on

tiptoes to taste his lips. He groaned and slanted his mouth over hers in full assault of tongue and teeth. His hand at her waist slid to her ass, lifting her against the rock-hard ridge beneath his fly. Desire ricocheted through her.

Not the time, Quinn.

Forcing herself to pull back, she whispered, "It's going to be okay." She landed one more kiss to his lips. "You have to trust me, Josh. Trust that I know what I'm doing."

"I do, but—"

"No buts."

A truck door opened and shut, then the gate at the back of the trailer clanged open. This was her chance to find a better vantage point.

"Stay here," she whispered.

"Fuck that. I'm coming with you."

"Josh, why can't you hear me? I need to know you're safe. If I'm worried about you, I'll make mistakes."

His thumb grazed her cheek. "And *I* need to know *you're* safe."

"I just want to see how many there are. I'll be right back."

"Sorry, wildcat. I'm not letting you out of my sight."

And he calls me stubborn.

"Fine but stay close and do what I say when I say, or you'll get us both killed. And don't get in my way."

He nipped at her bottom lip. "Yes, ma'am."

His grip on her ass loosened, and as Harper slid down his body to her knees, she couldn't help but think about how this scenario would play out if they were anywhere but here.

He grunted, as if his mind had gone the same direction.

Harper smiled up at him but couldn't see if he returned it. Her smile faded as the loading ramp thudded to the frozen ground, and she made her move. Sitting back on her haunches, then rising on the balls of her feet, she stayed low to cut across a swath of light and into the cover of darkness again.

Josh followed close on her heels as she made her way around the U of trees protecting the herd from the biting wind. Progress was slow. Every crunch of their boots on the frozen leaves and grass reverberated through the trees. She stopped every few feet to reassess the situation, Josh pressing in behind her.

"I only make out one guy," he said as the silhouette of a man unloaded a horse and tied him to the side. He pulled something from the back of the trailer.

She lifted a hand to shade her eyes. "Me, too. What's he doing?"

"He's assembling rails at the back of the trailer to create a makeshift chute."

"We need to keep moving."

Harper wove through the trees another twenty feet before she broke free of the blinding light. The truck became visible. Her gut clenched. A maroon 4-door dually.

She turned to Josh as he settled next to her and focused on the scene. His brows furrowed in confusion, then shot up in shock and disbelief.

"I don't understand. Why would he—" The pain etched on his face shredded her heart. His Adam's apple bobbed, and his shoulders sagged. "This doesn't make any sense."

No, it didn't. Reed was Josh's friend. They'd grown up together.

She laid a hand on his knee. "I'm so sorry."

His eyes turned cold as anger settled over him like a mantle. "Not as sorry as *he's* going to be."

He started to rise, but she tightened her grip. "No, Josh. We have to wait for backup. We have to do this by the book."

Jaw clenched, he nodded, his attention never wavering from the man expertly cutting his South Poll from Peterson's Herefords and herding them through the chute and into the trailer.

Harper pulled out her phone and texted Mealer.

Harper: *How far out are you?*

Deputy Mealer: *About a mile.*

"Oh my god, Ellie!" Josh vaulted to his feet and was gone before Harper finished reading the message.

"What the fuck?" Harper stood and drew her weapon, then blinked as Ellie ran across the field, wielding a rolling pin, her white nightgown billowing behind her, her head wrapped in a foil helmet. "Fucking hell."

So much for waiting for backup.

Chapter Nineteen

Josh sprinted along the edge of the herd. Never in a million years would he have thought Reed would steal from him, just like he didn't think Reed would harm Ellie, but Josh wasn't taking any chances. He had to get to her before she got to Reed.

Thank god, Reed hadn't seen her yet. The son of a bitch was too busy rustling cattle.

My cattle.

As Josh crossed between the herd and the truck, the headlights temporarily blinded him, forcing him to stop. It took a second for his eyes to adjust. A second that cost him.

A streak of white flew at Reed. "Get away from my cows."

"What the hell?" Reed grunted as Ellie slammed the rolling pin against his thigh.

His horse danced sideways into the trailer. The cows he'd been herding scattered, one almost knocking Ellie over. The rest of the herd shifted restlessly, bellowing at the disturbance.

"Fuck, Ellie." Reed slid to the ground and strode toward her. "It's me. Reed. I was just checking on Aaron's herd."

"You can't fool me." She stood her ground. "I know why you're here."

Josh emerged from the shadows, blocking Reed

from reaching for Ellie. "We both do."

"No, Bernard, don't believe him." Ellie tugged on Josh's coat with one hand and held her foil hat tight to her head with the other. "That's not Reed. It just looks like him. That's one of them aliens that butchered those cows near Houston. I heard about 'em on TV last year."

"I've got this, Ellie. Go back to the house." Eyes on Reed, Josh reached back to pry her hand loose.

Reed shook his head. "She's crazy, Josh. You can't listen to her. Shit, she thinks you're her dead husband."

"He ain't dead," Ellie screeched as she darted around Josh and flew at Reed again.

Josh tried to catch Ellie, but Reed shoved her. She flew backward, crashing into Josh. He lost his footing on a patch of ice. Her arms flailed as they fell. He took the brunt of the impact on the hard ground. Air rushed from his lungs. The back of her head slammed into his nose.

Bone crunched. Light exploded behind his eyes. Pain splintered through his face. The taste of copper filled his mouth as he tried to sit up, but Ellie's limp body and dizziness weighed him down.

Her tin hat covered his eyes. He shoved it aside. "Ellie?"

She didn't respond, but through the ringing in his ears, Josh heard Reed's tormented voice. "Fuck, man, I'm sorry."

"Ellie's hurt." Blood gushed from his nose and ran into his mouth. Cradling her against him, Josh pushed upright and checked for a pulse. Faint but steady. He looked up at Reed and into both barrels of a shotgun. "What the hell, Reed?"

"God, Josh." Moisture brimmed Reed's eyes. "I

never meant for this to happen. All you had to do was file a claim, and it would have worked out for both of us. No one was supposed to get hurt."

"And no one has to." He wiped his coat sleeve across his mouth and under his nose and winced. "Just put the gun down."

"I can't." Reed paced away from Josh, then turned back around. "Jesus, what am I supposed to do now."

"You can take the cattle. I'll file a claim. No one will know."

"She'll know." Reed tipped the shotgun toward Ellie. "She'll blab to everyone who'll listen that an alien who looks like me stole your cattle. Sooner or later, someone, like that pretty new sheriff, will look into it." Reed shook his head again as tears rolled down his cheeks. "My plan was working just fine until she started poking her nose into everything. When I heard she was out here yesterday, I knew that once she talked to Aaron about the trailer I sold him, she'd put it all together."

From the corner of his eye, Josh caught movement near the herd. He didn't know if it was one of the cows or Harper moving in. He had to keep Reed talking. "Look, I don't care about the cattle. I'll help you move them. Hell, I'll even help you sell them."

"I should have moved them earlier," Reed waved a hand at the herd, "but the storm hit, and Evan was here, then Sheriff Jenkins, and now you. What the fuck are you doing here?"

"I came to check on Ellie after the storm." The lie came easy. He would have come tomorrow.

"You always did have a soft spot for her."

"So did you." They all had. What had happened to

the man he'd grown up with?

"Fuck, Josh, why do you think this is so hard?" He rubbed his wet cheek against his shoulder and sniffed. "This wasn't supposed to happen."

"Talk to me, man. What's going on?" Josh asked. "Why steal from me? Why steal at all?"

Reed's bark of laughter roused Ellie. As happy as Josh was that she was awake, she'd be easier to manage unconscious. No telling what she'd do.

"Gambling." Reed shrugged. "Got myself in deep with a loan shark. I sold the trailer and a few head of Granddad's cattle, but it wasn't enough. I knew you could sustain a hit. Nobody else around here could. It wasn't personal. I just needed the money. They'll kill me if I don't pay them back. They threatened to kill Granddad, too. He's a bastard, but he's the only family I have."

"Why didn't you come to me?"

"Believe me, I thought about it." Reed snorted. "But if Granddad found out I borrowed money from a McNamara, it would kill him. At the very least, he'd disown me. Any way I looked at it, I'd lose everything—the only family I've ever known, my home. I wouldn't be able to hold my head up in town."

The desperation rolling off Reed had Josh gently laying Ellie on the ground beside him and rising on his knees. He had to be ready for whatever Reed planned next.

"Let's get Ellie to a doctor," Josh coaxed. "Then we can figure a way out of this."

"We both know there's no way out.

"So, you're going to kill me?" He couldn't believe Reed could do it.

Reed braced the shotgun against his shoulder. "It's you or me. I'm fucked either way. There's no good solution."

"Drop your weapon." Harper's voice, calm and deadly, startled both of them. She walked slowly forward, both hands gripping her gun as she aimed it at Reed.

"What the— How—" Reed swung the shotgun in her direction. "Don't come any closer."

Fury and fear drove Josh to his feet, his fingers curling into fists.

Reed turned the gun back on Josh, which was right where he wanted it.

"Put the gun down," she demanded again.

Reed swallowed hard. "I can't."

She inched closer. "Reed, listen to me. You don't want to do this."

"I don't have a choice."

"Right now, you do," Harper said. "Right now, you're only facing ten years max for theft of livestock. You'd probably get less, and if Josh talks to the judge on your behalf, maybe only a couple years. But if you pull that trigger, I'll be forced to pull mine, and I don't want to do that."

Once more, Reed aimed the gun at Harper. "I could kill you first."

"It'll be the last fucking thing you ever do," Josh growled. He didn't even recognize the man he'd called friend his whole life. What the hell had happened to him? When had he changed?

And how did I fail to see it?

"You don't want to kill anyone, but killing me," Harper said, her tone steady, keeping Reed's attention on her, "puts a needle in your arm."

"I'm a dead man anyway." Reed shook his head at Josh. "I'd kill myself, but we both know I don't have the guts."

"Josh?" Harper said his name softly, drawing his gaze. "Get Ellie out of here."

"Move, and I'll kill her for sure," Reed spat.

"Josh? Are you *hearing* me?" Harper urged. "Ellie needs you. No *buts*."

Her message came through loud and clear. If she was worried about him and Ellie, she'd make mistakes. He had to trust her. She knew what she was doing. He got it, but how could he leave her behind?

Josh looked at Harper. Really looked at her. Her feet planted shoulder width apart. Her weapon and her deadly focus trained on Reed. She was every inch the sheriff of Stone County. Hell, she'd probably disarmed suspects like Reed every day and twice on Sundays as a Houston PD officer. Josh had no idea what her plan was, but it didn't matter.

"I hear you, Sheriff." He blotted under his nose in the crook of his elbow, his gut twisting, torn between getting Ellie to safety and leaving Harper with Reed. "No buts."

Everything after that happened in slow motion.

Josh pivoted toward Ellie.

Reed swung the shotgun toward Josh.

Harper lunged for Reed.

Josh dove, shielding Ellie with his body as Harper slammed into Reed, knocking the barrel upward. They grappled against the side of the trailer for control. A shot blasted into the night sky.

Ellie flinched beneath him and reached for her

head. "Wha—"

Hooves stomped the ground around them as Josh gathered Ellie in his arms and ran toward the truck, dodging a wild-eyed calf. He tore open the passenger door and set her on the leather seat. Her feet were bare, caked with mud, and ice-cold. Her teeth chattered.

"Fuck, Ellie." He checked the backseat for a blanket or something to cover her. Nothing. He peeled off his gloves and slid them as far over her small feet as they would go, then took off his coat and wrapped her in it.

"No," she pushed his hands away, along with the coat.

"Shh, it's me. Josh. You have to keep the coat on."

She gripped his hand. "J-Josh? What's happening?"

At least she recognized him this time. That was a good sign. "I'm just trying to get you warmed up."

Ellie settled, burrowing into the coat.

Spotting Reeds keys on the console, Josh shut the door and ran to the driver's side to start the engine. As soon as he got the heater going, he sent a text to Evan.

Josh: 911 Ellie's hurt. Need Shayna.

He didn't wait for an answer. Didn't need to. They'd come.

Josh patted Ellie's hand. "Stay here."

He hated to leave her alone, but Harper might need him. Reed wasn't as big as Leon, but he outweighed her by a good seventy pounds.

Josh shut the driver's door, and another loud crack split the air.

****

With the echo of the second gunshot ringing in her

ears and both chambers empty, Harper focused on her assailant rather than his weapon.

She let go, and Reed stumbled backward, freeing up enough room for her to drive a palm up and under his chin. As soon as his head snapped back, she rammed a knee into his groin.

With a grunt, he relinquished the gun and reached for his balls, folding in on himself.

"Bitch," he coughed then dropped to the ground and rolled to his side.

Harper kicked the shotgun under the trailer and pressed a knee into his shoulder, forcing him on his stomach. Spinning to exert her weight on his lower spine, she forced one arm behind his back, then the other, and quickly secured him with cuffs.

"Reed Mills, you're under arrest for theft of livestock, assault with a deadly weapon, assault of a police officer, and whatever the fuck else I can come up with. You have the right to remain silent…"

As she finished reading Reed his rights, she stood and turned to find Josh beside her, his face a bloody mess.

"Are you okay?" he asked, concern rushing his gaze over her body, searching for injury then landing on her face. His frown deepened. "Your head is bleeding."

Harper dabbed at the cut near her hairline where the butt of the shotgun had tagged her during the altercation with Reed. "I'm fine."

"Are you sure?" His fingers closed around her arms, warm and enticing. "Did he hit you?"

"No." She ached to lean into him, to feel the beat of his heart against her palm, but she'd struggled to keep it together from the second she'd gotten close enough to assess the scene and saw him on the ground, his face bloody. If she accepted the comfort he offered, she'd fall apart.

Instead, she pulled away as the crunch of approaching footsteps sounded in the distance. "Where's Ellie?"

Josh must have heard them, too. He retreated a step and stuffed his hands in his jean pockets. "In Reed's truck."

Fuck, he wasn't wearing gloves. Or a coat.

Of course, he wasn't. He gave them to Ellie.

"There's an ambulance en route," she assured him. "Get them to check you out."

"I'll carry her up to the house. They might not be able to get back here."

She shook her head. "I'll get Dollins to bring his truck."

"Harper, I'm—"

"Sheriff," Mealer called out, trotting toward them. He glanced at Josh, then at Reed, still moaning on the ground. "Holy shit, Reed Mills."

"Let's get him up." She turned back to Josh, but he was already heading for Ellie. She wanted to follow him, to know what he wanted to say, but her priority right now was to update the team and secure the scene.

How fucked was that?

****

It was midnight and the temperature had dropped below freezing before Harper left Mealer in Ellie's back pasture. Dollins had driven his four-by-four out to pick up Josh and Ellie, then returned to help Mealer preserve the scene until morning. With her stomach in knots, Harper made a beeline for Ellie's house. She needed to get to the hospital.

The only way to stop fear from strangling her was to see Josh. Tonight could have ended much differently. The vision of him lying on the ground with Reed standing over him with a shotgun would haunt her forever. In that moment, she'd almost lost control. Her finger had itched to pull the trigger and blow the motherfucker's head off.

Now, her fingers played around the brim of Josh's hat. She'd found it not far from where he'd fallen.

The front of the house was a circus of flashing lights. Two sheriff department vehicles were parked near the gate to the pasture. Ackerman sat behind the wheel of his car with Reed slumped against the window in the back. Why wasn't he back at the station already? Was he waiting for instructions?

He could wait a few more minutes.

Two ambulances lined the drive. She'd expected them to be gone as well, but word had come to her that they were late on the scene due to the weather. The former sheriff's truck—of course, he'd be here—was parked in the yard, along with a silver Mercedes she didn't recognize and a truck she'd spotted as she and Josh had left his house earlier. Probably Evan's since it hadn't been there during the search.

Harper headed straight for the ambulances. The back doors of one rig opened. Her heart tripped as an EMT inside climbed out, revealing Josh sitting on a gurney, cotton stuck up his nose and a patch of gauze taped across the bridge. He was talking to someone.

His gaze shifted and locked on hers. The corner of his mouth tilted upward, and just like that, the knots in her stomach loosened. Her nipples tightened.

I'm so screwed. His smile alone can turn me to jelly.

And how the fuck could he still be that gorgeous with a busted nose?

Harper smiled back at him. Their connection felt good and so fucking right.

"Sheriff Quinn," someone called out to her. *Radcliff?*

She ignored him and quickened her pace.

"Harper." Radcliff came out of nowhere, blocking her path. "I need an update on the situation."

"Not right now." She tried to move around him, but he sidestepped in front of her.

"I'm getting calls from Mrs. Butts' neighbors, and I need to put together a press release."

Of course, you do, you fucking troll.

"I'll get you one as soon as possible, but I need to check on Jo—Mr. McNamara and Mrs. Butts."

"I've already done that. The medics are working on them. We'll know more after their assessment."

She glanced over Radcliff's shoulder. Josh's sexy grin had twisted into a snarl, his eyes narrowing on the mayor, but then his gaze returned to her. He gave her a resigned nod as if to say it was okay. He understood.

"Fine," she snapped. "We'd finished up with the McNamara search, and—"

"Not here. Let's talk in the house where it's warm." He struck off, and she had little choice but to follow. Fucking hell, she hoped the asshole didn't get re-elected.

As they entered Ellie's living room, Harper was shocked to see Shayna in the dining room. She looked just as surprised to see Harper and entirely at home here in her jeans and sweatshirt, her dark hair pulled into a ponytail.

Bloody bandages and various medical supplies littered the table. Was the blood Josh's? Had she treated him and Ellie before the ambulances arrived?

Radcliff's mouth moved, but Harper couldn't hear a word as Shayna's dark eyes held hers for what felt like the most awkward moment of her life. Here they were, two women who'd fucked the same men—brothers.

She was always Evan's.

Josh had said so, and Shayna was married to Evan, but did she secretly love Josh, too?

Shayna removed the stethoscope from around her neck. "I'll be out of your way in a minute."

"What?" Radcliff blinked at Shayna as if just noticing her. He surveyed the table and her medical bag. "I'm sorry, nurse. Can you give us the room, please?"

Harper tried not to roll her eyes. The fucker was so full of self-importance, and he obviously didn't realize who she was. "Mayor Radcliff, this is Shayna McNamara. She's Josh's sister-in-law. There's nothing you can say she doesn't probably already know."

"Very well." He focused on Harper. "What happened?"

Harper gave him a quick rundown of the night's events, and he left with a smile on his face while her heart broke for Josh and Ellie and, fuck it, even Reed and his grandfather.

"Come sit. Let me take a look at you," Shayna said when they were alone.

Harper scanned the table. The bloody bandages

were gone. The surface had been wiped down. In their place sat fresh rolls of gauze and a suture kit.

Had she stayed for my sake?

"I'm fine. It's just a scratch."

"I'll be the judge of that." Shayna smiled. "Besides, Josh would never forgive me if I didn't take a look."

"Did he ask you to?" Harper wasn't sure how she'd feel about that.

"No, he was too busy telling Evan what happened. Did you really wrestle Reed for a shotgun and take him down with a kick to the balls?"

Working her fingers around the brim of Josh's hat, Harper hesitated, wary and ever suspicious. And exhaustion would hit the second she sat down. There was still so much to do.

A hand on her shoulder pressed her into the chair, and gentle fingers removed her beanie then brushed back her hair. Harper let her, only because she was curious about Shayna and her motives for helping her.

"It's not just a scratch, but I don't think it'll need stitches. Just a butterfly." Shayna poured alcohol on a cotton ball. "This might burn, but it needs to be cleaned."

"Mmm."

Shayna dabbed at the cut, but the discomfort was slight. She backed away, then moved in again. "Wow, you're a rock star. I've had grown men cry over a little sting."

Harper shrugged. "I have a high tolerance for pain."

More like a fetish, but then she couldn't say that. Or maybe she could.

She looked up at Evan's wife—his collared sub by the looks of a delicate silver chain around her neck—and wondered what kind of pain she liked and if Josh had enjoyed administering it.

Harper grimaced. He must have if he'd gone looking for more at The Arena. *Where he met me.*

"Guess you're used to it," Shayna said, her cheeks flushing red as if her mind had only just gone to the same place as Harper's. "In your line of work, I mean."

Tilting her head back, she searched the woman's face for signs of malice and found none. "Why are you being so nice to me?"

Shayna sifted through a box of bandages. "Because Josh loves you, and I want him to be happy."

"Doesn't it bother you that..." *Because it sure as fuck bothers me.*

"A little, yes, but I was no nun before Evan and I got back together. I had other partners." She selected a bandage and faced Harper. "Besides, I love Evan, and I trust that he loves me, too, and that he wouldn't lie to me." She opened the seal on the tiny butterfly package. "Now, if I thought that night with Evan meant more to you than a session between a Dom and sub, I'd have a problem, but I don't. I've been that sub. I know the dynamics of a threesome." She shrugged. "I can also see that you care deeply for Josh, so..."

"Thank you" Harper stood as soon as the butterfly was in place. "I need to get back out there."

Shayna caught her hand, then let it go. "Harper, I know it'll take time, but I'd like us to be friends."

Harper nodded, not sure they could. Shayna was part of Josh's family, though, and what was Harper going to do? Ask Josh to tell Evan he couldn't bring his wife to the ranch? Make herself scarce when they visited? Fuck that. She'd worry the whole time about what they were doing. That was no life for either of them. He'd feel torn and come to resent her.

No, if she wanted Josh, she had to try…for all of their sakes.

An EMT met her on the porch. "Sheriff, can you speak to Josh? He won't let us take him in until he's talked to you."

She hid her smile. "Right behind you."

Mealer trotted up beside her as she made it to the sidewalk. "Sheriff?"

"Can it wait?"

"Um, sure. Just wanted to run something past you."

"You could have just called."

"Yeah, but if it's okay with you, Dylan said he'd swap places with me. I can't do anything but sit around tonight, and I'd rather be the one to take Reed in. I want to be closer to Lori if she needs me."

Harper stopped to focus. "Right. Sorry. I should have thought of that."

He waved off her guilt. "You have a lot on your mind."

A lot more than the job.

"Is it okay then?"

"It's fine, but I'd like to change it up a bit. Dollins should be okay on his own out here. I want you to follow Ackerman to help him with Reed. He might not go easily. Afterward, you can go home and get some sleep. We've got a full day tomorrow. I'll be in as soon as this place is cleared out. I expect you to be gone."

"Got it." He veered toward the house.

"Mealer, your car is that way."

He blushed. "My bladder shrank the second I stepped out of Dollins' truck."

"TMI, Deputy."

"Sorry, Sheriff. You asked."

Was Mealer actually teasing her? Nothing like solving a case to bring a unit together.

She smiled as she continued down the walk, but the light feeling of camaraderie died as she knocked on the back door of the rig. Defining her relationship with Josh might not be as easy, but if it went as she hoped…

The door opened, and Josh stepped down. He shrugged into his blood-stained coat. His nose was still plugged with cotton. The swelling beneath his eyes had turned a purplish red. His breath billowed from his mouth like clouds of steam.

They should be doing this in the house, where it was warm and offered more privacy, but to do that they'd have to walk back across the yard, and someone was bound to pull her away. She needed this…Josh. He needed her, too, if he was willing to hold up an ambulance and suffer with a busted nose.

She handed him the Stetson, looking a little worse for wear. "I found this and thought you might need it."

He threaded his fingers through golden waves, smoothing them into place, then settled the hat on his head. "Thanks."

"How's Ellie?" she asked, wanting to feel him out before she jumped right in.

"She was a little hypothermic, but they got her body temp up, gave her oxygen, and she was alert when they left. They think she might have a concussion from knocking into my hard head. They'll probably keep her overnight. I'll stay with her for a while after they fix my nose."

So, this was it. She would be busy for no telling how long with *sheriff stuff*.

"You know," he went on. "I'm almost glad for her condition. She doesn't remember anything, and it's going to break her heart when she finds out about Reed."

Which was one reason Harper had wanted Josh and Ellie out of the way. Not just for their safety, but in case things went sideways, and she had to shoot Reed. "I'm sorry it was Reed. I know he's your friend."

"*Was* my friend," he bit out. "If it was just the cattle, I could forgive him, but he crossed a line when he threatened you and Ellie. I can't forgive him for that, and I'll never forget it."

Josh was angry right now, but he wasn't the kind of guy to hold a grudge. She'd bet her badge on it.

Changing the subject, she pointed to his bandaged nose. "Does it hurt?"

"A bit. Shayna says it's broken, so I'm sure it'll hurt like a motherfucker when the ED doc realigns it, though they said there would be drugs." He glanced at her forehead. "Did Shayna take care of you?"

Harper touched the butterfly bandage. "Yeah."

"How was it?"

She lifted a shoulder and let it drop. "No stitches."

"No, I mean being around Shayna."

"Oh." Why were they talking about Shayna? "Awkward."

Like now.

She glanced around the yard. The ambulance with Ellie had left while she was inside the house. Radcliff was still here, talking to Jenkins. Ackerman was waiting for Mealer. Evan was on the porch. Waiting for Shayna?

"Harper?"

"Yeah?" she answered, suddenly realizing this conversation was probably better left for another time and place.

"Harper?" he said again, his firm but insistent tone drawing her gaze back to him. "I'm sorry I put you in danger. I saw Ellie, and I panicked."

"It's okay."

"No, it's not. It was stupid, a mistake I will forever regret and wish I could take back. I should have trusted you and let you handle it. I—" He swallowed hard. "I could have gotten you killed. I could have gotten us all killed."

"But you did trust me, Josh, when it counted most." The back of her eyelids burned. Her nose prickled. "It... It means a lot to me that you did."

He nodded. "Where does all this leave us? Do you still want there to be an us?"

A tear rolled unchecked down her cheek. "I do, but can you really get past me being with Evan?"

"I don't give a damn about all that shit. All I care about is you. I love you, Harper." He reached for her but froze halfway and cast a glance around. With a sigh, he once again relegated his hands to his coat pockets, leaving her aching for his touch. Always aching.

No more.

She propped her hands on her hips. "Take your hands out of your fucking pockets."

His head reared back, dark brows diving inward. "Huh?"

"Just do it."

Confused, he did as she asked, his arms awkwardly hanging at his sides. "I don't understand."

She scoped out their surroundings. Mealer walked out of the house onto the front porch. Evan and Shayna were heading to Evan's truck. Everyone else remained where they'd been before. She didn't care.

Stepping forward, Harper stood on tiptoe, gently placed her hands on his cheeks, and pressed her lips to his in a light kiss. "Now, put them on me where they belong. No more hiding."

He cocked a brow. "You sure?"

"I'm sure that I want to be with you, and I don't fucking care who knows." Harper hoped her admission would be enough…for now. She was pretty sure she was falling for Josh, but she'd said the words before and hadn't really understood what they meant. She had to get it right this time.

Stormy blue eyes held hers for a long moment before his lips split into a wide grin. "Then let's put on a good show."

His arms slid around her waist, gathering her against his hard body as his lips opened over hers in a slow and very steamy kiss. The cotton in his nose grazed her cheek as one hand fisted in the hair at her nape, giving her a taste of what she could look forward to later. His other hand flattened against her spine, and the evidence of his need for her prodded her belly.

And the zombieflies flew.

Epilogue

Three months later…

Harper jumped as the screen door banged shut, announcing Josh's return from the barn to check on Star. She rinsed the last plate from their dinner and placed it in the drainboard. Her pulse thrummed. She couldn't look at him, or she'd lose her nerve.

I'd have to fucking have it to lose it.

His hands slipped around her waist and under the faucet, trapping her as he washed up.

"She might foal early." The low rumble of his voice tugged at her lower belly.

"Hmm." Closing her eyes, she savored the feel of his hard body against hers, the heady scent of his cologne and a hard day's work, and his stiff cock grinding into her ass. He nuzzled her ear, his stubble catching in her hair. Her nipples drew taut, and arousal dampened her panties.

She stiffened. *Don't get distracted. Stick to the plan.*

As he reached for a towel, she ducked under his arm and made her escape, pretending she hadn't already wiped down the table.

"What do you think about going to the Rusty Nail again?" he asked, watching her as he propped a hip against the sink and dried his hands.

Not far from the auction barn, the bar and grill had a small dance floor and drew the locals on Saturday nights.

"Maybe Texas and Jarod will be there," he added.

Harper had never had girl friends. Growing up, her brothers were her friends, and she'd always found it hard to relate to women. But Texas wasn't all glamour and gossip, like a lot of women Harper's male counterparts dated or married. Texas felt like one of the guys, and Harper enjoyed her company. "Maybe."

"You had fun last weekend," Josh persisted. "I mean, yeah, it was hard to watch Will pretending not to be jealous. I swear, if he doesn't make a move on Texas soon, he's gonna lose his chance with her."

"Probably." Harper circled the table to avoid having to step between it and Josh. He never missed an opportunity to put his hands on her.

He grabbed a plate from the drainboard and began to dry. "Did you get the rest of your signs out?"

"Yeah." Elections were only three weeks away, and though she was running unopposed, she still had to campaign. She hated that part of being sheriff, but she loved the rest. Mealer, Kelsey, Dollins, and Ackerman had become like family, and they'd accepted her relationship with Josh without comment.

Even Radcliff had kept his mouth shut. Josh denied warning him off, so maybe the motherfucker was just happy with the arrest. He'd certainly enjoyed his fifteen minutes of fame.

The sleepy little town of Stone Creek had awakened with a giant roar at the scandalous news of Reed's arrest. The press had invaded but quickly crawled back under their rocks after the TSCRA Ranger left the sheriff's department to close the case because Josh dropped the rustling charges.

Aaron Peterson hadn't pressed charges against Reed, either. As it turned out, Reed had taken advantage of Peterson's absence and "borrowed" the trailer he'd sold him to steal Josh's cows.

Reed had taken a plea deal for the remaining assault charges, denying the town the drama and excitement of a trial. He'd be out in less than a year.

"Are you okay?" Josh asked, startling her.

"I'm fine." *Coward. Quit stalling.*

"Are you still thinking about the call from your dad?"

"No." She'd been shocked when her father called the week after the commotion died down to congratulate her for making headlines. He'd called again yesterday after the sentence hearing just to check in. Something was wrong. Patrick Quinn never called his kids unless it was to bitch about something they'd screwed up. She'd check in with Mickey tomorrow. If any of her brother's knew what was up with the old man, it would be him.

"Did something happen at work?"

"Hmm? No." *Just fucking tell him.*

She opened her mouth, but before she could get the words out, he said, "Walter Mills came by this afternoon."

Her head snapped up, and for a second, she almost forgot the litany she'd rehearsed and how, once spoken aloud, the world as she knew it would forever be changed. "What the fuck did he want?"

"To apologize for Reed."

"Hmph." She threw the rag in the sink and opened

the cabinet to put away the dishes he'd dried.

Who knew the old man had a fucking heart, that he loved his grandson, and hadn't disowned him, after all? Instead, he'd gotten Reed a top-notch lawyer. And *now*, he'd crossed enemy lines to apologize. Would wonders never fucking cease?

"He offered to sign over a parcel of his land to pay me back for covering Reed's gambling debts."

"And?"

Josh shrugged. "I declined."

Not surprising to hear. Josh had made it clear the day of Reed's sentencing that he'd only done it for the boy he'd grown up with, not the man Reed had become. They would never be friends again.

"On a brighter note," Josh said, his gaze following her every move, "I went by to see Ellie this morning, and she's doing great. Clear as a bell. No confusion."

Harper hugged the last plate to her chest and peered around the cabinet door. "She mentioned you'd been there when I stopped by on my way here. She looked good."

During Ellie's hospital stay, tests revealed one side of her diaphragm had collapsed, preventing her chest from expanding properly, which caused her CO_2 levels to rise. Due to Ellie's age, they didn't suggest a diaphragm plication, but as long as she stayed hooked up to her oxygen tank, she'd be fine. So far, she was following doctor's orders.

Josh reached for Harper's hand, but she dodged his touch to slide the plate on top of the others and closed the cabinet door.

He folded his arms across his chest. "What's going on? Are you mad at me?"

"Why would I be mad?" *Shit, this is going all wrong.*

"I don't know, but you're acting like my mom when Dad did something to piss her off, and I've been trying to figure out what I might've done."

Harper shook her head. "I'm not pissed. You've done nothing wrong."

"Wait. Are you—" He pointed back and forth between them. "Do you not want to do this anymore?"

"What? No." Her stomach twisted. "Why would you think that?"

"Jesus, Harper, you haven't looked at me since you got here, not really. I can't get more than one god damn syllable answers out of you, and you shy away every time I try to touch you."

"It's not what you think."

"Then what is it? Is it because Shayna and Evan were here again this week for the sentencing? I thought you two were thick as thieves now."

"I wouldn't say that, but yeah, we're friends." Like Texas, Shayna had surprised Harper. Hell, she'd surprised herself by how quickly she came to like Shayna. Over the last months, they'd defined boundaries and stuck to them. "We've found common ground."

"Is it the club? Do you miss it? Do you want to go back?"

"No." They'd gone back to The Arena a couple of times, and both agreed the club didn't offer anything they couldn't get from each other, but if he'd changed his mind… "Do you?"

He straightened and stalked toward her. "I've already told you, Harper. You're all I need."

"Don't touch me," she warned, retreating. If he did, she'd forget everything but the feel of his hands on her skin. "Not yet, anyway. I can't think when you touch me, and I have a lot to say."

Throwing up his hands, he backed off. "Then start talking."

"Okay but sit down. Please."

His jaw ticked, and for a moment, she thought he'd refuse, but then he pulled out a chair. As soon as his ass hit the seat, his head popped up. "Are you pregnant?"

A giggle bubbled out of her. "Um, no."

With a snort, he sat back in the chair and crossed his arms. His legs stretched into the aisle. "I wouldn't mind having a baby with you."

"You're confusing *having* a baby with *making* one." Still, the thought of having a child with Josh made Harper's insides feel warm and gooey. They hadn't used a condom since the night she'd kissed him by the ambulance, but she'd had the shot.

His hungry gaze roamed over her. "Could I suggest practicing?"

"Stop it." Harper planted her hands on her hips. "Stop looking at me like that, or I'll never get through this."

Brows furrowed, he nodded. "Sorry, go ahead."

She took a deep breath and exhaled slowly. Her feet began to move, taking her from the back door to the threshold leading to the hall and back again. "So, every day the evidence has been piling up."

"What kind of evidence? Is there a new case I don't know about?"

She held her finger to her lips. "Shh. Just listen."

He twisted his fingers in front of pursed lips as if

he were turning a key in a lock.

"Okay, here goes." She held up a finger. "I think about you all the time. While I'm driving, when I'm at work, in the shower, buying groceries." She ticked off another finger. "My tummy flutters every time I see your name on my phone when you text or call me. I love that, not only did you resurrect my moldy, old zombieflies, but you've transformed them into living creatures of color and light."

His upper lipped curled into a snarl. "What the hell is a zombiefly?"

"The butterflies you get when you see someone you're romantically or physically attracted to."

"I know what butterflies are. I've just never heard them called that." He scrunched his nose, which had healed perfectly. "Are you saying the feeling you get when you see me is moldy and old and zombified?"

She rolled her eyes. "My butterflies were dead when we met. I hadn't felt them in years. You brought them back to life. Feel better now?"

His teasing grin told her he did and that he'd been pushing her buttons.

Asshole. Two can play at that game.

"Let's see. Where was I?" She unbuttoned the top button of her shirt and stripped it over her head, leaving the new bra she bought for tonight—cherry red lace.

Josh's groan pebbled her flesh.

"When you look at me," she went on, "like you're doing right now, with that hunger in your eyes, I feel like I'm the only woman in the world. And the way you run your hands over my skin as if you're memorizing every curve"—she trailed a finger over the swell of her breast—"makes me feel worshiped, cherished. Your touch sets my skin on fire, and I get all hot and needy."

"Harper, baby, come here." He crooked a finger.

This wasn't her plan at all, but trying to make the moment serious hadn't worked. She should have known letting Cherry out of her cage would calm her fear. Cherry could tell him how she felt in her own way.

But Cherry was a relentless brat.

Harper shook her head and pulled the snap on her jeans. "I love how you care about Ellie, the guys who work for you, the whole damn town." She lowered her zipper, giving him a glimpse of red lace. "I can't go anywhere without someone asking about you. You're a good man, Josh. The best man I've ever known. And you're all mine."

"Hell, yeah, I am."

Smiling at his enthusiasm, she toed off her boots and pulled off her socks, then hooked her thumbs in the waistband of her jeans and dragged them over her hips and down her thighs. They slid the rest of the way to the floor, and she stepped out of them. She wiggled her toes, drawing his gaze to the fresh red paint on her toenails. Shayna's influence. Strangely, the thought didn't bother her.

"I love your crooked, sexy smile. Yes, that one." Harper laughed. "I love it. And god, I love that you can make me laugh like this. It feels so good."

"I love hearing it."

Harper closed the space between them and straddled his thighs. "Yes, you've told me that, and I believe you now because *your* laugh warms my soul."

His hands fell to her hips and tugged her onto his lap, adjusting her until her pussy nestled tightly over his cock. Bending her over his arm, he lowered his lips to the swell of her breast. "Tell me more about this evidence."

She drove her fingers into his hair as he opened his mouth over her nipple and sucked her in, lace and all. Her hips bucked. "Mmm, I love that you let me pull your hair."

His teeth dragged on the taut bud.

"Fuck, yeah, I love that, too." Harper hissed out a breath and yanked him away to whisper against his lips. "Let me finish, and you can do that again. Whatever you want."

A growl resonated from him, but he didn't argue.

She rocked back to look at the beautiful man who'd tamed her. "I love that I know you'll never lie to me. I love that I can be vulnerable with you, but you still let me be strong. *You* make me stronger." She swallowed against the rising tide of emotion. "When you make love to me, your eyes are the darkest blue, and they're so intense. The feelings inside me are just as intense, so extreme that it hurts. Sometimes, I can't breathe. And then you say those three little words, and I'm complete."

Placing both hands on his face, she brushed her lips over his. "I've known that I love all these things about you, Josh, and many more, and still, I didn't know if I loved you. But then, I'm the sheriff, and after looking at all the evidence, I can only draw one conclusion."

"And what's that, wildcat?"

"That I am hopelessly, emphatically, and irrevocably in love with you."

His gazed held hers, and her heart melted at the raw emotion living in those ocean blue depths. "I know."

"How could you know when I didn't."

"I saw it in your eyes the night you told me my hands belonged on you. I've been waiting for you to figure it out." His fingers fisted in the hair at her nape. "Now, say the words."

The words he wanted to hear tumbled freely from her lips. "I love you, Josh. I love you. I lo—"

His mouth brushed over hers, his tongue gliding between her lips. She answered with her own and rolled her hips. Tingling heat rippled from her center each time her clit rocked over his granite length.

She broke away to draw a deep breath. "I need you."

"Hold on." He sat back. "I have something for you."

A laugh trickled from her throat as she ground against his cock. "Mmm, yes, give it to me."

"Hold that thought." He reached into his pocket.

"Wait." Harper sobered. "Please don't tell me it's a ring. I—I just got on board with the whole love thing."

He dangled a key in front of her. "I was going to ask you to move in, but if you'd rather just have it for when you want or need it, I can live with that...for now."

"I'll take the key and think about the rest." Moving in was a big step, but she spent most of her free time here anyway. Her laptop sat on his coffee table. Her toothbrush and various other toiletries were scattered across the counter in his bathroom, and half her closet was in his.

"That's fair." A frown creased his brow. "I think we had our first fight tonight."

"Where've you been." She shook her head. "I'm

pretty sure we've been fighting since we met."

"Yeah, but we're good at making up." His words feathered against the side of her neck, making her shiver. "Let's go upstairs and make up some more. And you can tell me all the other things you love about me."

Harper rolled her eyes but squealed as Josh hauled her over his shoulder, slapped her ass, and trotted up the stairs. "I love it when you toss me over your shoulder like a caveman, then throw me on your bed and eat my pussy until I see stars."

"I know you do, wildcat," he growled. "I know."

Thank you for reading *Taming the Wildcat*.

Darah would love to know what you think, so please leave a review or just a rating or contact her on social media. *https://linktr.ee/darahlace*

For a glimpse of Harper's past with Evan and Clay, you can find *Between Two Cowboys* (Darah's contribution to *Tempted for More*—a collection of short stories) at *https://www.darahlace.com/.*

Darah Lace

About Darah Lace…

Multi-published author of spicy contemporary and paranormal romance, Darah Lace lives in Texas where she enjoys a simple life with her husband and two dogs. She loves sports, music, watching a good romance, and penning scenes that sizzle. When she isn't writing, she's scouring bookstores for her next adventure.

Connect with Darah on social media:
darah@darahlace.com
www.darahlace.com
www.linktr.ee/darahlace
https://www.amazon.com/author/darahlace
https://www.goodreads.com/darah_lace
https://www.bookbub.com/authors/darah-lace
https://www.tiktok.com/@darah_lace_author
www.instagram.com/darahlace/
www.facebook.com/darahlace
www.facebook.com/DarahLaceAuthor
https://twitter.com/DarahLace

Sign Up for Darah's Newsletter
https://www.darahlace.com/newsletter/

Also Available

Texas Two-Step
Cowboy Rough Book Five
By Darah Lace

Texas Tallulah Taylor never thought she'd be turned on by a dirty text from a stranger, one that leads to a naughty texting session with her best friend. Nothing can come of it though. She's lost everyone who's ever mattered in her life. She refuses to risk losing him for a single night of pleasure.

Will Sanderson has loved Texas since they were kids, but she's kept him in the friend zone. But after her texts turn heated, he's willing to throw caution to the wind. He'll show her he's the only cowboy who can give her the ride of her life…for the rest of his.

~*~

Dear Reader,

Texas Two-Step was previously published as *Sexting Texas* but has been revised to fit into the *Cowboy Rough* series by changing the location to Stone Creek and including Harper and Will and other characters from *Taming the Wildcat*.

For those of you who have read *Sexting Texas*, I hope you'll enjoy the following excerpts from revised scenes.

For anyone who hasn't read Will and Texas' best friends to lovers story, perhaps a small glimpse of their romance might peak your interest.

(Excerpt from the opening scene of *Texas Two-Step*)

With a mental sigh, she focused on the man who'd been her rock more times than she could remember and tried to think of something other than her need for sex. "You got a good price for your bull."

"Yeah, I did okay."

His spur of the moment addition of fifty head of cattle to today's sale had thrown her. That and the sudden private sale earlier this week of his prize-winning bucking bull. Crusher was Will's pride and joy and had earned the Double A Ranch a hefty purse last year. He was sure to have done the same this year. She couldn't imagine why Will would want to sell the big guy. Unless he needed the money.

"Is everything okay? With the ranch, I mean."

"The ranch is fine." He turned to face the mirror again, his gaze catching hers then flitting away to follow the couples on the dance floor.

She twisted on the high-back stool to see who he might be checking out, but the crowd was a little thin and a lot older tonight except for the newly elected sheriff, Harper Quinn, and her deputies. Texas and Harper had become friends shortly after Harper's arrival back in January, but Texas didn't want to intrude. Sheriff's Dispatcher Kelsey Price had passed the state licensing examination to become a Peace Officer, the first step on her way to becoming a deputy sheriff, and they were celebrating.

Texas looked at Will again. Nah, Harper was taken. She and Josh McNamara were engaged and planning their wedding, and hooking up with women in committed relationships… That just wasn't Will's style.

Which, come to think of it, she wasn't quite sure exactly what his style was anymore. He hadn't dated anyone since he and Krystal split up a couple of months back. Not for lack of willing women. Will was a catch—good-looking, wealthy, a generous heart, and a sense of humor. But he hadn't looked twice at anyone, at least not that Texas had seen.

~*~

(Excerpt from the town meeting in *Texas Two-Step*)

Will stepped out of the row of metal folding chairs to make room for her to claim the seat he'd saved, but as flustered and turned on as she was—oh, hell no, not going to happen.

"JD, you sit with Will." She looked to the rear of the small hall. "I see a spot in the last row."

Without another word, Texas skirted both men as Mayor Radcliff asked everyone to take a seat. She'd lied of course. There was no seat in the back, so she'd have to stand. She glanced around for a place to light. Jarod propped against the wall on the opposite side of the room, and she thought about joining him, but she didn't want to encourage him by seeking him out. The state she was in, best to keep to herself.

"Texas." Sheriff Harper Quinn waved her over. She stood next to Josh opposite Jarod. They scooted over to make room.

"Thanks." Texas leaned against the wall beside Harper and crossed one booted foot over the other.

"Standing room only, tonight," Harper whispered.

"The expansion has a lot of people worried," Texas

said. "I'm only here because I promised Will."

Harper nodded. "I wish I didn't have to be. Radcliff loves the sound of his own voice."

The vibration of her phone had Texas plucking it from the rear pocket of her jean skirt.

Will: JD smells like mothballs.

She tucked her lips between her teeth to keep from smiling and typed a reply.

Texas: Be nice. JD is family.

The meeting was called to order and the crowd quieted. Texas listened for a whole three minutes before she tuned out Mayor Radcliff's voice. From her position, she could see the back of Will's head, his shoulders, and part of one long leg stretching into the aisle. He wasn't paying any more attention to the council than she was, with his head down, probably nodding off.

Harper's shoulder nudged Texas' as she leaned close. "You and Will having a good time?"

A flush warming her from head to toe, she stared to Harper. Had she seen Will enter her house Saturday night? "What do you mean?"

"Just that you two have been out and about a lot since you and Jarod broke up. I saw you at the Rusty Nail the other night."

Texas shrugged. "We're just hanging out until he finds a new girlfriend."

The words left a bitter taste in her mouth, but it was only a matter of time before they were back to friends with zero benefits.

Harper nodded but didn't look convinced.

Will: Bored.

Texas: No kidding. They talk in circles.

She didn't have to listen to know half the town wanted the growth the expansion promised, including fast food chains and department stores. Others wanted to retain and promote the quaint, small town, rustic theme of family-owned shops and restaurants.

Will: Help me stay awake.
Texas: JD's snoring will do that.

She recognized the soft wheeze she'd come to love over the years as it competed with the arguing council. Will gave the older man a gentle nudge, and JD's snoring quieted.

Will drew his leg from the aisle and leaned forward, his elbows on his knees, head down, almost disappearing from view. Her phone signaled the arrival of a new text.

Will: Send me a pic of your tits.

She blinked at the explicit words. The heat in her face had just cooled, but now it flamed. Good thing she wore a leather vest over her T-shirt or anyone within six feet would have seen her nipples rise and pucker as if they preened for Will's attention. Shit. She hadn't expected him to continue sexting as part of the friends with benefits arrangement—a simple "hey, I'm horny" maybe. She certainly hadn't expected him to choose a time when she was cornered in a public place.

Yet, she couldn't deny the same lust enthralled her now as it had two nights ago. And she was stone cold sober this time. Her hands shook as she thumbed a reply.

Texas: My breasts are not for your entertainment.
Will: IDK, I've entertained some damn naughty thoughts in the last 24 hours and most of them

starred those pretty tits of yours.

The traitorous "pretty tits" grew heavy, tingly, and ached for his mouth. Her chest tightened, and her breathing turned shallow and rapid.

Texas: Tell me.

God, she was insane, but anticipating his response made her heart pound.

Will: I want to lick the valley between your tits, get them all wet, and squeeze them together.

The taut cord from her breasts to her clit twanged like that of a guitar, and moisture pooled in her panties. She felt reckless, out of control…alive.

Texas: More.

Will: Then I'll slide my dick through the silky vise.

The throbbing in her pussy intensified. She straightened against the wall and pressed her thighs together, but the friction only increased her need. She swallowed a moan and gave him a texted version to let him know she liked his fantasy.

Texas: Mmmmmm.

Will: The head of my cock will tap your chin. You'll open for me and wet the tip with your tongue.

Every nerve under her skin sizzled, and she struggled not to squirm. Her mind was fuzzy, making it difficult to form a response. Luckily, she didn't have to because he didn't wait for one.

Will: Your nipples are plump little berries. I want you to pinch them while I fuck your tits.

She sucked in a breath and blew it out.

Texas: OMG, yes. I'm pinching them hard. I want to come.

No lie there. One touch. That was all it would take.

Will: You will. You'll scream my name. I'll fucking lose it and cum will shoot from my cock onto your throat.

"Mmmahh." The sound erupted before she could hold it back.

"You okay? Harper asked.

Josh's gaze shifted from Will hunched over his phone to the one in her hand. A knowing smirk tilted his lips.

"I'm fine." She pressed the phone to her chest and scanned the room to see if anyone else had heard. If they hadn't, she was sure her face and body betrayed her sexually needy state just as easily.

Will was probably waiting for her to text him back. Another survey of the hall showed everyone's focus on the platform, except Jarod's. He was watching her, eyes narrowed as if he knew the dirty things Will said and her perverted reaction to them.

Shit. Her gaze dropped to her phone again. Big mistake.

Will: I need to fuck you. Now.

"Oh, my god," she muttered under her breath, both panic and lust wrangling for control. This was insane. She had to get out of here. She needed air.

Movement from her left had her head snapping up. Jarod had pushed off the wall and taken a step toward her. That was all she needed to get her feet moving. No way was she in the mood to deal with Jarod, and one word from Will and she'd jump his ass.

~*~

If you've made it this far, here's another bonus.

I've added an epilogue to *Texas Two-Step* that will reveal more fun facts about some of the Cowboy Rough family. You can also find it on my website (*www.darahlace.com*) and in my February newsletter *(https://www.darahlace.com/newsletter/)*.

Also Available

Bachelor Unmasked
Preston Brothers Book One
By Darah Lace

He wears a disguise to discover the truth.
She wears one to keep secrets.

After a long business trip, the last thing Spencer Preston wants is to attend a masquerade party. However, an encounter with a hot she-devil changes his mind, especially when the woman behind the sequined mask is the prim and proper, no-nonsense, secretary he's been fighting an attraction to for months. Suspicious of her dual lifestyle, he slips on his mask and sets out to discover her secrets.

Melody Jamison hates hiding behind her plain-Jane persona, but her last job ended in sexual harassment. To get a promotion at Preston Enterprises, she needs to show Spencer she's more than a pretty face. The problem is, she's hot for her boss. When a friend suggests a masquerade might be the perfect place to let her hair down without revealing her secrets, she agrees to a night out. But she never dreams she'll meet a masked stranger who makes her body hum like only Spencer can.

There's a corporate spy running loose at Preston Enterprises, Melody is at the top of the suspect list, and Spencer must continue to hide behind a mask in order to uncover the truth.

Other Books by Darah Lace

COWBOY ROUGH SERIES
Saddle Broke
Bucking Hard
End of His Rope
Taming the Wildcat
Texas Two-Step
Deal with the Devil (Coming 2025)

PRESTON BROTHERS SERIES
Bachelor Unmasked
Bachelor Auction
Bachelor Bad Boy (Coming Fall 2024)
Bachelor Betrayed (Coming 2025)

MACTYRE VALLEY WOLVES SERIES
Claiming Sophia
Embracing Everly (Coming 2025)

STAND ALONES
S.A.M.
Getting Lucky in London
Dragon's Bride
Yes, Master
Game Night
Wrong Number, Right Man
Yesterday's Desire

Printed in Great Britain
by Amazon